THE HAUNTING OF ROAN MOUNTAIN

THE PARANORMAL ARCHAEOLOGIST: BOOK 2

S. A. JACOBS

To my daughter Abby.
May you always continue reading... Even if you don't agree with
a character's choice in clothing.

PROLOGUE

APRIL 22, 1905 - Cloudland Hotel

ROBERT MASON RETIRED to the sitting room in the hotel after hearing Samuel's grand plan. He walked into the quiet room and over to the dark mahogany end table where there was a crystal decanter filled with whiskey. He turned over one of the glasses on the table and pulled the stopper from the decanter.

The reflection of flames from the fireplace danced on the sharp edges of the crystal as Robert slowly poured the amber liquid. He returned the stopper to the decanter and sighed deeply as he picked up the glass. He gently swirled the whiskey and walked across the room to the window. At first, all he could see was the reflection from the fireplace and the lamps in the room. He unbuttoned his jacket and rested his arm on the top rail of the lower window sash.

Now, close enough to see beyond the room's reflection, he gazed at the mountain outside. It was a peaceful night. The stars shone brightly and extended to the very edge of the horizon where they met the rolling peak of the neigh-boring mountaintop. He stood stoically for a few minutes and took a deep breath followed by another large swallow of whiskey. As the fiery liquid ran down his throat, a sound drew his attention away from the window.

Across the room, the doorknob began to turn. His eyes bore down on the door with great intensity. It swung open and three men walked in, all dressed as finely as Robert was. It was his brethren—John, William, and George. The three of them were discussing the meeting they'd just had with their leader, Samuel. Robert was genuinely uninterested and turned back to the window.

"Robert, what do you think of Samuel's plan?" George asked, heavily slurring his words.

Robert didn't move. He continued swirling his glass of whiskey, his eyes intently focused out the window.

"Samuel is too full of himself to recognize what a damn fool he really is," Robert said in a stern voice.

The room fell quiet. The only sound was the ticking of a large clock in the corner.

"He still makes a point though," William said tentatively. "Surely you can agree that a paper map is not the safest course of action."

Robert took another sip of his whiskey. "You are indeed correct, William. A map will never preserve what we have hidden. Samuel's flaw is his hubris. His wife should not hold the key. As much as he believes he has full control over her, he does not."

He turned around to address the room.

"Surely you understand the purpose of these maps is to secure the future of our society beyond our years. If we were only planning for the foreseeable future, no map would be necessary as we know where we have hidden our hoards.

However, we know not when that time will come. So, we are securing our future beyond our years. As well as we have hidden everything, you must all acknowledge that our treasure also needs to be protected."

"We know that. Why else would we have Sentinels stationed across the country protecting it?" George retorted. "You are as crazy as Samuel!"

"You idiot! Yes, they are hidden and yes, they are protected. They are protected by Sentinels today, but what about tomorrow? What about one hundred years from now when we are all dead and gone? We are the architects of the future of the Sovereign Lords. We secure the future of this leadership. How can we guarantee that the Sentinels of generations to come will provide the protection we require? My portion of our hoard is right there, nearly visible from this window. Yes, someone looking for it would need my instruction, but what is to stop someone from happening upon it? Say twenty years from now someone wants to build another hotel, like this one, on that very spot. It will be found. I fear the Sentinels cannot be our only protection for the long-term future."

"You're correct," William said. "We do architect the future of the Sovereign Lords. We direct every action anyone within the KGC takes, including the Sentinels. So, we can ensure the ongoing protection of our hoard."

"We can suggest it. We can even demand it. But can we really ensure it for generations to come? No matter what you, I, or even Samuel want for the future, we are not completely in control of it. There is risk. That is a risk I am not comfortable with."

"What are you suggesting?" John asked.

"We all need to take our own steps to secure our maps and instructions. Samuel has chosen his path... no matter how misguided I think it is. I have my own approach to securing my map and my instructions. I urge you all to do the same." Robert swallowed the remainder of his whiskey and turned back to the window. "For protection, we need something we can count on no matter what happens...a different kind of Sentinel required to keep everything guarded long after we are gone."

PART I

1

I TOSSED my backpack on the ground and took a seat in the wooden rocking chair. I welcomed the fact that the Seattle-Tacoma Airport had these instead of the usual airport seating. Sadly, that rocking chair was the closest thing to home I'd experienced in weeks. Had it been two weeks prior, I would've gladly welcomed the moment of respite. That day though, I was waiting to go home. There was one flight standing between me and getting there, a flight which was delayed again for the fourth time.

I had just finished up a long stretch of recordings for the second season of Paranormal Archaeology. The show was a success. I had money and was doing what I'd always dreamt of...at least in theory. In reality, I just wanted to be home so I could live my life. The last shoot of the season had featured the haunted Cadillac Hotel of Seattle. As great as it was to have the production wrapped up, the fact that it was one in the morning and my flight was still not even close to boarding drove me crazy.

A month later, I would be going into post-production with the show where I was scheduled to spend two months going through the hundreds of hours' worth of video. We would isolate the small moments that most felt like there was a ghost present and then build a story around them. Until then, I got a well-deserved break. A break I needed more than anything.

Before long, I started to doze off. With my eyes closed, it was so easy to feel as though I was sitting in the rocking chair on my own front porch. I could hear the birds chirping. I could feel the warm Tennessee sun on my face. That was also the precise moment that someone felt the need to vacuum the terminal's carpet. Frustrated with this interruption, I grabbed my backpack and headed to the only store still open in the terminal.

I brought an overpriced bag of Cheez-Its to the counter and started fishing cash out of my front pocket.

"Excuse me, are you David Spur?" the cashier said.

I looked up to see the young woman standing at the cash register, staring at me with wide eyes.

"The one and only," I said trying to harness my perpetually happy, fan-friendly voice.

"Oh my God! I cannot believe it's you!" she said. "You need to talk to my brother! He has this house, and there is some absolutely crazy stuff happening there. It might be on an Indian burial ground or something. I'm telling you, the stuff he talks about makes the places on your show look like nothin'. If you want, I can call him now."

Here we go again, I thought. Nothing was a magnet for people with ghost stories like being the face of a paranormal investigation show. Everywhere I went, someone would approach me with a brother, an uncle, a best friend's uncle's sister's boyfriend who knows this guy who has a haunted house. Apparently, everyone assumed we were looking for locations despite the fact that we had at least four seasons worth of locations already being researched.

"Oh wow, that is really interesting, and I would love to speak with him," I said, trying to sound interested. "It's just that, well, the production company has to go through everything I look into first. I kinda signed my rights away with them. So, unfortunately, my hands are kinda tied on this. But tell your brother to go to the website and submit a request. I'm sure I will be talking to him soon once that happens."

I hated bullshitting people, but I didn't really have a choice anymore. I couldn't be honest with them because that would be the fan who posts something on Twitter, and the next thing you know my whole show would be canceled. Of course, sometimes I thought that the show being canceled might not be such a bad thing at all.

By the time I got back to my choice of rocking chairs in the terminal, I was even more frustrated. No longer hungry, I put the Cheez-Its in my bag. I grabbed my ear buds and turned up some classic jam-band music to relax me. I pulled my University of Tennessee cap down, partially covering my eyes, and said goodbye to the world around me.

I was accustomed to being exhausted. Before TV, when I would work my cases, the emotional level was so intense that it often took me a week of seclusion to recover. Now, life was just as draining, but on a completely different level. It was more mechanical. The crazy hours, endless nights in a hotel, and the constant need to keep up my appearance all took their toll.

As the music took over, I thought back to the girl at the shop. I was simply too beat and too tired to really even entertain a conversation with her. That fact annoyed me. I loved the paranormal world. I loved the history. I loved the way everything was intertwined. The show was none of that. On the last recording alone, we spent days filming one of the most haunted locations in Seattle, but the TV approach wasn't real. We were not there to help someone. We were not there to really understand everything that had happened. Sure, there were some shadows there, and it certainly was haunted, but everything we did was just so removed from my normal approach.

I began to realize how much I missed my pre-TV life. There was something fulfilling about working with real people, helping them understand and appreciate the history and helping them to eventually put their hauntings at bay. If I wasn't so tired, I might have gotten up and gone back to talk to her further.

After an hour of shallow sleep, my phone jolted me awake with an alert that my plane was finally going to board. It was time to stop thinking about that crap. I was finally going home! It was time to recapture my life.

TEN HOURS LATER, I was nearing my home. Fortunately, I'd been able to sleep through the entire flight. Though I was still exhausted, I was awake enough to drive. With every passing mile, I felt more alive. As I navigated my old pick-up through the mountain hollers, I had to keep reminding myself that I hadn't driven in a month and should proceed with a bit of caution. It was hard. I was finally home, and navigating these backroads was the surest sign of my arrival.

As I headed into Erwin, I decided I might as well stop by the post office and pick up the mail that must have piled up in my absence. Besides, there wasn't a better place to get a dose of local gossip. It would be great to just get some confirmation that this place was indeed still home. I walked inside and spotted Sue Ellen wearing her readers behind the counter. It wasn't until I was about five feet away that she recognized me.

"Well, look what the cat dragged in. If I didn't know better, I would say David is back." She looked at me with some reservation.

"Hi Sue Ellen. What did I miss?" I asked.

"Why, look at you, Mr. Hollywood. What happened to your hair, dear? You look like a damn fool walking in here like that."

I ran my hand through my hair and looked down at my Italian dress shoes against the white industrial tile floor. The show's production company had convinced me to change my look a bit. I had gone on a massive diet and training plan. They'd purchased my clothes without my input. My hair—which I'd never paid any attention to—was now dyed and styled.

"Yeah, well, I'm home now for awhile," I said. "This will disappear soon enough."

"Good thing if you ask me. Bad enough they're fixin' to put in one of those Starbucks over across the tracks but then to have you running around looking like Hollywood is too much." She turned and yelled across the room. "Greg, can you fetch David's mail, hon?" Then she turned back to me. "I don't suppose you have talked to Mel, have you?"

"No, I haven't talked to too many folks. I...hell, I haven't heard from her since she married Austin years back."

"Oh dear, what a mess that turned out to be." She shook her head sadly. "I always knew that boy was up to no good. He had that poor girl move away, and then he left her. Damn shame, him leaving her after uprooting her from her family. She was back here not long ago, living with her mom up on

Banner Hill. Last I heard she was getting back on her feet and moving over to Roan somewhere, but she came here 'bout a week ago asking about you."

"She was asking about me?" I raised my eyebrow.

"Yes. Seems she was looking for you and didn't know if you had up and moved away or if you were coming back here. I wouldn't worry 'bout it dear, but you probably should give her a call when you get a chance."

"I will definitely look her up," I replied, not knowing if I would or not.

Greg stepped out of the back room and handed me a large plastic bin full of mail. I got a stern warning from Sue Ellen to return the bin and to look like my old self when I did. I loaded the mail in my truck and headed home.

After a couple of miles, I pulled up to my house. I lived in a small brick ranch on the end of a one lane road surrounded by woods. Everything looked to be just as I'd left it. It felt so good to be home. I unlocked the door and wheeled my suitcase inside, leaving it in the middle of the family room. The house smelled a bit musty from being empty. I went through the house, opening the windows to get some fresh air flowing. With no motivation left, I lay down on the couch.

I lay there enjoying the moment. There was something truly intoxicating about being home and being alone in my house. My eyes wandered to the framed newspaper hanging on the wall. It featured the front-page article about my work with Murderous Mary. I thought about how hard I had worked to be successful outside this town. But now, I wondered why. The TV show was what I'd wanted at the time, but the reasons felt so distant.

As my thoughts drifted, a single word appeared in my mind: *Melanie*. There had been a time when Melanie and I were inseparable. It was impossible for me to not smile while I thought back to those school days. That was so long ago and so much changed since then. The more I thought, the more those images became cloudy. I wondered if Melanie had been a catalyst for my wanting to get away from here in the first place.

It seemed a bit ironic that she'd gotten divorced and still didn't look me up until I was on TV and appeared to be very successful. I probably looked like the perfect mark for her. Someone who wouldn't question her motives, blinded by the fact that she was paying attention to me. I wanted so badly to push all thoughts of her out of my head. The couch I had longed for became terribly uncomfortable. I changed positions over and over trying to get comfortable.

I eventually decided I might as well drive back to town and pick up some groceries. If there was anything left in the house, it wouldn't be edible anymore. Either way, I just needed to distract myself from thoughts of Melanie. My first day home shouldn't have been filled with thoughts of what might have been and what never was.

THE NEXT DAY, I headed out to the office, the small building I'd leased out to run my investigations from years ago. Despite not actively working in that capacity after starting with the show, I kept the lease...just in case. As I unlocked the glass front door and walked in, it was clear that in my absence Linda had taken over decorating duties. The previously dingy, fluorescent-lit conference room now looked like a Hookah lounge. The beige walls and ceiling were covered with brightly colored fabrics. A set of lamps in the corners had replaced the fluorescents. It wasn't really my look, but it certainly looked better.

Linda had been an associate of mine since the beginning. She wasn't exactly a co-worker or a friend. She possessed a talent set that complemented mine, and we just naturally worked together on cases. When I got the office, I set her up with a space of her own. It seemed logical. When I started the TV thing, I let her have the run of the office so she could continue with her work.

I sighed deeply and rolled my eyes in playful amusement before heading to my office on the far side of the building. Surely my office would still be safe. I opened the door, turned on the lights and set down my box of mail in the corner. The room was small and plain. Stained beige walls surrounded the small window high above the desk. The metal desk with its worn, fake-wood top, was just as I'd left it, cluttered with stacks of papers and books. My giant CRT computer monitor, yellowed with age, blended perfectly with the desk.

Before settling in, there was one more thing I needed to do. After all, I had been gone for a while, and I needed to reassure myself that it was still there. I opened the closet and stooped down to reach the safe on the floor. I quickly dialed in the combination and opened it.

There, right on top, was my Grimoire, safe and sound. The Grimoire, "Münchner Handbuch der Nekromantie," was my most sacred possession. It had been gifted to me by my best friend Jim after I helped him with some nasty spirits. In monetary terms, the book was simply priceless. Most believed it didn't even exist. When Jim found the book, I'd quickly realized that the spells inside were simply too powerful to be available to the public. That was why it resided in my safe and not a museum. Of course, it didn't hurt to have it as a retirement plan in case my television career didn't work out.

Outside of Jim and his wife Kat, no one knew I had the book, not even Linda. Comfortable in seeing it was still present, I shut the safe, spun the dial, and closed the closet. I took a deep breath and sat down on the old fabric office chair behind the desk. I started to thumb through the files of paper with no real purpose. It just felt nice to sit there in the same way I used to. Back then I had so much drive. I'd spent nearly every night in that office feverishly seeking any small nugget of information I could find for a case. Now I was fighting to even remember those days. That passion was gone, and I missed it.

I glanced over to the old phone and answering machine on the corner of my desk and noticed the flashing red light. I pressed the play button and the ancient mini-tape in the machine started to rewind and shift into gear. Soon, the message played, e static in the background making it sound strange.

"Um...hi David. This is Mel. Look, I know it's been awhile, and I don't even know if you check this machine anymore, but I need your help. Please give me a call, and I can explain."

As she gave her number, I feverishly scribbled it down on a Post-it note. It was Melanie. It had been years, but her voice was still unmistakable, even through all the static. I put the Post-it down on my desk and stared at it. Part of me wished I had a newer answering machine with a date stamp, but that was silly. I mean I had what, one message after a whole month of being gone. I pulled out my cell phone and started dialing her number.

With my finger hovering over the call button, I hesitated. I was simply not ready to call her. I saved her number to my phone instead. I wasn't afraid of calling her, but I wanted to know why she was looking for me. I wanted to think she was actually just looking to reconnect with me, but she said she needed my help, and I couldn't imagine what that would be for. It had been years since we even talked. Even if she was going through some stuff, I didn't see how I would be on the top of her list of people to ask for help.

I continued staring at my phone, debating whether or not to call. Before I made up my mind, the jingle of the sleigh bell attached to the door disturbed my thoughts.

"David, my dear, where are you?"

It was Linda. I stood up to exit my office when the door flew open, and she walked in. She wrapped her arms around me.

"I see you redecorated the place Linda," I said, flashing a sarcastic smirk.

"You really didn't think I could keep it like it was. At least I left your office this miserable shade of vanilla." She waved her hand dismissively at my mess of an office. "So, have you decided to leave that TV show behind and come home?"

"What? Nah, I'm just in between taping and post-production with a few weeks off. I figured I would make sure everything is good here."

"David, David, David." She shook her head. "You forget who you're talking to. You really think I can ignore that blatant lie?" She looked at me with sincere concern.

I silently cursed myself for playing coy with her. I knew better than to think that might get by her.

"I'm just beat from the whole damn thing. I want to be myself again for a bit."

"Oh the life of a two-bit paranormal investigator in a one-horse town," she said. "C'mon dear, you were lucky to grab that last paid gig. Without the TV show, you were gonna have to get a real job or something."

"You're right. I just never thought doing this would become one of those jobs. You know, the jobs people sleepwalk through while saving their real lives for when they clock out."

"David, everything has a price. You know that better than anyone. What you don't know is if the price of financial stability is worth the price you are paying. You answer that, you know what to do. Find yourself, find your answer."

2

I WENT home with Linda's voice echoing in my head. I'd sat on the opposite side of the table a thousand times listening to her spew that kind of crap to clients. But now to me? Worst of all, I understood what she was saying. She was right. I needed to find myself and realize what I really wanted to do. I was far better at solving other people's problems than I was at understanding my own.

I fished out the piece of paper where I'd written Melanie's number and just stared at it. I ran through all the possible reasons she may have called, realizing the only way I would get an answer was if I asked her. I took a deep breath and dialed the phone.

After a couple rings, she picked up. "Hello?"

One word was all it took for visions of her to come flooding back into my head.

"Melanie? It's David. I got your message. What's going on?"

"David! Oh my God! I can't believe you called back. I kinda assumed you would never get the message. Look, I really need your help. Um, professionally. There are a lot of weird things going on here, and you were the only one I felt like I could call."

"Wait, like paranormal stuff?" I asked, feeling a bit taken aback.

"Yeah, of course," she said. "Listen, I'm at work and don't really want everyone here knowing about all that. Are you home now?"

"Yup, I'll be home for a few weeks," I replied.

"How about you come meet me so I can talk about this?"

"Uh yeah....sure. When and where?"

"How 'bout you meet me up at the Carvers Gap, where we used to go hiking, tonight around six?"

"Damn, I haven't been up there in forever. Sounds good. I'll see you then!"

"David, thank you," she replied. "You have no idea how much this means to me."

"Don't worry about it. I'll see you tonight." I hung up the phone.

That explanation for the call was not what I'd been expecting; deep down I'd hoped it was something else. *Eh, it's easier this way.*

A few hours later, I started getting ready. After putting on my jeans and hiking boots, I spent almost ten minutes picking out a shirt. I realized I'd spent more time looking in the mirror than I did when getting ready for a recording. I felt foolish. I splashed some water on my face and tried to tell myself not to think about her. This was a gig, nothing more.

Soon, my truck sped out of Erwin en route to Roan Mountain. Despite all the games I was playing in my head, I was excited about this. I used to spend so much time up at the Gap hiking the Appalachian Trail. Simply going up there would be a welcome reprieve from the life I had been leading.

It was a beautiful afternoon. The sun shone brightly across the pavement. After navigating the switchbacks, my truck finally reached Carver's Gap.

Despite the near perfect weather, there were only a few cars up there. It was the highest parking area on the mountain, as well as the trailhead for the Appalachian Trail and various other paths across the mountain balds. I was a little early, so I parked the truck and stepped out. Even there, away from the trail, the fragrance of the rhododendrons in bloom was overwhelming. It was truly a beautiful area.

I made my way to the trailhead of the current Appalachian Trail and entered the canopy of trees surrounding the trail. It always amazed me how the temperature dropped so much in the wooded trails. The sun was blocked out, and it was cool and dark. It was like stepping onto another planet. As I headed up the first part of the inclined trail, I marveled a bit at how easy the walk was. Years earlier, it had been far more taxing for me. I realized that all the work I'd done to get in shape for my on-camera life had its benefits.

With that new-found energy, I didn't want to stop. I wanted to take on the trail. I paused to look at my watch and realized it was time to head back to the parking lot and meet up with Melanie. I took a deep breath as apprehension started to sink in and made my way back.

I slowed my pace as I neared the trailhead. The canopy of trees started to open up, and I began to get a line of sight to the lot. I saw a car parked in the lot that hadn't been there when I'd started on the trail, a black Jeep Wrangler. Melanie leaned against the fender, her long dark brown hair blowing in the breeze. She looked gorgeous.

"Melanie!" I yelled as I clumsily stepped off the trail into the parking lot.

As her name left my mouth, I realized that for all the time I'd spent honing my laid back and suave persona for the TV, I was clearly still the same clumsy odd kid as back in high school. I forced a deep breath to try to harness my more refined persona.

Melanie slowly turned around to face me and a smile appeared on her lips. As clumsy as I was, Melanie was equally cool. Whatever happened, she had always taken it in stride. She was a bit of a tomboy, a jeans and a t-shirt kinda girl, but there was a natural beauty in that. No, she'd never been the prom queen. At the same time I'd always found her to be more beautiful than any prom queen I'd ever seen. Her green eyes had always stood out to me, and on that day it was no different. Of course, I couldn't help but notice her perfect figure. All these years later and even now, the sight of her still took my breath away.

As I neared her Jeep, she walked around it to greet me.

"David! Thank you so much for coming," she said as she greeted me with a hug.

"Like I'm gonna miss an excuse to come up here," I replied.

She looked me up and down cautiously.

"Uh, I didn't mean it like that. It's good to see you, just surprising after so long," I said realizing that didn't sound any better.

"David, it's fine. It has been forever. I get it. I'm just glad you showed up."

Rather than prolonging the awkwardness any longer, I decided I should get to the point. "So what can I help you out with?"

"Shit, I don't know where to begin." She bit her bottom

lip in distress. "Look, the last few years have been a bitch. We'll just leave it at that. Then, I finally got my shit together, finally bought a house. I was standing on my own for the first time in like twenty years, and then this house starts messing with me."

"I'm sorry Melanie. I really am. Tell me about this place."

"It's an old tiny home, but every time I step inside, I feel like someone is watching me. I'm constantly looking around for someone. I'm constantly hearing things. I can't sleep. Hell, I can hardly go back there, but I have nowhere else to go." She put her hands on her head as if she were fighting a headache.

I'd witnessed a lot of different reactions to the supernatural. Some ignore it and pretend like it's nothing. Some get angry. Some start sobbing during our first conversation about it. I knew Melanie, she wouldn't cry. However, it was clear that she was in pain. I put my arms around her in an attempt to comfort her, but her body was rigid.

"Okay, it's alright," I said. "We'll figure this all out."

Looking at her, conflicting feelings washed over me. I knew there'd been a divorce. I saw the strange tattoo of a clock on her wrist. So much had changed since I last saw her, but it was still Melanie. I realized no matter how far we had come in life we were still the same people at our core. That put me in a very difficult spot. She was calling on me for help, but what if her problems had nothing to do with the paranormal? Half the time, people imagined these things in a subconscious attempt to excuse or explain every unresolved issue within their psyche. If that turned out to be the case here, I didn't know if I would be able to tell Melanie that.

"Listen, I want to help you, but you should know upfront I may not be your best choice on this."

"Are you fucking kidding me?" she said, not hiding her annoyance. "What the hell do you mean you're not my best choice? This is your world. I spent days on end listening to you ramble on about this crap. I can't even turn on my TV without seeing you wearing night vision goggles while walking through some old hotel. Now you're back here, and you can't help me?" She turned and started walking back towards her jeep.

"Jesus, Melanie! That is not what I'm saying. I'm here because I want to help you."

She stopped and turned to look at me.

"Then just tell me what you are trying to say....'cause it sounds like you're blowing me off. Just like everyone else has."

"Listen, these things are not always simple. It isn't a matter of throwing some holy water around and being done. It takes time. I am here right now but will be leaving again in a few weeks for post-production. I am only concerned I might not be able to see it through. Not to even mention that no one can know I'm doing this. My contract forbids me from even having this conversation without clearing it through the production company."

I felt horrible saying that. I hadn't lied. They were all true statements. However, my deepest concern was the potential that the problems might not be paranormal at all.

Her eyes softened a little as she thought through what I'd said. "Look, I am sorry. It's just after the last few years, I really needed this house to be a fresh start for me, a chance to let go of the past and start new, but from the moment I moved in... well...it's been a nightmare. I'm getting close to losing it here."

She stepped closer to me. "I get it, you have your life and every-thing else going on. But you're David, the kid I grew up with, the guy I spent countless days and nights with up on this mountain. I don't know. It just felt like if anyone could help me with this, it would be you. I just need someone to be honest with me. There is no point having someone come in there and string me along on this. I can't afford to leave, but I also know that if I do have to leave, you're the one person who would tell me that."

As she said those words I realized just how judgmental I'd been. She needed my help, and I was not being the friend she always had been to me. I was treating her like that woman in the airport.

"You're right," I humbly replied. "I'm sorry, Melanie. I come home from the show, but I guess I don't really let go of being the person on the show. I forget sometimes that here, I need to let go and be me. That isn't right. If you want my help, you got it."

For a few moments, she didn't respond. She just looked at me. After what felt like minutes, she jumped up and wrapped her arms around me. "Thank you!"

For the next half hour she gave me a bunch of completely vague descriptions of what was happening that did little to quell my reservations. It was hard to form an opinion without being in the house and feeling it. Yet, it was good to talk to her. It helped break the ice after the turn the meeting had taken. We agreed that I should take a look at the house itself. We got in our cars, and I followed her down the mountain to her home.

As we descended the mountain, I replayed our meeting in my head. Typically, I didn't get emotionally involved with my cases, at least not at the beginning. I was able to approach them objectively. That was not the case with Melanie.

I replayed the range of emotions and reactions I'd had since receiving her message. Those thoughts unnerved me. She meant something to me. That much was clear. I knew I had to separate those feelings from the case itself. I hoped I would be able to.

After a few minutes, we had made it down the mountain. I followed closely as her Jeep slowed to pull off onto the short gravel drive. The drive led to a set of cabins. She pulled to a stop in front of the second small cabin. The cabins were old but held a certain charm. There was a wide front porch extending across the entire windowed front. It was the image of a cozy mountain cabin.

I parked my truck and got out, looking at the beautiful scenery.

"Wait, you didn't tell me this is where you lived," I said. "Damn, I've been by these places a thousand times. Didn't they used to be vacation rentals?"

"Nobody has vacationed here for a long time. They were owned by a father-son combo for a few years. They kinda trashed the place. Anyway, they came on the market not long ago. Given the size and condition, it was about the only place I could afford without moving back to Erwin full-time with my mom." She paused. "So how does this work? I've seen your show. Do you camp out with a bunch of equipment or something?"

"Hell no! That show, well that isn't what I do. This... this is a little more personal. I'm less concerned with making interesting TV than I am with feeling what this house has to say to me," I replied.

"Well, come on in then, I guess. I'll get you some tea."

She walked up the steps to the porch, waving for me to follow.

Getting my first glimpse of the small cabin, I quickly took in the layout. There was a main room that served as both a kitchen and family room. Of course, no cabin would be complete without a stone fireplace. A small hallway led to the bedroom and bathroom. There was a vaulted ceiling over the main portion of the house, and a loft above the bedroom in the back, creating another space usable for a bedroom.

Whenever I first walked into the location of a supposed haunting, I tried to get a feel for the energy present. Sometimes, it was overwhelming, like a thick fog. Other times it was completely tranquil. This cabin was neither of those extremes. There was certainly some energy present. However, it didn't feel particularly strong or menacing.

Melanie hurried to the kitchen and pulled out a pitcher of tea from the refrigerator. The cabin was clean and neat. There wasn't a speck of clutter. It took me a moment to realize why this stood out to me. Then, I realized that it wasn't just the lack of clutter, but the lack of anything personal. There were no pictures on the walls, no magazines or books on the table. It was sterile, like a vacation cabin, not a home.

"How much time do you spend here?" I asked.

"I try to stay out as much as I can. When I first moved in, I was here all the time, but it's hard. I can't stand being alone here with all this stuff going on. It is completely unnerving to be alone and feel like someone is watching you. Lately, I pretty much only sleep and shower here. Other than that, I'm up on the trails or at work." She poured the tea into two glasses.

"I'm sorry. I didn't realize it was that bad."

She shot me an 'I told you so, asshole' look as she handed me a glass of tea.

"Okay, where in the house is it the worst?"

She casually sat down on the couch and sipped her tea. "It seems to be the worst in the bedroom. I don't even sleep back there anymore. But I don't feel comfortable anywhere in here, if that is what you're asking. This room is tolerable, I guess." She motioned to the pile of blankets and pillows on the couch.

"Okay, what about the loft?" I asked.

She sighed. "Who knows? I haven't had the nerve to go up there since I moved in."

"Do you mind if I have a walk through the place? I'm not going to go too deep. I just wanna see what I can feel in the different rooms."

"You're the expert," she said with a smile. "Have your way with the place."

With some trepidation, I stood up and began to walk through the house.

The bedroom was stark and plain., containing only a queen sized bed and a pair of old dressers. It reminded me of a hotel room when you first check in. Furnished but empty of anything resembling a life. I walked over to the half-open closet. Inside, a pile of folded blankets sat alone on a shelf. There were no clothes, no jackets, not even a box of knickknacks.

More concerning to me was the fact that Melanie claimed that room seemed to be the center point for the activity, and I was not feeling much of anything. I decided to make my way back to the main room. Melanie was sitting on the edge of the couch, nervously swirling the ice around her glass of tea and staring off into space. When I approached, she blinked and jumped slightly.

"So, is it hopeless?" she asked.

"None of this is hopeless. I've been in places far darker than this, and once we figured out what was going on, they became as peaceful as any other home. But we do need to figure it out." I sat down on the couch with her. "Listen Melanie…"

"You won't ever call me Mel like everyone else, will you?" she interjected.

"I never have. Just because I haven't talked to you in forever doesn't mean I'm starting from scratch. You are still Melanie to me." A slight smile crept onto my face.

"You always were a little different," she said now, looking almost cheerful. "Look David. I'm sorry I never tried to keep in touch. Austin would have killed me. Still I should've reached out to you. Anyway, I am sorry. I'm very glad you came out here today. It means a lot to me."

"I'm glad you called," I said uncomfortably. "I hope I can help you out in some way."

As I looked at her, I was pleased to see that she had finally let her guard down. She appeared so vulnerable, her big green eyes staring at me with so much hope. It really reminded me of the Melanie I knew so long ago.

"I think it would be good for me to spend some time here on my own," I said. "Any chance I can come back here tomorrow while you're at work or something?"

"Yeah, I'll throw a key under the mat," she said with a smile. "But let me know what you're up to. I don't think I could handle walking in on one of your creepy investigations."

3

LATER THAT NIGHT, I was sitting on my couch, staring idly at my laptop, my mind elsewhere. Melanie had gotten into my head in a bad way. This was highly unlike me. Sure, there had been women in my life... women who had typically ended up being second on my list of priorities behind my work and research. However, there was something about Melanie. She was the one person I could imagine becoming my priority.

It really wasn't a surprise; it was simply frightening. Truth was that I had always been like this with her. She was that girl that I had always been close to but never had the guts to ask out. I stood idly by, safe within the friend zone, as she dated boy after boy. Then came Austin, the self-proclaimed guitar prodigy who stole her heart. When they got married, we went our separate ways. I thought we had moved on forever. But after seeing her, I'd realized I hadn't moved on so much as I had simply ignored anything I felt for her.

I resisted the urge to dig out my old high school year-book just to read the note she'd written me. I needed to

clear my head. I decided to focus on researching the house.
The first thing I needed to do was to figure out when the
cabin had been built and look through police reports and
newspapers for anything that might have happened on the
property. If that failed to yield any clues, I would have to
research the history of the land where the house now stood.
This was always a last resort as records that far back were
usually scattered at best.

From what I could tell, Melanie's cabin was built in 1915,
along with two other neighboring cabins and a small barn.
It changed hands a few times up until 1956 when it had been
purchased by a man who'd owned and operated the property until fairly recently. If I could track down anyone from
that family, they would likely be a great resource. The big
downside of the property was the fact that for most of its life
it had been a vacation rental. Much like hotels, places like
that could held an immense amount of residual energy,
making it impossible to pinpoint. The story changed from
day to day, week to week, with every new patron.

A standard house was pretty easy. I only needed to
follow the history and the stories of the people that lived
there. Sure, there were always good and bad times, but the
happenings that led to strong energies were pretty easy to
spot. An asshole wife-beating husband, or a kid that tragi-
cally died, or whatever. But with a property like Melanie's,
the story and the people were constantly changing. There
could have been a murder committed by an out of towner
who covered his tracks well, and that would never appear in
any newspaper.

As I thought about it, there was one other hurdle I saw
in researching this case...its location. To some degree, Roan
Mountain was a typical small mountain town. Like most
small towns, Roan had a very insulated feel, and towns like

this tended to be guarded when it came to historical research. Here in Erwin, I could go to the library, the police station, just about anywhere and easily get help from almost anyone, but I had grown up here. Roan... well, Roan, despite how much time I'd spent there, I was an outsider. I was sure that my new found fame would just add to the town's trepidation in assisting me. There would be the constant fear that I was trying to exploit them for my show.

I sat and thought about where I would start. I knew I had to go to the house tomorrow. Hopefully with Melanie not there, I would be able to focus and get a better feel for the place. Beyond that, I was really not sure. I had to get Linda involved. Along with her unique abilities in the field of spiritualism, she was the best resource for small town gossip. Unlike Sue Ellen at the Post Office, Linda didn't share gossip freely, but she absorbed everything. She shared only what she needed to in order to keep everyone else sharing.

I decided to get ready for tomorrow's visit. I went to my closet and pulled out a large plastic case and tossed it on my bed. Unlocking the hinges, I pulled it open and took a look at the contents. My old investigation equipment, secured tightly in foam. I'd never been one to rely on equipment for my research. For me, it was all about what I felt, and backing up those feelings with historical information. However, sometimes I found my feelings to be too easily manipulated, so the equipment helped to back them up.

My rig was pretty simple compared to what I used on TV. I had an EMF meter, a few digital recorders, and a thermal imager. TV.... well that was TV. It wasn't about the history or what I felt. It was all about what we could show the audience as proof. This simple setup was all I needed for Melanie's place.

I inspected the equipment, changed batteries, and made sure everything was ready for tomorrow.

———

THE NEXT MORNING, I arrived at Melanie's house. It was still early, but the sun was shining brightly on the face of the cabin. I walked up to the porch and found the key under the mat along with a Ziploc bag with a piece of paper in it. I opened the bag and took out the paper.

David,

Thank you again for coming out. I really appreciate your help. Send me a text so I know you made it in okay.

- Mel

The attention from Melanie brought a smile to my face. I folded the note and put it in my pocket. Once I was inside the cabin, I texted Melanie as she'd requested.

The cabin was still cool from the night. Everything was silent and still. As I strolled deeper into the house, I realized it looked exactly as it had when I'd left the previous night. That wasn't surprising except for the fact that Melanie lived there. The blankets were still folded near the couch. In the sink were the two glasses we'd used for tea but nothing else. It felt almost as if she'd left the house minutes after I had.

I set my case on the couch and began to unpack it. I took out the digital recorders and started setting them up. I put one in the bedroom, one in the loft, and one on the kitchen counter. Those three would be able to cover the entire house. I got out a clipboard with a notepad on it. I took off my watch and clipped it to the board so I would have a constant visual of it and began to note the time. The most important thing, especially with the audio recordings, was to log everything I did and the exact time. If I walked across the room, I had to note it. If I sneezed, I had to note it. If I didn't, it would be impossible to review the audio recordings and make a distinction between subtle noises I'd made versus something else.

I got my thermal imager and slowly walked through the house, taking a cursory scan and logging the time and temperature of each area. I wanted a baseline to compare any anomalies with later. Finally, I did the same with the EMF meter. The process took about an hour, and during that time I didn't see any reading that caused me any concern. With my baselines complete, I could focus on the energy I felt in the house itself.

It was proving to be more difficult than ever. In most cases, I never had to focus. I didn't have to work at feeling things at all. I just felt them. It wasn't that I couldn't feel them now. It was more that I was thinking about Melanie. I couldn't clear thoughts of her out of my head enough to feel the house. After sitting on the couch for a few minutes, I got fed up. I logged my departure on the clipboard and walked straight to my truck. I opened the glove box and started going through the mess of its contents before pulling out an old smashed box of cigarettes.

I hadn't smoked in at least a year, but I needed something to clear my head. As I lit the cigarette and inhaled the stale smoke, I burst into a fit of coughing. I immediately felt a chill come over my body, while hot streams of sweat ran down my forehead. It was clear that my body had moved on from smoking despite my assumption that it would help me relax. I started to walk around the property, puffing but trying not to inhale the smoke.

The cabin sat nestled in between two identical cabins. The others were a decent distance away but still visible through the trees. The cabin closest to the main road appeared to be empty. There was no 'For Sale' sign to indicate it was available, but the gravel drive was becoming grown over from disuse, leaving the cabin looking forgotten with its curtains drawn tight. I made my way back to the main drive and threw out the cigarette. I walked past Melanie's cabin toward the third when a voice stopped me.

"Whatcha lookin' for there, buddy?" the voice asked in a less than friendly tone.

It took me a moment to place where the voice was coming from until I saw the rocking chair on the porch of the third cabin.

"Sorry, I was just having a look around," I replied.

"Yeah, well the trail and shelters are up the road a piece. This is all private property!"

Despite the warning, I kept walking towards the third cabin.

"Nah, I'm a friend of Melanie's. She asked me to take a look at her place for her." I hoped my calm tone would appease the stranger.

I turned the corner to get a clear view of the cabin unobstructed by the trees. The cabin was an identical twin to Melanie's. The rocking chair on the front porch was occupied by a younger man wearing a white tank top and jeans. He had shaggy brown hair, and it looked like it had been a few days since his last shower. There was a blue Igloo cooler next to the rocking chair, a much more comforting sight than a shotgun sitting on his lap, which I'd expected. I raised my hands in a feeble attempt to show that I meant no intrusion.

"Can't say I know any Melanie. Then again, I can't say anyone has been all that neighborly here," he said in a much calmer voice. "I've actually never met anyone living down here." He stood up and opened up the cooler, retrieving a beer, and walked to the porch's railing. "I s'pose since you're the closest thing I have seen to neighbors, I best give you a beer." He held out the wet can.

"I certainly appreciate it," I said with a sigh of relief.

I walked forward the final few steps, reaching out my hand to accept the beer.

"Name's Zeke," he said as I took the beer.

"David," I replied.

"Who did you say lived there? Melanie? I haven't seen anyone up there except an older guy."

"Well, I know Melanie bought the place about six months back. I guess I'm not the one to comment on the company she keeps." I opened the beer and took a swallow.

"If you don't mind me askin', what exactly are you doing at the place then?" he asked with a suspicious tone returning in his voice.

I cursed myself for not knowing how to answer. It wasn't like I could say I was hunting ghosts.

"Aw well, nothing really. She was having trouble with her window getting stuck and asked me to swing by and help free it up." I hoped he didn't catch me looking at his open windows for inspiration. "Kinda curious though, what do you know about this old guy over there?" I asked both out of genuine interest as well as to change the subject.

"I don't really know anything. Like I said, I haven't exactly met anyone out here except hikers looking for a place to sleep. Just saw him a few times in the upstairs window as I drove by is all." He raised his beer to take a sip and stopped just before the can touched his lips. His hazel eyes bore down on me. "Wait a second, I know you! You're that guy on TV chasing the ghosts, right?"

"You got me." I held my hands up in mock surrender.

"Well, that is me for about half the year. The other half, I'm down here in Erwin."

"No shit. Well, come up here and have a seat. I sure as hell didn't expect a TV star to be wandering up to my place today." He paused. "Hold up. You're not out here looking for ghosts, are ya?"

"Why, you know some?" I asked, trying to play it all off.

"I dunno man, I wouldn't say ghosts, but this place sure is weird."

"I take it, you're not from Roan," I said with a chuckle.

"Nah, I'm from Louisville. I needed to get out of the city and this seemed to be the perfect spot. But then, a couple weeks after I moved in, I lost my dog. Wasn't like he just ran off either, far as I can tell. I went to bed, and the next morning he was just gone. Looked everywhere for that little guy. Set up a bunch of trail cameras and everything. I dunno, I guess I have been less than thrilled about this place since then."

For over an hour, Zeke and I talked and drank. I learned about how he moved here a year ago. How he made his living doing some computer stuff all from in that little cabin. It was really nice to chat with someone. It was something that I hadn't done in a long time.

Our conversation was not without me subtly prying and trying to learn a few things. Despite his belief that there was nothing supernatural happening here, his stories of 'weird things,' as he put them, seemed to paint a different picture. His story about his dog was a concern, but not unheard of in these parts. What worried me more was the man he had seen at Melanie's place. Sure, maybe she was seeing some-one, but it seemed odd that he had only seen him in the upstairs window. Melanie had told me she never went up there.

The fact that he had never seen Melanie at all was concerning in a different way. As I'd noticed, her cabin didn't appear to be occupied. I was beginning to question my own sanity. I began to wonder if Melanie was nothing more than a ghost or a figment of my own imagination. Maybe I was starting to lose it. I pulled the note she wrote me out of my pocket to double check that it was real.

After I finished my beer and said goodbye to Zeke, I picked up my clipboard from my truck and headed back into the still cabin. I decided to walk through the place with the thermal and the EMF meter again to see if there were any substantial changes. I made my way through the house but nothing stood out. As I headed upstairs to the loft, the readings grew higher, but nothing off the charts. As I walked, eyeing the meter, I noticed that the closer I got to the walls, the higher the readings became. The walls of the loft were wooden paneling. In the far side of the room, the ceiling angled downward. The far wall was only about three feet high where it met the sloping ceiling.

The readings continued to rise as I stepped over to the side of the loft. I set the thermal imager down and ran my fingers across the walls until they came to a gap in the paneling. Just as I'd suspected, there was a small room there. I pulled open the door, and when I did, I was hit with a blast of icy cold air. I moved the EMF meter into the room and the readings went off the chart.

As the cold air surrounded me, I could feel the energy rising inside my chest. I took a deep breath and closed my eyes. The energy was strong but not overwhelmingly negative. There wasn't malice or spite, but loss. It wasn't sadness. I didn't sense the loss of a person or lover. It was less emotional than that. It was a loss of something, though. I could feel it in my bones.

"What are you looking for?" I whispered to the dark room.

As the words left my lips, the wave of energy spilled out of me like a geyser. In an instant, the cold and the energy were gone. As if blown by the wind of that energy, the door to the room slammed shut. I was left panting for air. My heart was beating out of my chest. I sat slumped on the floor, needing a minute to recover. At least I knew that I wasn't losing it. There was something there, that much was for sure. I just needed to learn what it was.

After recovering, I stood up and began to pack up my equipment. As I reached for the digital recorder I'd set up in the loft, I hesitated, considering leaving it there. That was me being less concerned about the paranormal and more about wanting some answers from Melanie. A ghost or not, that didn't explain the emptiness of the house or the fact that her next door neighbor, who apparently drinks on the porch all day, had never seen her. I begrudgingly powered the recorder off and brought it downstairs.

I knew it was none of my business, but it bothered me for some reason. The voice in my head turned into a childhood punk that kept telling me that I liked her. So what if I did? It wasn't like she was interested in me. Those thoughts shut the voice up for the time being. I was annoyed with myself. I hurriedly packed up my stuff and left the house.

It was just after three in the afternoon. I decided to head straight to the office in hopes that I could catch Linda there. Just over a half hour later, my truck rolled into the parking lot of my office. Fortunately, Linda's trademark VW beetle was there, complete with the bright blue Coexist bumper sticker on the back. I shook my head looking at it, questioning not only how that old thing still ran but how it even had enough power to make it up the hills around here.

I stormed into the building, anxious to talk to Linda. As I walked through the entry area, the strong smell of burning incense hit me. Linda sat cross-legged on the floor in the corner of the conference room. Her face appeared completely peaceful, and it showed no sign that she even realized I'd walked in.

"Linda, we need to talk," I said in a much harsher tone than I'd intended.

Her head gently turned to the side as she opened her eyes. They bore into me for a moment, not with malice or even concern. I knew immediately what was happening. She was reading me. Linda had an uncanny ability to understand all the emotions a person carried with just one penetrating look.

"David, my dear, what is troubling you?" she asked.

4

I PULLED up a chair and sat down next to Linda. A wave of trepidation ran through me. I'd sat in that room countless times watching Linda read people, and within minutes, their deepest concerns and secrets flowed out of her mouth like a river. But now I was in that seat. My palms began to sweat as she gracefully stood up and sat in the chair across from me.

"How did you become so lost?" she asked.

I stared blankly at her, unable to compose a response. She was right. I was lost.

"Is this about your case, the girl, or the general confusion as to your place in this world?" she asked.

"Stop for a second. I don't need you to rip apart everything going on in my head, Linda." I shifted in my seat, trying to avoid the conversation. "Tell me what you know about Melanie. I am not talking about your feelings or my feelings, or any of that. I need to know what you *know* about her. From the world of gossip."

"David, you know I am not one to gossip," she replied with a look of mock surprise.

"You know just about everything about everyone in this town. Cut the crap and tell me." I was becoming agitated.

"Pretty simple...married, realized her husband was nothing more than a wife beater, divorced, moved out to Roan, but you know all that. Why don't you ask me your real question?"

"Okay, something isn't right about her. I don't know what it is. I spent the morning at her house, but it doesn't seem like she lives there. It doesn't feel like a home. It's more like a hotel room before she even brought in a suitcase. Hell, I talked to her next door neighbor, and he had no clue she even lived there. He thought the place was owned by some old man."

"The old man is the answer you are looking for, David. You know how this goes...but Mel...is a different story. You've spent the last several years of your life solving puzzles, finding the key that unlocks every mystery. Sometimes people are not a puzzle. No amount of research or information will help you understand a person. If you want to understand a person, talk to that person."

We sat there silently as I tried to make sense of what she was saying. Her words swirled around in my head.

"What are you saying?" I finally asked.

"The case is a puzzle. If you are seeking to solve that, treat it like one. How often have you ever cared about the comings and goings of a client? You don't because it has nothing to do with the puzzle you are trying to solve. Mel, she is not a part of the puzzle. Yet you are treating her like she is. Her history, her actions, have nothing to do with that house. Yet, you want to know and understand all of it. Not because it will help you solve the puzzle, but because you are interested in her as a person. The only way you can understand her is by talking to her, not me."

I leaned back in my chair and stared at the purple fabric Linda had draped over the ceiling. It had taken her less than five minutes to rip apart everything that was going through my head. I knew she was right. I leaned forward and again eyed Linda.

"I don't know how to talk to her," I replied.

"Excuses, David. Are you looking for me to spell this all out for you?"

"What do you mean?" I asked.

"Talk to her. Of course, I would say you must first come to terms with the fact that you are interested in her...but we'll take baby steps here. And you *do* know how to talk to her. I know that much. You two were inseparable for how many years?"

"Linda, so much has changed since then," I stated matter-of-factly.

"Excuses again!" she insisted. "Look, you are the same people you were then. Sure, life moved on and put you in different places. If you could talk to her then, you can talk to her now. Now stop making excuses, and just do it."

I rolled my eyes in defiance. I knew she was right, but I was certainly not going to admit it. As if sensing that very fact, she smirked at me and leaned in close, like she was going to tell me a secret.

"Enough of this now. I would have become a high school counselor if I wanted to do this all day. Why don't you tell me about something that really interests me? Tell me what you felt in that house."

I wanted to take a moment and lick my wounds. It wasn't easy to get such blunt advice from someone. Unfortunately, Linda knew I'd experienced something at the cabin. It was time to shift gears and chat with her about it.

"Do you know anything about the cabin?" I asked.

"All I really know is that everything out there tends to be far more than what it seems," she replied, pausing as if she was holding something back. "It is clear your connection with this runs very deep... and I am not talking about any connection you may have to Mel."

I took a deep breath and told Linda everything I knew and everything I'd experienced with the cabin, including my conversation with the neighbor. It was the type of conversation I was used to having with Linda, and it was far more comfortable than my talk with her about Melanie. When I finished, she set her palms down on the table and stared as if she was reading me for a moment.

"Well, you are far from finished there, David," she said.

"Where do you think I should go next?" I asked.

"The same place you do with all of these cases—the history. Unless there is a direct message from the entity in that place, the history is the only thing we can use to piece the clues together."

"I figured as much," I replied with a hint of defeat. "There are typically no shortcuts on these things."

With a lot on my mind, I headed home. There, I grabbed a beer and went out to my back porch. As I sat on the rocking chair, I was surrounded by the sounds of the forest around my house. I silently gazed into the trees as if looking for something to guide me. Never had I been so out of sorts. I certainly had never needed Linda to ground me like that. My life up to that point hadn't been anything particularly spectacular, but I always moved forward with a sense of true direction. I was losing that.

With a deep sigh, I pulled my phone out of my pocket and texted Melanie.

Spent day at your house and observed a bit. Tomorrow I will

be heading to the library to research the history of your property.
If you need anything, give me a call.

I set the phone down on the table and took a long sip of
my beer. Linda's voice replayed in my head, telling me to
talk to Melanie. I knew she was right, but the idea was terri-
fying for no reason I could comprehend. Part of me knew it
was the Melanie I always had talked to, and there was no
reason to worry about it. Then there was the other part. I
felt guilty for many things. It was a small town; everyone
knew Austin was a piece of shit and on bad days would take
his frustrations out on her. Yet I had never been there for
her. I sat ignoring everything because she chose him. Just as
my thoughts began to dive deeper, my phone started to
buzz. Melanie's name appeared on the screen. I took a deep
breath, preparing for the call.

"Hi Melanie," I answered, trying to sound cheerful.

"Hey David, how'd it go today?"

"Oh, pretty interesting. You were right. There is definitely some energy in that house. It seems to be centered in
the loft. I still haven't put together all of my data, but there is
something there for sure. The trick now is figuring out what
and why."

"Um, okay. Look David, I don't really know what that
means. I guess I'm asking, is it safe for me to be there?"

I paused for a second. Part of me wanted to respond with
brash sarcasm, informing her that it didn't matter because
she was never even there. Then, I realized she was trying to
get some peace. I needed to bite my tongue and help her.

"Oh...yeah it's safe. I mean...you may hear some sounds
from time to time, but I have seen nothing to make me think
it's anything malicious."

"Not sure I like the idea of hearing things in the night,"
she replied.

"Hey, I got an idea!" I said with unmistakable enthusiasm. "I don't want to cleanse the house yet since I'm still learning why the spirits are there in the first place, but I could confine them to the loft. That way you can have some peace while I work through this."

"That would be great," she replied.

"I can even do it tonight if you want. We could meet up for dinner somewhere, and then I could come by and confine everything up in the loft."

"That would be really great, actually. Wanna meet me at the BBQ place in downtown Roan at six?"

"I'll see you then!" I said, unable to contain my excitement.

I set my phone down with a smile and took a sip of beer. My eyes fell upon my ridiculously overpriced watch.

"Oh shit!" I yelled to no one.

It was already five, and I was meeting her in an hour, plus I still needed to shower. I stopped for a second, asking myself if this was a date. I didn't know. Either way, I wanted to look my best. That of course brought up the question of what to wear. Did I go Hollywood David, or Erwin David?

I ran into the house and took a quick shower. I ended up splitting the difference on my clothes. I wore a designer pair of jeans and a Columbia buttoned shirt. I looked in the mirror, satisfied with my choice. I ran to the spare bedroom and threw open a bin in the closet, pulling out a couple boxes of sea salt and a smudge stick. I threw them in a backpack and ran outside to my truck. My watch said 5:33 pm. If I drove just fast enough, I would make it.

A gas station was up ahead on my left. I realized I needed to stop and buy some gum. I couldn't believe myself as I pulled over. I hadn't ever worried about my breath, and here I was buying gum like my life depended on it. I was out of my comfort zone in every way possible. Thankfully, everything was moving too quickly for me to overthink my actions.

I pulled into the parking lot of the rustic looking BBQ restaurant right on time. I spotted Melanie's Jeep already parked under the sign, which couldn't be missed thanks to the old lights of a patrol car on top. I checked my hair in the rearview mirror and headed inside.

The place was fairly busy. Inside, the walls were covered in wood paneling, and proud taxidermy trophies adorned the walls. My eyes wandered to the counter where a few people stood in line to order. Melanie must have spotted me a second before I saw her. She stood up and walked towards me.

She looked amazing. Her dark, slightly curly hair fell elegantly on her shoulders. She was dressed casually in jeans and a nicer shirt, but she pulled the look off perfectly as she sauntered up to me. There was a smile on her face. I was just opening my mouth to say 'Hi' when she gave me a hug.

"Thank you again, David," she said, releasing me from her arms.

"I haven't really accomplished anything worthy of thanks yet, but I'll take it," I replied with a smirk.

"Well, why don't we get in line and order?" she asked.

"Sounds good," I said, my attention moving toward the menu board.

"Ribs or pulled pork?" I asked.

"Well, this place is supposed to have the best sandwiches anywhere, but just about any place with a smoker claims that down here."

We ordered our food, went back to the table and sat

down. She eyed me cautiously while swirling her straw in her drink.

"Why are you here David?" she finally asked.

I gave her a puzzled look. "I'm here to help you. Maybe we haven't talked much, but I still consider you a friend. That's just kinda what I do."

"Not here and now. I mean in general. How are you still hanging around these mountains?"

"I dunno," I replied, still unsure of what she was trying to get at. "This is just home."

"Look, before we kinda drifted apart, we were best friends. It's been awhile, but we still know each other, right?" She paused and looked at me with her soft green eyes. "You know what I remember most about you? Well, about us?"

"What?" I replied.

"Both of us wanted to get out of here more than anything in the world. No, we *needed* to get out of here. We plotted, schemed, and dreamed of ways of leaving these small towns behind and starting a new life. We were going to find treasure and leave, never looking back."

"Well, that was a while ago," I replied.

"Of course it was! But you made it!"

She was right. I had made it. Yet, the further I got from home, the more I wanted to come back.

"Look, I get it," she said. "I placed my bet on a guitar player who was gonna make it big, and I lost. So yeah, I'm stuck here for now. But you...you made it. You got out, and yet...here you are."

I looked at her, stunned. I was trying to come up with something to say when I heard a booming voice. "David, your order is ready." I was saved for the moment.

"Hold that thought," I said.

I returned a few moments later with two trays of food and still no clue how to respond.

"Look," she said cautiously, "I didn't mean for it to come out like that and put you on the spot. I just... well, as much as I hoped you would call, part of me was hoping you wouldn't. For you. I just hoped one of us was living out those dreams we had."

"I get it." I said as I grabbed a couple of fries. "You know, I never really thought about it. I guess at some point I stopped dreaming of ways to get out of here and just focused on the day in front of me. On some level, I have kinda been drifting in the wind, I s'pose."

As I spoke those words, a light bulb went off in my head. I wasn't going to say it, but it was her. Those dreams just kinda stopped when she took off with Austin. After she got married, I stopped dreaming of leaving town. Maybe those dreams had been ours together, and they just weren't the same solo.

"You ever stop and consider the fact that you cannot get BBQ like this anywhere else?" I said trying to add some levity to the conversation. "Maybe I'm here because of food like this."

"This place is good, but not that good," she replied, now smiling again. "It's no Ridgewood or anything,"

"I can't tell you why I'm here," I said. "The fact is, I don't know. I fly all over the place and live out of hotels for half the damn year, and it's always nice to be back here. I don't know that it is anything in particular beyond the fact that it's just comfortable."

She nodded in agreement as a large clump of slaw from her sandwich ran down her chin. I grabbed a napkin and gently wiped her face.

"I see you still make a mess of your food," I said.

She took a moment to swallow. "Yeah, well. you're still short!"

"You know, you can still get out of here, too. What's holding you back?"

"Please, like that can happen," she said, waving her hand dismissively.

"Seriously," I replied.

"C'mon, I can barely afford a roof over my head. A roof of a tiny haunted cabin, no less. I never went to college. I could barely hold the shitty job I have. How am I gonna get out of here?"

"To hell with that," I said. "You can do whatever you want. For what you spent on that haunted cabin of yours, you could have gotten a place nearly anywhere. You say your job sucks. Well, so do most of the jobs everywhere you go. Look, I'm just trying to say, nothing is stopping you from getting out of here either."

She shrugged. "I guess I just envisioned being in a different financial situation when I left. Same reason I guess I expected you to bolt out of town as soon as you landed that TV gig. Maybe we are both stuck here. It was all so much simpler back then. Adult life sucks sometimes."

For the first time, I started to see how she'd changed. She was still the same Melanie I'd always known, but now she was lonely. So was I, when I really thought about it. I was lonely when I was on the road longing for home. After being home for a couple weeks, I'd long to get back on the road. I was leading a nomadic existence.

We moved the conversation away from the topic of being trapped in a small town and just enjoyed each other's company. Making jokes, sharing memories, talking about the life we'd shared years ago. It was the most enjoyable time I'd experienced in years.

We finally made it out of the restaurant with our stomachs full and our to-go cups in hand. I followed her to her cabin. Once there, I headed up to the loft while she stayed on the couch. I started by putting a line of salt on the window sills and in front of the door to the attic. I put another line on the top of the stairs and along the entire length of the open wall that looked over the living room.

Once complete, I headed downstairs and lit the smudge stick. I slowly walked from room to room, speaking softly to the spirits, forbidding them from these parts of the house. I extinguished the smudge stick and placed it in a zip-loc bag.

"Okay, at the very least, this should keep the spirit contained to the loft, as long as you, or someone else, doesn't break the line of salt. Any break in it and all bets are off. We will get to cleansing the house later. For now, I need to understand it better."

"Wait, so you're saying that all this activity will be trapped up in the loft, and thus will be more powerful?" she asked.

"Well, I suppose that is one way of looking at it. I cannot believe they will be thrilled about being stuck up there. So yeah, maybe stay out of the loft for now, but the rest of the house is clear. You should be able to sleep peacefully."

I grabbed my things and started heading towards the door. "Look, it's late. I better let you be. But thank you. It was nice to spend the evening with you again."

"David, wait!" she said as she stood up and walked towards me. "I should be the one thanking you."

Catching me completely off guard, she wrapped her arms around me, giving me a hug. Impulsively I wrapped my arms around her as well, dropping my backpack. Without even the slightest thought, I kissed her.

5

I COULD TASTE her lips on mine the entire drive home. Her taste, her smell...it was intoxicating. The kiss only lasted for moments, but it was overwhelming. I spent far too much time cursing myself for not staying longer and making the most of the night. Deep inside though, I knew I couldn't. I needed to savor every moment with Melanie. I'd waited nearly twenty years for that kiss.

Despite the ecstasy of that moment, it also raised a whole slew of questions I couldn't begin to answer. Did it mean we were dating? Should I be texting her constantly? I had no clue how to move forward with her. Give me a haunted house, and I could take care of shit like no one else. Give me a relationship to navigate, and I needed a roadmap.

There were still countless unanswered questions about her house, but I couldn't take my mind off her for long enough to focus on that. At the end of the day, I chose to simply send her one text before heading off to bed.

Thank you for an incredible night!

Sleep overtook me before she responded.

I woke up to a simple winky face response. Like I had

any hope of understanding what was really implied by that. Still, I knew I had to respond.

Heading to library today. I'll let you know if I find anything, I sent back.

I got cleaned up and packed my backpack. Soon, I was on the road to the Roan Library, only stopping for a couple energy drinks along the way. I pulled into the sleepy, nondescript one-story building that housed the library. There was only one other car in the parking lot, but given the fact that it was the middle of the week, it wasn't much of a surprise. When I walked in, the library was absolutely silent and the familiar scent of musty books hung in the air.

"How can I help you this morning?" a voice said.

My gaze moved over to the front desk where a middle-aged woman sat amidst a pile of books, a stamp in her hand.

"Hi, I'm doing some research on a house in the area. Where could I find the local archives?" I replied as cheerfully as I could manage.

The woman paused and looked at me, her eyes inspecting every inch of me.

"How far back you looking to go?" she asked, with a slightly cheery voice.

"Starting in the early 20th century, up through the mid 1990s."

"You'll find everything we have in the far back corner. Property records, newspapers, etc. But sadly, I don't see many people like you going through that stuff, so nothing is digitized. If you need any help at all, please let me know."

"It shouldn't be a problem. Thank you for your help," I replied as I headed to the back of the library.

I decided I would start with the most recent set of ownership records, knowing that would give me the best hope of finding someone I could speak to in person. After poring through papers and documents, it was proving to be difficult. One family owned the property from 1956 on. Unfortunately, there was no documentation on their sale of the property. While I had the family name, a search on the internet proved to be a complete black hole...as if that family had disappeared.

Feeling frustrated, I decided to go back to the beginning and work my way forward. At least there, I had a bit of a paper trail to follow. I learned that the cabin was built in 1915 by a Johan Sellmer. Sellmer was apparently a bit of a real estate investor back then. Not only did he build those cabins, but he also built a number of houses in Roan and neighboring communities between 1915 and 1923. By then, the cabins were all used as a rental property, and most of the houses he built were sold immediately.

Following his death in 1947, the cabins were sold off by his son William. The younger Sellmer was born in 1918 and was married with three children by the time he sold off the cabins. His oldest son, John, would have been about ten years old at the time. As luck would have it, it appeared John was still alive. Subsequent research showed him living in a small local retirement home. As this was the best lead I had so far, I figured I should follow it.

I packed up my things and bid the librarian a farewell as I stepped out into the hot day. The retirement home was only a couple miles away. I was starving but anxious to talk to John Sellmer. I stopped off at a gas station and picked up a couple of Snickers bars, eating one and throwing the second in my backpack.

The retirement home was a small, one-story building. It

looked more like an old apartment complex. I walked into the main entrance. Once in the vestibule, the door was blocked by a glass pane with a hole to speak through and another hole to slide documents through. A young woman in light blue scrubs glanced my way only to say, "Deliveries are made to the dock out back."

"SORRY, no, I'm here to visit a resident," I replied.

"Who are you visiting?" she asked.

"John Sellmer."

"Family?"

"Uh no. I'm looking to speak with him about some property he used to own," I replied sheepishly.

"I'm sorry sir. If you are not family, you need to be registered and approved by the resident," she said with a matter of fact tone.

"I'm sorry, Susan," I said reading her name badge. "Believe me, I understand protocols and completely respect that. It's just, I don't know how to reach him any other way. Would it be possible for me to give you my name and the nature of my visit so you can see if he would be willing to meet with me?"

She looked at me, a slight smile on her face. "You know, John doesn't get many visitors. It would probably do him some good. Let me go ask, as long as you promise not to upset him."

I wrote my information on a slip of paper and gave it to her, hoping she wouldn't recognize my name from that damn TV show. I sat in a plastic chair, feeling restless.

A few minutes later, Susan returned. "David? John agreed to see you. Please come this way."

After being buzzed through the main door, Susan led me down the wide beige hall which smelled like urine. We passed a recreation room of sorts. Glass windows surrounded the small lounge where a handful or residents slept or watched soap operas. A few doors later, we reached John's room. He sat in a recliner near the window. His gray hair was neatly combed. He was wearing khaki slacks and a sweater. Clear tubes ran from his nose down to the beat up green oxygen tank next to the chair.

"Hi, John. Thank you for seeing me." I extended my hand to him.

He didn't reach for my hand. He looked at me for a moment and then over to Susan. He nodded to her as if to tell her to leave. She nodded in reply and walked out.

"David, is it?" he asked in a gruff voice. "Shut the damn door and then come sit down."

I did as he said and sat down on the chair across from him.

"Let's get a few things straight," he said. "I don't know you. Yet, you seem to want some information from me. So, I assume you will be compensating me for my time."

"Uh, well I suppose that depends on how much money you want."

"I don't want your money. Money does me no good in here. You want me to talk, you will bring me things I can't get on my own."

"Okay, what do you want?" I asked with some hesitation.

"Well, I would say cigarettes and women, but I will just get caught with those. I don't s'pose you have any whiskey in that bag of yours."

"Uh no, sorry. I don't." I considered how I could appease him. "I do have this." I pulled the Snickers bar out of my bag and offered it to him.

John eyed the plastic wrapped candy bar.

"That will do, but if you need to come back here for another visit, I expect whiskey."

I handed him the candy bar. He quickly hid it in the side pocket of his slacks.

"What would you like to bug me about?" he asked.

"I was wondering if you knew anything about the three cabins your father used to own."

He sighed and looked at me for a long moment as he scratched his chin. "Ahhh, the rental cabins. Well shit, I was just a boy when my dad got rid of them. Damn shame too. He was sitting on a gold mine there with three cabins completely paid for on the edge of the National Forest."

"So, you do remember them," I replied, trying to coax more from him.

"Yeah, I remember them. We stayed there every summer. Well, until my grandad passed. I always loved that place, but my dad was too short-sighted. I look back at all the money we could have made by keeping them and renting them out. My dad, well, he didn't care about that. He hated that place."

John went on to talk about how his dad had only went there because his mom wanted the family to. After his grandpa passed, his dad had listed them for sale within a week of his passing. There was certainly something about his father's revulsion of the property. Yet, it was also clear that John never understood it.

"Those cabins were my Grandad's pride and joy. He built a lot of houses, but those were the only ones he hung onto. Used to talk constantly 'bout how he built them with his own two hands. He talked about how it took him a month to haul the wood for them down the mountain until he had enough to build them. He designed them himself. He truly loved them."

"I'm sorry, did you say he hauled the wood down the mountain?" I asked.

"Oh, hell yes! There was some place up on top of the mountain that was being torn down. He bought all the wood for next to nothing. The only catch was that he had to get it all down the mountain... no small task back then."

As he spoke, I could feel the hairs on the back of my neck stand up. I didn't need to ask another question. I knew without a doubt where that wood came from. 1915 would have been only about five years after the Cloudland Hotel closed its doors. That was the only considerable construction up on that mountain.

I'd always felt connected to Cloudland. One of my first cases involved a possessed table from the Cloudland dining room. Then, we uncovered the sinister plots of murder involving the KGC, which manifested in the nastiest case of possession I'd ever witnessed. Thankfully, I was able to vanquish those demons and cleanse a Chicago mansion owned by my friends Jim and Kat. Yet, it was still a surprise to realize, once again, I would be battling the demons of Cloudland.

John continued to speak, although I'd stopped listening to much of what he was saying. I was consumed with thoughts of this new revelation. Soon, there was a knock at the door followed by Susan entering the room.

"I'm sorry John, but David really needs to be leaving," she said sweetly.

John sighed. "Yes sweetheart. Look David, if you decide you need some more information about that place, let me know. You are always welcome here." He smirked as his hand patted the pocket where my Snickers bar now resided.

I FELT giddy as I stepped out of the retirement home. That was a bigger break in the case than I'd ever anticipated. I took out my phone and texted Melanie. *Got a big break with some information on your house. Would you mind if I swung by and checked out a couple of things?*

I started up my truck and blasted the AC as my phone buzzed with her reply.

Sure, but I was hoping you would wait for me to be there. ;)

How about we meet up tonight then. Maybe up at the Gap. We could get to the bald before sunset, I replied.

6, you bring the beer :), her last text read.

I headed straight to her cabin. Her key was tucked under the mat, and I let myself in. As I set my case of gear on her couch, I realized that I still hadn't analyzed any of the audio from yesterday. I was getting behind, but I felt so close that I had to continue with my current line of investigation. I could analyze the audio later. I took out my thermal imager and flashlight. I headed up to the loft.

Taking care to not disturb the line of salt, I entered the loft. I turned on the light and slowly padded across the room. Immediately, I realized something was different. My eyes scanned the room trying to place it. Then, I spotted it. There was a stack of blankets and a pillow in the corner of the loft. I knew those had not been there the day before. Confused, I walked back downstairs and looked next to the couch. The blankets that had been there before were gone.

"Did she sleep up there after I sealed it off?" I said to myself.

The conversation with her the day before ran through my head. It was Melanie who made the observation that, with the rest of the house sealed off, the presence may be more concentrated in the loft than before. I felt a hard pit forming in my stomach. There was something not right about all of this. I was concerned. I realized I needed to talk to Melanie. Unable to do that now, I headed back to the loft.

I gently brushed away the line of salt in front of the attic door so that I could open it. As I did, I felt the temperature drop. Nervously, I unlatched and opened the door. I got down on my knees and crawled inside. I could see my breath in front of me as I entered.

I turned on my flashlight and scanned the interior. Thankfully, the attic was empty. As I looked closer, I saw what looked like writing on the timbers. The timber closest to me was covered with signatures. Some were dated. The dates were all between 1890 and 1908. I couldn't place why they were there. It was almost as if visitors to Cloudland had all signed their names. I moved the flashlight to the next beam. It was more of the same.

I decided to use my thermal imager. As I scanned the attic, it mostly displayed bright blue, showing the frigid temperature. Then, as I moved it along the beams, it showed a bright pinpoint of red. I stopped and moved to bring the imager closer. As I did, the point of red started to move. There, on the screen of my imager, I saw a slow gentle motion of a signature writing itself. When it was done, a single name shown in bright red. I moved the flashlight to illuminate the beam behind the imager. The name 'Robert Mason' was clearly visible.

The image took my breath away. All of a sudden I was dizzy. The attic started to spin around me. In a flash, I saw the attic door slowly closing. I closed my eyes and shook my head violently, trying to get my bearings. As I opened my eyes, I saw a sliver of light from the door and dove for it. I shoved myself through just before the door slammed shut.

I took a deep breath and slowly crawled out of the attic. I spun, shut the door, and latched it behind me. Without even taking another breath, I moved to brush the line of salt back in place once again, trying to keep whatever was in the attic from getting out. I lay on the floor, exhausted from the encounter. The name Robert Mason shot into my head again. It was one name I didn't need to research. I knew exactly who Robert was.

Robert Mason was a member of the KGC or Knights of the Golden Circle. No, he wasn't just a member, he was a leader. He was one of five people known as the Sovereign Lords. I didn't know many details about him aside from his position. I did know that my last run-in with one of these Lords, Samuel, was one I didn't care to relive.

Samuel, as it turned out, was as much of an asshole in spirit form as he'd been in real life. I could only hope that Robert would be a much nicer spirit. Samuel's spirit had nearly killed my friend Jim in an epic supernatural show-down at his mansion, with me standing nearby. While the experience ended in the best outcome possible and brought me much success in life, it was also an experience I didn't want to repeat.

My mind immediately turned to Melanie. Despite my initial feeling that the energy in her home wasn't malicious, knowing who was the cause of it made me rethink that. To make matters worse, I cared about her. As much as I'd initially tried to separate my feelings for her from the case, she was far more than a client to me. I was concerned for her safety.

I glanced at the pile of blankets in the loft, and it unsettled me. I needed to warn her. I needed to make sure she was aware of what we were dealing with.

6

My truck tires screeched as I skidded to a stop in front of my office. I stormed inside, seeing Linda in some meditation pose in the conference room.

"You think you could've fucking told me my connection was another damn Cloudland case!" I shouted.

"Breathe, my dear David," she said as she stood up and walked toward me.

"How many cases am I gonna have featuring these damn Sovereign Lords?"

"Well, by my math you only have two more after this." The sarcasm in her voice was as thick as the smoke in the room. "You are connected to them. There is something drawing these to you. All is connected, nothing by accident." She was even more zen-like than normal.

"Yeah, yeah. I get it. But Melanie? Really? I can't get her involved in this. What if this one turns out like Sam?"

"What makes you think you have any control over her involvement? So far no one has chosen to be connected to them. Yet, they all have been."

"Just stop!" I snapped at her. "I just wish you would have given me a heads up is all."

"David, you know as well as I do, I didn't know what your connection was. But now, your concern...that is much clearer to me." She gently put her hand on my shoulder. "Please listen. You need to separate your feelings for Melanie from this case. Yes, your feelings for her are strong, but you must draw a line. You must understand that her being involved is beyond your control. You are not there to keep her from this. That die is cast. You are there to help finish things."

I let out a deep sigh. "Dammit, Linda. You're right, I know that. I just wish you weren't sometimes."

"And David...I am glad you have decided to explore the possibilities with her. You both deserve that."

"Jeez, is it that obvious?" I asked.

"Let's just say that there is an aura around you I've never seen before." She smiled and gave me a hug.

I walked out and back to my truck. Having a clairvoyant as the only person to turn to was difficult at times, especially when it came to relationships. I hated how she saw right through me while still unable to really offer direct advice. In the end, it felt like she oozed common sense. Yet, so often, that was exactly what I needed.

On my way to meet Melanie, I stopped off at a liquor store to pick up some beer. Walking through the store, a display of Jefferson's Small Batch Whiskey caught my eye, and I picked up a bottle. I stashed the paper-wrapped bottle in my backpack and headed for a quick stop at the retirement home. This time, I had no issue getting to John's room.

"You know I'm not saying a word until I'm paid." John said.

Looking over my shoulder to make sure no one was around, I retrieved the paper bag and put it in his hand.

"That's more like it," he said. "With that, what would you like to know now?"

"Absolutely nothing," I said with a large smile. "I just felt like I should repay you for the last time we talked. Enjoy!"

Without another word, I turned and left.

I made it to the Gap about ten minutes early. The day was hot. I could feel the heat radiating off of the blacktop parking lot. I opened the gate of my truck and sat down, pulling a beer out of the cooler in the back. I observed the people coming and going. A family was taking their photo in front of the National Forest sign. It was a few peaceful minutes for me to try and collect my thoughts. As I closed my eyes, the bright sun bled through my eyelids, and I could see Robert Mason's signature slowly appear and burn into my mind. My eyes snapped open, and I shook my head to hit reset. As my eyes adjusted to the bright sunlight, I spotted Melanie standing in front of me.

"Wake up!" she yelled.

I jumped, startled at the sight of her. I'd only closed my eyes for a second. She walked up and took my hand as I jumped off the back of my truck. She pulled me straight into her arms and greeted me with a quick kiss. The show of affection was amazing but also left me unsure of how to respond.

"If I knew that was how you were going to greet me, I would've tried to meet you this morning," I said, smiling.

She stepped to the side and grabbed my open beer from the truck. She took a swallow and turned away, walking towards the trail head.

"So are we doing this or just sitting in your truck?" she asked looking over her shoulder at me.

"Hang on, I'm coming!" I quickly threw some beers in my backpack and hurried to catch up to her.

From the trail head, it was just over a half mile trek until the canopy gave way to the bald of the mountain. The canopy provided a respite from the heat of the day. As we walked, I started to explain the basics of what I'd learned at the retirement home. She seemed to be genuinely interested. Unfortunately, while hiking, I was behind her and unable to really gauge her reactions. Also, my mind had started to drift elsewhere.

While behind her something caught my eye. On here orange backpack was a small, one-inch pin. It was black with a white drawing of an eagle skeleton on it. I immediately recognized it. I'd given it to her years ago.

About midway through the hike, the trail passed a large boulder. She stopped, seemingly to check and make sure I was keeping up. She leaned playfully against the rock, shaking the empty beer bottle.

"I think it's time for a refill," she said, biting her lower lip.

"Funny, considering you took my drink."

I took her empty bottle and replaced it with a new one.

"So, if you learned everything from that guy, why'd you return to my place?"

"I wanted to see if I could pinpoint the energy to the actual structure before I go jumping down the Cloudland rabbit hole." I took a swallow from my own beer.

"Well, Cloudland is waiting. Let's get up there." Without another word, she started hiking again.

I couldn't help but feel like she was leading me like a little puppy. Although it would've been a lie if I said I didn't enjoy it.

As we neared the end of the tree-covered section of the

trail, I felt conflicted about where to take the conversation. I wanted more than anything to bring up the fact that I'd noticed she was clearly not living at the house. Yet, I was having fun with her. I knew bringing it up had the potential of derailing the light-hearted nature of the walk. For the moment, I remained silent.

As we exited the canopy, the beauty of the mountain opened up. It was always an awe-inspiring vantage point. She led me along the trail to the crest of the hill.

"Why so quiet? Too much of a hike for the city boy?" She smirked as she looked back at me.

"Oh please. You think just because it's been years, I can't still out-hike you?"

"Based on what I'm seeing, I think you're working far harder than I am."

As we reached the crest of the mountain, there was a spot where the lush grass gave way to rocks. We stopped at an uncovered rock and sat down.

We sat silently for minutes, observing the world from that peaked vantage point. I put my arm around her, and she shimmied closer to my side.

"You remember the last time we were up here together?" she asked.

Of course I remembered that night. That was the last evening I'd spent with her. It was just after she'd gotten engaged to Austin.

"Yeah, I certainly do." I paused for a moment, unsure of where to go next. "No offense, but I like this hike much better."

"This may sound silly," she said, reaching over to her backpack, "but that night you gave me this."

She pointed to the pin on her backpack. The tiny pin was scratched and worn.

"Yeah I remember that. I can't believe you still have it!"

"This was your most prized possession! You spent forever trying to find this on eBay. It was from some band that played on the Warped Tour, but only overseas. Then you gave it to me. I still know nothing about the band or what the pin was, but it has been with me ever since. It has been my link to you."

I couldn't help but smile. Looking back on it, maybe it was silly. I had given it to her while saying something about it being a symbol of my always being there for her. I hadn't thought about it in years, but seeing it now, I realized just how much she took those words to heart.

"Well first off, it isn't just some band. It's the pin of Die Toten Hosen who did perform on the European and Australian leg of the Warped Tour. But yeah, I gave it to you hoping you wouldn't forget about me. I'm surprised to see it again. I thought we'd drifted too far apart."

We did... well I did. Look... I've made a lot of mistakes. I'm sure you know the rumors about Austin and me. None of that is ever what I wanted. It's taken me a long time to get away from him and finally start to pull my life together. I guess I just wanted to say that I never forgot who we were back then. The fact that you are here shows me you haven't forgotten either. I'm just thankful that we could be here again together."

She was right, we had both come a long way since then, but we were still the same people. As much as I wanted to dive headfirst into these memories, I needed to clear the air first.

"So... I got a question for you, something that has been nagging at me since I was at your house." My heart sped up as the words left my mouth.

"Go ahead."

"I couldn't help but notice that it doesn't really seem like you're living in the cabin." I could see her smile fading. "So, what's the deal with that? I mean, I ran into your neighbor, and he had never even seen you."

She took another sip of beer and set it down with a sigh.

"Sorry," I said trying to retreat. "It's none of my business. Forget it."

The few seconds of silence before she spoke felt like an eternity.

"I haven't really moved in. I'll give you that. Most of my stuff is still stored at my mom's. It's just that when I first moved in, it was so uncomfortable. The combo of being alone for the first time in years and then this ghost or whatever...I just never felt like I could stay there."

"I get it, Melanie." I squeezed my arm around her a little tighter. I still wondered where she was living, since it wasn't her cabin, but didn't push for more information.

"What about you?" she asked, clearly ready to change the subject. "How the hell did you end up on TV?"

"I don't know. I just kinda fell into it. I mean, after I got the press coverage for putting the ghost of Murderous Mary to rest, I started getting contacted left and right. I didn't know it, but there were enough people around here dealing with hauntings for me to do it full time. Then came Jim's estate in Chicago. I had no idea what I was getting into there, but apparently the right people learned about it, and next thing I knew I had a production company calling me."

She turned to face me. The right side of her mouth curved up slightly into the cute smile I remembered. "Tell me about this place in Chicago."

I retold the story of Jim and his inherited mansion, and the hauntings that went on there. I spoke about how Jim ended up being the reincarnated son of the estate's original owner.

"It was the most intense, yet rewarding, experience I've ever gone through," I said.

"So, do you like the show?" she asked.

"I have kinda a love hate relationship with it. I mean, the money is great! So is the freedom to do whatever, when I'm not working. The show itself is really the opposite of what I want to do. Like your house, for me it isn't about experiencing the fact that something is there. It's about understanding why and how I can help free whatever is stuck there. In the show, there is no history, no story. It's whatever can be done to get compelling video footage."

"Well, since you brought up my house...I know you said it was built from Cloudland wood, but so what? What does that fact really mean?"

"That's what troubles me. Cloudland alone is nothing. I mean, in reality, it was an amazing place and, historically speaking, it should be remembered in that light."

"Ohhhh...I feel a but coming here." She smirked at me.

"Yeah, for sure. Cloudland has been tainted by a few really shitty people that spent a lot of time there."

"Wait! Are you telling me my house is connected to the KGC?" She stood up. I couldn't tell if she was just anxious or excited. "After all of those wild treasure hunts for KGC gold you dragged me on when we were kids, how do I end up living in a house connected to them?"

I stood up with her. Her eyes were wide as she fidgeted with her hands. I told her about what happened when I went back to the house earlier that day, about the name I'd seen and who he was.

"This is a clue to the treasure, isn't it?" she asked.

"Wait a second! I wouldn't go that far. Yes, Cloudland's

history is intertwined with the KGC. But that certainly doesn't mean anything in relation to treasure.

"Oh c'mon. If you taught me anything it is that any visible connection to the KGC is meant to be a clue."

"All I know is that for some reason Robert is stuck there. It could be treasure, I suppose, or something completely different."

"So now, we have to find out why he is there?"

"That is certainly the plan."

I was so enthralled in the conversation I failed to realize that the sun was now starting to set. I looked out over the horizon as the sun painted the mountainside in fiery red and orange light. Melanie noticed my gaze and looked back at me.

"You know, being here with you just feels right," she said softly.

I turned to look at her. The reflection of the sunset created a fire in her eyes. Looking at her left me paralyzed. Her hair was being tossed in the breeze. Her face, her soft lips, and her bright eyes were the last thing I saw as I put my arms around her and kissed her. As our lips touched, everything else faded away. There was nothing on top of the mountain at that moment. There was nothing in the world around us. All that existed was us connecting in a way I had never experienced.

The vibrant sunset had given way to a still, blackened-blue horizon. Melanie and I were still locked in our embrace.

"You do realize I'm not letting you run home this time," she whispered.

She took a small hiking tent out of her backpack, and we began setting it up while we still had a tiny amount of light to work with.

"You should have been a scout 'cause you have this preparedness thing taken care of for sure," I joked.

"Let's just say I spend a lot of time up here, and the tent is more attractive than finding my way down the trail in darkness just to get back to a haunted house."

With the tent set up, we bid farewell to the darkened mountaintop as we closed the tent and embraced each other.

SLEEP DID NOT COME for us that night. We lay there holding each other. When we did talk, it was a light-hearted blend of reliving our childhood together and discussing the future that lay before us.

With her head nuzzled in the crook of my arm, her eyes sparkled. My fingertips gently walked across her shoulder.

"You know, it would be a lie if I even tried to pretend I hadn't dreamt of being with you like this forever."

She smiled as I said this.

"It would be a lie if I said I hadn't dreamt of it as well," she replied. Then, her eyes dropped from mine. The smile disappeared. "David, I gotta tell you something."

Here we go. Nothing good could follow a statement like that, I thought.

"What is it?" I asked.

"So, I haven't been completely open with you about all of this...I mean, I haven't lied, but there is more to it that you need to understand."

"About what?"

"Ugh, about the house."

I stayed silent and let her speak.

"You already know that I don't feel comfortable in that

house. What I didn't tell you is that, when I moved in, I started having these super vivid dreams."

"What kind of dreams?"

"I'll get there. I haven't been sleeping in that house. I hardly go there except to shower. I've been sleeping up here, on this mountain. Here, come walk with me please."

She threw on some clothes and then stepped out of the tent. I followed her lead until we were standing hand-in-hand outside the tent on the top of the mountain. There was a silence and stillness in the air. It was dark, but my eyes had adjusted to the darkness. I could actually make out a lot of the landscape by the moonlight.

"Come this way," she said, grabbing my hand.

We walked silently across the mountaintop, eventually stopping on an unidentified area.

"Here, right here," she said. "Let's just say I wasn't at all surprised when you connected the house to Cloudland. Right here was the western edge of the building. It is the exact vantage point from my dreams. Every dream was exactly the same. I would be standing here, looking out over the horizon. But there was something out there, like a spot of light glowing in the distance. I would try to move my head, and I could see a little of the inside of Cloudland. No matter what I did, this glowing spot of light would always be in the distance."

She let go of my hand to point.

"It is out there, I can feel it," she finished.

I stood there in silence, partially because I was trying to take in what she'd said but also because I really didn't know how to respond.

"Look, I know I sound completely insane," she said, "which is why I didn't tell you in the beginning. Maybe I needed to hear you say that there was something there to believe I wasn't crazy. I don't know."

"You are not crazy. This doesn't change anything."

"Are you serious? I just told you I spend every spare moment I have running around this mountain trying to find something I've only seen in a dream, and you can really say I'm not crazy?"

I gently grabbed her shoulders and turned to face her. "You are not crazy. Sure, this isn't exactly a normal thing to do, but you were reacting to what you experienced the best way you knew how. The only thing this changes is the importance of getting to the bottom of it."

"Thank you for not thinking I'm crazy." She kissed me. "Oh, there is one more thing."

"And what might that be?"

"I have been sleeping out here pretty much every night... but last night I slept at home, and not just at home. I slept in the loft." She stared at her feet like a kid caught sneaking cookies. "I know you spent all that time trying to make things safer for me there. I'm sorry, but I had to try."

"What do you mean?"

"When you explained it, how the spirit or whatever would be trapped in the loft, I guess I thought if I slept up there, the dream would change. It might show me more. I have been hiking all over, and I just can't find anything."

"So, I take it your plan didn't work."

"Nope, same dream."

"You know, this stuff is often like a puzzle. Your dream is a great piece, but not the full picture. We have work to do. We need to figure out what will release Robert. Right now we don't even know what is out there to find. For all we know, there is a body out there."

She took a deep breath and looked at me. A few seconds later, I saw the corner of her mouth turn up slightly.

"You promise you will work this through with me?" she asked.

"As long as you don't hold back anymore, then I am on your team."

I wrapped my arms around her and held her close. It felt right. My questions were answered, albeit differently than I would have ever expected. But this was good. Under the blanket of stars, on a still night, with Melanie in my arms, everything felt like it was exactly where it was supposed to be.

"You know, if I'm not allowed to hold back anymore, that might be a problem for you," she whispered with her head buried into my chest.

"How's that?"

"See, I'm pretty sure I wore you out once already tonight. I don't know if you can handle me not holding back."

I laughed. "I really don't think you need to worry about that one bit."

She moved to kiss me slowly on my neck. Her hand slowly grazed down my chest. At that moment, she had me completely under her control. I ran my fingers through her hair and leaned in to kiss the top of her head. She responded by forcefully pushing me away. Confused, I looked at her to see her smile turn sultry.

"Then, you better get that ass of yours back to the tent and prove it."

She grabbed my hand and led me across the mountaintop to where her tent was waiting for us.

7

As AMAZING as it was to wake up with the sun rising over the mountaintop and Melanie in my arms, it quickly turned disheartening. The abruptness of her needing to get ready for work and having to hike a couple miles was jarring. The next thing I knew, I was pulling into my driveway. I was glowing from the night before but also exhausted.

I was too keyed up to sleep. So, I sat there unsure of what to do. I pulled out my laptop and began to research Cloudland. To some extent, I was already an expert on its history. Everything I knew was more about the essence of the hotel... the history and the people. Now, I wanted to learn more about the location. If Melanie was seeing a vantage from the building itself in her dreams, I needed to know what that was and, more importantly, what lay in the distance from that view.

I slammed the laptop shut as I realized I had all the materials I needed at the office. When I'd researched the table from the Cloudland dining room years ago, I had come across an old set of plans for the building. I needed to see them now. There was an urgency rising in my chest as I drove to the office.

It was a relief that Linda wasn't there that early. I went to my back office and started digging through the pile of boxes until I found the plans I was looking for. I brought them into what remained of the conference room and spread them out on the floor. Melanie had mentioned the western edge of the building, giving me a starting reference point.

According to the blueprints, the hotel was three stories tall. The western edge was massive. That didn't narrow things down too much, but it was a start. I could see that the first floor was split in half. On one side was the lobby, along with dining and sitting areas for guests. The other half was the kitchen and rooms for the staff. The second and third floors were all guest rooms. Assuming I was looking for a guest room, I started scanning the second floor of the building. I realized almost immediately that what I was looking for was not on the second floor. Those were all standard guest areas. Small rooms with shared bathrooms throughout the entire floor.

I moved on to the third floor. This floor was much more interesting. Here, the northern half contained standard sized rooms just like on the second floor. However, the southern half was comprised of much larger suites... suites appearing to contain private sitting rooms. Additionally, there was a massive library off these suites.

If Robert was staying here with his buddies, surely it would be in this area, I thought.

On the western edge was one massive room with a private bath and sitting room. I figured that had to be what I was looking for. Robert would have been staying in one of those rooms, and the view of that one room appeared to align with Melanie's dreams. If that was the room, then I needed to know what Melanie was seeing on the horizon. Pondering that for a moment, I realized I needed to match it up with a map. I rummaged through the box until I pulled out a topographical map with the footprint of the hotel on it. I needed to match that up to a more expansive and modern map.

I sighed at my realization because it meant I'd have to pay another visit to the Roan library. That was where my energy ran dry. I packed up the plans and brought them back to my office. I settled into the chair, which still fit me like a glove, and I drifted off.

I was jarred awake at the sound of the sleigh bells on the door. Opening my eyes, I saw Linda sway into the hallway.

"Did you come back for more of my advice, dear... or did you figure this out and start working the case?" she asked as she opened the door across the hall.

"I'm good, thanks," I called back. "I don't need another dose of you reading me."

"Don't be mad at me. You know I have a gift. When someone is in need, I share. Believe me David, you were more in need than anyone I'd seen in a long time."

"Stop. Just come in here and talk... but don't read me again. You know that shit freaks me out when I'm not on the other side of the table."

She stepped in and sat down in front of my desk. Her eyes moved up and down, looking at me. A large smirk appeared on her face. "Okay, so just so I understand... You want to talk to me, but you want me to ignore the fact that I can see you had a very interesting night?"

"Stop already. I wanted to talk about the case."

Linda looked at the box I'd been rummaging through. "I suppose you don't want me to say 'I told you so' either."

I slammed my hands on the top of the desk. "What now, Linda?"

"Nothing. I was just reminiscing about the day I found you packing up this very box. You were so full of determination to put the Sovereign Lords behind you."

"Yes, and true to your nature, you told me that bit about the cases choosing me... I remember."

"You may remember, but you still aren't listening to me," she said.

I ROLLED my eyes and leaned closer to Linda. "Alright, I'm listening now. What do you care to share with me?"

"Think about your case in Chicago. We sat in this office and dissected Jim's and Kat's connections to the experiences they were having."

"Of course we did!" I interjected. "That is what we do!"

"David, please! Their connection was to the family of one particular Sovereign Lord. Yes, they were, in part, connected to Cloudland and of course the Lords themselves, but that connection was secondary. It wasn't about the KGC directly. Now, I will ask you one simple question. Why were you called for that case?"

"They called me because I acted like I knew everything about that house on some website. It's that simple."

"Is it that simple? My dear, please take a step back for a moment. If your client was answering you in the same manner you are responding to me, you would force them to dig deeper and look at the bigger picture. You are connected, not to Jim and Kat's house, but to the bigger picture. Why did you even post on that website about a house hundreds of miles away?"

I started to absently play with my watch as I listened to her. "I was simply interested in it. That's all."

"Of course you were. As long as I have known you, you have been fascinated by the legends of the KGC and their lost treasure hoards... but if a client of yours were to say that, how would you respond?"

"I get it. You are telling me that I am connected to the KGC. This connection of mine has driven me to focus my efforts into it... you know, you could have just said that!" I was agitated.

Linda didn't respond. She didn't have to. She said everything she needed to with the smile that appeared on her face.

Linda was right. If a client of mine had come in to tell me that they had spent so much time obsessing on a subject which now tormented them, I would certainly see a connection there. An underlying reason they started to obsess in the first place. It was almost never just an interest. It was the fact that they were drawn or directed there. I'd always been drawn to Cloudland and the KGC, and Linda obviously felt that was how I'd always found myself tangled in the web of the Sovereign Lords.

"You've known this all this time? Why the hell wouldn't you tell me this before now?"

"I tried as much as I could without forcing the knowledge on you, but you were never open to it. I knew we'd circle back to it somehow. I assumed at some point you would take a step back and realize this on your own." She leaned back in her chair.

My head spun. I couldn't imagine how I would be connected to the Sovereign Lords. I wasn't related to any members of the KGC that I knew of. Beyond that, I felt ashamed and embarrassed.

"How could I not even sense this in myself? Am I really that much of a fraud?" I asked.

"My dear, you are not a fraud. I have seen your talent firsthand. You... you just never looked at yourself the way you do everyone else. Really, there was no need. The point is, you know now. This knowledge wouldn't have changed anything in the past cases. They were finished the way they needed to be."

She stood up and reached for my hand.

"David, now you know. Come with me. We have much work to do."

She led me out of my office into the conference room. I followed with no reservation. I still felt too embarrassed to even think about what she had in store for me.

Linda instructed me to sit on the floor in the center of the room. I obediently did as asked. She then walked over to the front door and locked it. Coming back into the conference room, she shut and locked that door too. As she walked through the room with her colored dress floating behind her, she lit a series of candles. On a small table in the corner of the room, she lit incense, which filled the room with its sweet fragrance. Finally, she turned off all the lights and approached me. She sat in a lotus position facing me. Whatever was about to happen was far beyond anything I'd experienced with her before. Typically, these connections were explored with objects that she could focus on.

"What are we doing?" I asked with some hesitation.

She didn't respond. She just sat there in her lotus pose with her eyes closed. It was dark except for the candle light. I could see her chest rise and fall with each deep breath. I was too impatient to fully relax. I wanted her to just tell me what she was seeing, but I also knew not to disturb her when she was focused. So, I waited. I watched the candle

light flicker and dance on her soft but intensely-focused
face.

She grabbed my hands. I felt my breath slowing. I closed
my eyes. She had lulled me into a deep meditation. I tried to
control my mind. I wanted to force it to focus on those cases.
I wanted to see the connection between them. The more I
tried to force the direction of my thoughts, the more they
went elsewhere. I was thinking about Melanie... thinking
about us now but also reliving all of my past memories with
her. My thoughts seemed to always come back to high
school when we were nearly inseparable. I relived the nights
we'd spent on the abandoned trail in Roan Mountain. We
would go there nearly every night.

A loud clap pulled me out of these thoughts and back to
the conference room. Linda was awake and now standing
over me. There was a look of concern on her face.

"What is it?" I asked.

"You need to prepare. You are not ready... not yet." She
grabbed my hands again and pulled me to my feet. "What
are your plans for the next few days? Is there anyone who
will miss you if you're not around?"

"Well, Melanie I s'pose. That's it though."

"Text her. Tell her you're working on a lead for the case
and cannot talk. That you won't be available for a couple of
days."

"What is going on? What's happening?"

"Do you trust me?" she asked.

"Of course I trust you Linda. It's just, I want to know
what the hell is going on."

"All will be revealed. Text Melanie. Then turn your
phone off and give it to me. Where we are going, you need to
be free from any distractions."

After I relinquished my phone to Linda, I was told that I needed to find myself. She asked me to get in my truck and follow her. We started driving in the general direction of Roan, but Linda was taking all side roads. Within a few minutes, I really didn't know where we were or where we were headed. I trusted her, but it had gotten a bit strange, even for my tastes.

After about an hour of driving, her Beetle pulled off on an unmarked dirt drive somewhere high in the mountains. I watched as her car bounced on the rough drive, expecting it to bottom out and get stuck. We were deep in the forest. Then, we reached a clearing. There was a massive octagonal cabin. *Is this where she lives?* I asked myself, realizing that I'd worked with her for years and had no clue where she actually lived.

She parked her car and gestured for me to do the same. I got out of my truck and marveled at the cabin before us. It was beautiful.

"David, welcome to The Sacred Walk Healing Center. This will be your home for the next two days."

"Healing Center? Linda, I don't need rehab for crissakes. I appreciate your help, but this is a bit much."

"This is not rehab. I told you we had work to do and that you must prepare. Here, your preparation begins."

I felt angry and resistant, but I trusted her. I pushed my apprehensions out of my mind and solemnly followed her into the healing center.

As we entered the cabin, we were greeted by an older man wearing only a white robe.

"Selestino, it is so great to see you again!" Linda said. "This is David. He will be staying here for a private session."

Selestino responded with a curt bow and gestured towards the room inside.

"Welcome to the Sacred Walk David. Let me show you around and help you get comfortable."

He walked me through the large room in the center of the cabin. That was the ceremony room. It was a large circle with a high ceiling filled with skylights. The floor was bare wood. Along the perimeter of the room there was a row of futons. I was informed that I could use this room whenever I wished for meditation, prior to tomorrow's ceremony.

He guided me through a doorway opposite the entrance. There was a hallway leading to a kitchen, bathrooms, and bedrooms. He led me to the first room. There was no door. Inside was only a hammock, a small table with an oil lamp, and a robe hanging on the wall.

"This will be your room," he said. "Please change into your robe, and we can begin the preparation."

"Hold up bro. Can someone just explain to me what is happening here?" I challenged.

"Please, change and get comfortable. I must confer with Linda first. Then, I will be able to speak as to the treatment process."

Selestino left the room. I was unsure of what was happening here. I knew Linda meant well, but this was taking things to a whole new level. I sat on the hammock to compose my thoughts. At that moment, all I could hear in my head was Linda saying I was connected. I realized that as uncomfortable as it all seemed, I did want to explore that connection. On the off chance this 'treatment' could help me understand, it might be worth the effort.

With newfound acceptance, I changed out of my clothes and put on the robe. Feeling like I was going to a toga party,

I walked out of the room to the kitchen area. There, Linda and Selestino sat talking.

"David, please have a seat." Selestino gestured to an open chair at the table. "Linda has informed me of what we will be trying to achieve here. This may be a difficult journey. It will be a very introspective walk. For that purpose, I must demand that we keep talking to an absolute minimum. I will be your guide. Therefore, I ask that you follow my instructions implicitly. Linda will be here to oversee the treatment but will be stepping back so that I can be your guide."

I nodded in agreement, assuming the vow of silence had already begun.

"The purpose of this walk is to help you reach the deepest recesses of your mind and achieve a greater understanding of who you are. In order to do that, we must first prepare and purge all the roadblocks you have created. Until the ceremony is complete, we will be meditating here. Your diet must also be controlled. The food here is to sustain the body alone. Drink plenty of water."

"Wait, what exactly is this ceremony?" I asked.

"The ceremony is a journey. We will begin with a series of meditation sessions between now and then. Once the ceremony begins, we have no control over where your mind will take you. This is why our meditation will put our focus into the areas we want to see in the ceremony."

Frustrated that I still had no answer to what it all was, I looked over at Linda. My eyes pleaded with her. I hoped she would jump in to offer something.

"David, the ceremony is a controlled meditation session. You will be taking in some herbs to enhance your introspective vision. Trust me, this will help you see everything you need."

"So... I guess we should begin then?"

"The sooner, the better." Selestino stood up and began walking to the ceremony room. "Please come with me, and we shall begin. Please understand I am your guide, and in order for this to work, I need you to follow all of my instructions."

8

OVER THE NEXT SEVERAL HOURS, I had three different meditation sessions. Each session began with a unique set of instructions. In the first session, I was instructed to clear my head and focus only on my own breath. That was the most difficult, as my thoughts always drifted. In the beginning, it was frustrating. As time went on, I was able to clear my head to a certain degree. When finished, I was actually more relaxed than I had been in a long time.

Following the first session, I went to the kitchen to discover that the special diet I was on consisted of raw vegetables. Linda refrained from speaking with me. I could only believe that she was trying not to distract me from whatever I was supposed to achieve there. With a few carrots in my stomach and some water, Selestino informed me that it was time to begin my next session.

As we began the second session, I was instructed to simply not interfere with my own thoughts. I was supposed to let my thoughts flow naturally in and out of my mind. Instead of directing them, I was asked to monitor them as if I was watching them in a movie. My mind of course went straight to Melanie. Then, while I sat there, I watched it shift from thoughts of romance to all of the apprehensions I had when it came to her. It was disappointing. I also began to question if any of my previous trepidations were truly appeased or if I had merely been ignoring them. When the session ended, I began to fear what else was in store for me.

The final session shifted gears. This time, Selestino asked me to simply focus on his voice. As we began, he softly spoke the word 'Cloudland'. He repeated that single word with regular cadence for the duration of the session. My mind traveled through the various cases involving the hotel. Then, I drifted back in time. My obsession with Cloudland had been a part of me for as long as I could remember. It wasn't Cloudland the place as much as it was the Sovereign Lords and the KGC treasure. My mind drifted back to times in high school when Melanie and I would go hiking, seeking signs of that hidden treasure.

At the conclusion of the third session, I was allowed to graze on some more vegetables before I returned to my hammock for the night. There, it felt like another meditation session. I hadn't done anything all day but sit and think. Now, I was wide awake and couldn't do anything but think even more.

The only nice part about being there was that I had no prompts or assignments. My mind was free to travel anywhere. I began to think about the last meditation session and my lifelong obsession with the KGC treasure. I had always considered it a simple fairy tale I chose to believe. I wanted more than anything to leave home and travel the world, which required more money than I could foresee having. It made the quick fix of finding treasure alluring. It was really hard for me to believe that there was anything more to it than that.

Linda, on the other hand, always looked for a meaning behind everything. In her mind, things just didn't happen. Logic was used only to explain away the questions we couldn't answer. I had logical reasons for my obsession with the KGC, but she would never listen to that reasoning. She believed there was a purpose and a connection for everything in our lives. While that often ended up being the truth in cases we worked on, it was different to look at my own life that way. I fought hard to believe that I alone controlled my path.

These thoughts left me feeling unsettled. I was fighting so hard against the idea that there was a deeper connection that I tired myself out. As I neared sleep, I felt lonely. I wanted someone there to confide in. I wanted a friend. I wanted Melanie. Being with her the last few days had made me realize how much I enjoyed and needed someone by my side. I'd led a pretty solitary existence in my adult life. I accepted it, but I never chose it. Now, having Melanie in my life, I realized I didn't want that solitary existence.

The loneliness intensified. I was there in an empty room. Worse, I wasn't allowed to even speak. I was just as alone as I normally was, but now I had nothing to distract me. There was no TV to watch, no case to research. It was just me and my thoughts. I became restless. Needing to stop the thoughts of loneliness, I got up and walked to the dark ceremony room. There, I found a futon and laid down. Under the skylights, I could see the stars. That was far more comfortable. Watching the night sky, I was able to finally drift off to sleep.

I AWOKE the next morning to a bright sunlit ceremony room. Selestino was in the center tending to a cauldron.

"I see you opted to sleep here rather than in your bedroom," he said.

"I just felt better being able to see the stars. I'm not used to everything being so quiet."

He stopped stirring the cauldron and looked at me. His face was serious but his dark brown eyes were warm.

"David, this journey can be trying. I understand, but you must stay focused. We are here to help you see things inside yourself...to bring a greater understanding of who you are. For that to happen, you must let go. We will continue our meditations throughout the day. Tonight, your focus and effort will be rewarded with knowledge and understanding."

I knew better than to respond.

"Please get some food and water. We will begin our preparations shortly."

I spent the day in various meditation sessions. At first, we repeated the same techniques from the day before. In the final session, I was instructed to visualize a large clock face. With every breath I took, I was to visualize the hands of the clock moving backwards.

The session lasted for hours. At the start of it, I was just seeing the clock. However, as the session moved forward, my mind transitioned into slowly walking back in time. Each image, each memory, went further back in my life than the last. I walked back through my recent years. The session kept going, and my mind kept going further back. I saw my parents and the home where I grew up. It was like I was standing there watching myself as a child.

While I witnessed an immense number of scenes from my life, nothing stood out to give me insight. It was all a history I knew. I was not taking a different perspective or learning anything. When the session ended, I was frustrated. I felt like the intention was for me to see something from my past in order to open the door and help me realize who I was, and I wasn't seeing anything like that.

Following that session, Linda joined me in the kitchen breaking the protocol of silence.

"I must say I'm impressed with the fact that you have been following along without giving Selestino any lip," she said.

"You asked me to trust you. That is exactly what I've done, but I have to say I'm not learning shit. You know me, I learn things by doing them, by experiencing them. This is...well it seems stupid."

"There is my David," she smiled. "This is only the preparation. Tonight, everything will come together."

"Fine. However, if it doesn't, then will you just tell me what you see? In real words?"

"I won't have to," she replied.

As the sun fell, I was invited back into the ceremony room. The room was only lit by candlelight. In the center was Selestino. He invited me to sit with him.

"As we begin, I must stress one thing. You must relinquish all control, physically, mentally, and spiritually. Here, you are safe here at all times. Linda will be here to coach you through the journey, but you must be willing to let everything take its course, whatever that may be."

I nodded in agreement.

Selestino then handed me a wooden cup and asked me to drink. As I brought the cup to my lips, the smell was overpowering. I took a deep breath and drank it. It was disgusting. I could feel the liquid slowly make its way to my stomach, creating a wave of discomfort wherever it traveled.

"Please, lie down and let it guide you," he said.

I made my way over to the futon where Linda waited. I laid down and Linda covered my body with a white sheet.

"Just relax," she said, putting her hand on my forehead. "There's nothing more for you to do but let go."

I lay there watching the sky above in a near sleep state. I was at peace for a long while. A numbness began to take over my body. My limbs felt like they were restrained. Sweat poured from my body. When I closed my eyes, I felt like I was lying on a raft rocking in the surf. The rocking feeling made me nauseous. With every breath, the feeling intensi-fied. I wanted to get up. I wanted to walk to the bathroom and splash cold water on my face, but I couldn't conjure the strength to move. Sweat continued to run down my fore-head while my body shivered. Then, with an instantaneous burst, I vomited. I was able to roll to my side, but barely. With each heave, I felt myself slipping deeper into darkness.

Linda was there. She helped me. She cleaned me. She put a wet towel on my forehead. I could barely even acknowledge her help. The nausea subsided but the discomfort escalated as my mind traveled deep into dark-ness. The candles projected lines of light everywhere. They started to move in patterns which slowly turned into a vortex. The vortex swirled faster and faster. I tried to hold onto the moment. I tried to focus on my surroundings. The harder I fought, the more powerfully the vortex pulled against me. With a deep breath, I let go. The vortex consumed me and pulled me into pure nothingness. My senses were completely devoid of input. I couldn't feel, hear, see, or even smell anything. The world went black.

———

I FLOATED IN COMPLETE EMPTINESS. After a while, a pinprick

of light appeared in the distance. I was drawn to it but unable to move. The light was coming to me. Gradually, it became larger and brighter. The light exploded. Shards of light shot through the air like broken glass until they completely overtook me.

In the wake of the explosion, I found myself in my home as a child. I couldn't move or change my perspective. I could only observe. I saw my younger self sitting at the dining room table doing homework. My dad was in the kitchen talking on the phone. He was dressed in his work uniform that matched the long curly green phone cord perfectly. He looked agitated. He was pacing back and forth, his boots clomping on the kitchen floor with every step.

"I don't know what the big deal is," he said. "We've rerouted the trail probably fifteen times since I've been here. No, there hasn't been a wash out. But look at the damn reports. I have five people hospitalized and one missing, all from the same stretch of trail, and you're going to tell me we shouldn't re-route?"

I looked over at myself. I appeared to be completely oblivious to the conversation my dad was having. I was focused on my homework.

"Listen, it is my call, and I say we are going forward with it!" My dad slammed the phone down.

As I heard the clang of the phone, my view shifted. The scene before me blurred and faded out. Once I was back in nothingness, a light appeared and the process repeated itself. This time the scene was outside. I immediately recognized it. It was the last time I went hiking with my dad. We were on an abandoned stretch of the Appalachian Trail, resting at a dilapidated shelter.

"Why is this closed down?" I asked, setting my backpack down. "It seems pretty safe to me, just overgrown."

"It's safe because I'm here," my dad said.

"Why is it safe with you and no one else?"

My dad reached into his pocket and pulled out a gold coin.

"Here, take this," he said, handing me the coin. "Carry it with you anytime you walk into this area of the forest. This will keep you safe. Never lose it and never come here without it. You must promise me that."

"I promise." I squeezed the coin tightly in my hand.

The scene faded. Then everything changed. In the emptiness, instead of a prick of light, I saw a snake. Its body slowly slithered toward me. The closer it got to me, the bigger it became. Soon, I could feel the cool, rough coils wrap around me. The scales covered my face. They squeezed tighter and tighter. I couldn't breathe. I tried to move, but I was still completely immobile. I panicked, struggling to breathe, struggling to survive. Just when I was about to give up, the tightness around me disappeared. The snake was gone and in its place was another scene.

While the previous scenes were interesting, this one I didn't want to see. It was the day Melanie told me she was getting married. I remembered it well. I tried to shut my eyes but couldn't. I used every ounce of energy I had to force against it like the snake. Then it was gone. Everything was gone.

I was back in the ceremony room. Linda was by my side, looking at me. I was out of breath and my head ached. I saw rays of sunlight coming through the skylights above.

"Welcome back, David," Linda said.

"What the fuck was that?"

"Don't worry. You are done. It's a lot to take in. We must not speak of what you experienced yet. You need time to process it."

I cleaned myself up and tried to reacclimate to the real world. The only thing I could see in my mind was that coin my dad gave me. I knew exactly what it looked like, but now I needed to see it again.

Linda told me I was finished at the center and returned my phone. I changed back into my normal clothes and thanked Selestino for everything. I was in a hurry to leave. Linda didn't want to talk until I was able to process everything, which was fine by me. I jumped in my truck and drove home. There was only one thing on my mind: getting that coin and seeing it firsthand.

I walked into my house and went straight to my closet. There was an old shoe box on the floor. I picked it up and started rummaging through it. That box contained everything I had saved from my dad. His badge, some photos, even his old wallet. Then, I found it. I picked up the dirty old gold coin and looked at it. It was exactly as I'd remembered... exactly as I feared.

On the coin was an image of an 8-point star. The star gave way to a larger cross. Around the edge of the coin were the words "GREAT SEAL OF THE K'S OF THE G C."

At that moment, I knew that my belief that my dad had found this coin in the woods was wrong. I knew it had been given to him. Someone gave it to him with a purpose the same way he gave it to me.

PART II

9

JULY 12, 1920 - Cherokee National Forest

It was a beautiful summer morning, and the sun shone brightly. Robert shielded his eyes to get a better look at the house as he approached it. The new modest house was embedded into the forest. Its freshly whitewashed walls stood out from the dense foliage around it. Robert climbed the steps to the front door and walked in.

"Just a minute," a voice said.

Robert stepped over to the grandfather clock in the sitting room. He instinctively pulled out his pocket watch to see if the clock was set properly. The sound of hurried footsteps broke Robert's focus. He turned to see a young man. The man was out of breath as he entered the room. He was wearing a freshly pressed olive peacoat and a tan, wide-brimmed Stetson-style hat.

"Robert," he said. "What a great surprise to see you. I apologize for keeping you waiting."

Robert turned from the clock and extended his hand. The young man eagerly shook it as Robert examined him.

"Please, have a seat," Robert said, gesturing to the chairs. "We have a few matters to discuss."

"But of course." he cautiously sat down.

"First, I want to thank you for your patience and allegiance. I know when I asked you to help me, this must have all sounded like a dream. Now, as you stand here in your new home, in your new uniform, with a new job and a secure future, I hope you can see I am a man of my word."

"Absolutely!"

"Good, then I will be direct with you. As you know, I pursued the creation of this portion of the National Forest in order to protect the land you have been watching for me. This of course gave me the ability to also recommend you for your new position. Do not make the mistake of thinking that your allegiances are to the National Forest. You are accountable to me and me alone."

"I understand, but I thought the purpose of all of this was to protect the land. That is what the National Forest will do. What more needs to happen?"

"Johan, it is protected from being purchased. It is protected from being disturbed to a degree. You are correct. But, it is not safe. I need you to take special care to ensure my interests remain secure. Do you understand?"

"Of course."

"Good, then there is something else I need to share with you. You are already well aware of the evil that lurks in that part of the forest."

Johan nodded in response.

"Which is why I came here today," Robert continued. "In order for you to truly protect that portion of the land, you also need to be protected from the evil which lurks there."

Robert reached into his breast pocket and retrieved a

small gold coin. He looked at it with a grin as he rolled it over his knuckles. He then handed it to Johan.

"This coin will protect you. It is a charm of sorts. Whoever carries it will be safe from the evil in the forest.".

Johan eyed the coin suspiciously. "I'm not sure I understand."

"You don't need to understand. Just as you don't need to know exactly what it is you are keeping secure in the forest. That was never part of our agreement. You keep that area secure, and I compensate you generously. While you may not understand how or why this coin will protect you, you need to trust me when I say it will. Keep it with you at all times. That is of the utmost importance."

"You have my word."

"Remember when I first gave you this task?"

"Of course."

"Then you will also remember that I made it clear that there is no expiration date on this task. The forest needs to be secured long after I am gone. Long after you are gone. With that, it is your responsibility to ensure that this allegiance is passed on. This coin must also be passed to whoever replaces you. That coin is the only way one can safely travel in that area of the forest."

10

I HAD NEVER SEEN another coin like this, however I'd never researched it either. I'd always assumed that this coin was a calling card of sorts for KGC Sentinels. Sentinels within the KGC were simply protectors. They were sworn to protect land and areas important to the KGC. They were not members of the KGC; their existence was completely secretive. They would typically identify themselves by using specific hand gestures only recognizable by members of the KGC. In my mind, this coin was a token of that position.

The coin was the only thing I could keep my attention on. The visions from the ceremony were too overwhelming. Even Linda said I needed to let them simmer. I was now considering the idea that my family, even my dad, were KGC Sentinels.

I picked up my phone and called Melanie. I didn't really have a plan for the conversation aside from letting her know that I was still alive.

"And here I thought I might've scared you off," she said as she answered the phone.

"Not in the slightest. It's a long story, but Linda locked

me up in this meditation center to find out something about your house."

"I wanna be jealous that this woman gets to take you away for a couple days, but I'm more curious about what happened and what you were able to find out."

"It's kinda hard to say. I'm still trying to process everything. Do you remember that shack we used to hike to?"

"You mean Spearfinger's Shack? Of course I remember that. Why?"

"Holy shit!" I yelled. "Spearfinger!"

"Uh yeah, that is why we went there. Remember, you were all into chasing down the haunts and lore."

"Sorry, I forgot about that. I just remember all the time we spent there. "

"Well, yeah. Once we realized there was nothing but stories out there, it became our secret place to be stupid kids and not get busted." She paused. "You know, I tried going there recently."

"What do you mean?"

"That shack. It... well it felt like maybe that was the direction of the light in my dream."

"But you never made it there?"

"No! That trail felt worse than my cabin. Every step I took, I felt like I was being followed. I guess I scared myself off."

"Oh my God! Melanie, I just figured something out! Any chance you can come to my office after work today? I really need to see you."

"Hmmm...you need to work on my house, or you need to see me?"

"Well, both really, but I mainly need to see you. I miss you."

"Okay, I'll text you when I leave. But just so you know, if Linda is there, I might take her out."

As I ended the phone call, memories flooded back to me. That day on the trail when my dad gave me the KGC coin, we were at the old shack-turned-shelter on the closed and re-routed stretch of the Appalachian Trail. That shack is where Melanie and I always hung out. Melanie was right. We went there under the guise of it being Spearfinger's Shack... but that wasn't exactly right. As I remembered, I may have embellished the Spearfinger story in a feeble attempt to get Melanie someplace alone with me, but the lore was there. I may have embellished it, but I didn't make it up.

I'd been awake for well over twenty-four hours, but my mind was racing. I needed to explore this. I got in my truck and headed to the office. As I pulled in, I saw Linda's car. I found her meditating in the conference room. Startled, she stood up.

"I didn't think I would hear from you for a while. Usually that experience takes some time to process." There was a look of concern on her face.

"I'm fine. Yeah, I'm connected. I'm a KGC Sentinel and have the coin to prove it. But that isn't important right now. I need you to tell me everything you know about Spearfinger!"

"Are you sure you're okay. Maybe you need some sleep."

"Like I said I'm fine. Just tell me!"

"I'm sure you know everything that I do. She was a shape-shifting demon according to Cherokee legend."

"Right, but that legend was way south of here. Plus, according to the Cherokee legend, she was killed...vanquished by the Cherokee people."

For the first time that I could remember, Linda looked confused.

"If that's all true, then how do the stories of her come back to Roan, back when I was a kid?" I asked.

She cautiously put her hands on my shoulders. "You know the answer to that, David. Spearfinger may have been a hundred miles away, but the forest is dark and scary. It's the perfect tale to tell around a campfire. I'm afraid Spearfinger in Roan could be just that, a campfire story."

I took a deep breath. "I know that Linda, but what I don't know is whether there really were stories of Spearfinger in Roan, or did I make that up myself as a kid?"

"I do not have an answer to that. Yes, Spearfinger comes up in stories all across these mountains. So, I can only believe that yes, at some point in time, people were recounting her story in Roan."

I sat down in the middle of the room and buried my head in my hands. There was something about that story... but I couldn't place it. Linda apparently couldn't either. Was it all some after effect of the ceremony?

I looked up at Linda, shaking my head. "I don't think that's it. I think she is real, again. I think she is a part of all of this somehow."

LINDA WAS CONCERNED ABOUT ME. She urged me to rest. As a way of appeasing her, I convinced her that I would take a nap there at the office. When I was sure she was gone, I pulled out the maps of Cloudland and went to work. I realized that my old topographic map would provide exactly what I was looking for. With the map, I would be able to identify if that shack was really the spot Melanie was seeing in her dream. I affixed the map to the white board in the conference room and then covered it with a clear piece of plastic. That allowed me to draw on the map without ruining it.

I first outlined the footprint of the Cloudland hotel in red marker. Next, I scrutinized the western edge of the map. After a few minutes, I found it—a square used to symbolize a structure. That was the building that became known as Spearfinger's Shack. I outlined it in red as well. Next, I used a straightedge to draw a blue line from the shack back to the Cloudland. Given the orientation of the map, that line would be precisely east to west. When I was done, I stepped back to look at it. It wasn't what I'd expected. In my mind, I'd assumed the line would connect straight to Robert's suite in the Cloudland, but it didn't. It didn't even touch the building.

So either, Melanie's dream insisting that the light was straight west of Cloudland was less than precise, or the shack was not the source of it as I'd been hoping.

"Of course it couldn't be that easy!" I yelled to the empty room.

I was tired and felt defeated. I curled up in a bean bag chair and stared at the map while I drifted off.

I had a dream of my own. It was short and precise. Clear as day, the only thing I saw was my dad on the phone saying, "Five people hospitalized and one missing."

There might have been more of that dream, but the next thing I remembered was waking up to the sound of sleigh bells on the door. I jolted up in a cold sweat and out of breath. I looked around the dark and silent conference room.

"David, are you here?" It was Melanie.

"I'm here. Hang on a second," I fumbled around for the light switch.

When I turned on the lights, she was just making her way into the conference room. She looked at me with concern before she ran in and wrapped her arms around me. It felt so nice to be in her arms.

After she let go of me, she looked at me with wide eyes as she raised her eyebrows.

"What happened? You look like you have been through the wringer. Are you alright?"

"Yeah, uh well, it's been a crazy couple days. I haven't slept much, but I am so glad to see you again."

"You scared me! The way you were talking on the phone about that shack. You sounded... I don't even know, but you didn't sound right."

"Sorry, I was just experiencing some revelations in my head and it got kinda intense."

She stood back, looking even more concerned. "Can you finally tell me what the hell has been going on?"

"Yeah, absolutely. But before I do..." I fished the KGC coin out of my pocket. "Do you remember this?"

She grabbed it from my hand and looked at it. For the first time since she arrived, I saw her smile. "Of course I do. You always had this with you. You told me this was your key to finding the treasure of the KGC."

"Yeah, that was my story back then anyway. Although, I learned over the last couple days it is a lot more than that." I pulled her over to the beanbag I'd slept in and told her everything I'd learned. When I first called her that morning, it was clear she was agitated by my disappearance. Now, she was in shock. She held my hands in hers as I spoke. When I finished, she put her arms around my shoulders and just held me.

Despite how on edge I'd felt since the ceremony, when she did that, I felt at peace. We kissed. I wanted nothing but to stay in that feeling for eternity. After a long time spent in that silent embrace, she was the first to speak.

"What is all this?" she asked, pointing to the map on the wall. "It looks like something out of a spy movie or something."

"Well, that was just a theory, I guess."

She looked at me quizzically. "It looks pretty involved for a theory."

"I s'pose. After talking to you, I had a hunch that you might have been right. That the point of light you saw in your dream was that old shack. But as you can see from the line, it isn't quite due west from the Cloudland."

I stood up and took a green marker and drew an X on the western edge of Cloudland.

"From what I can tell, this would be pretty much exactly where Robert's room would have been and thus his vantage point."

She joined me by the board and picked up the straight edge and drew a line from the 'X' to the shack. Then she stepped back and looked at it.

"No, that definitely isn't it," she said. "I mean it is kinda the right direction but not really. Listen, I know you are... well, focused on this right now, but you look like hell. Maybe you need to just step back from this for a moment. I dunno, maybe hit reset for a bit."

She was right. Not only was she right, but she was also the perfect distraction from it all, despite the fact that it was her case. She decided to drive me back to my house where she would make me dinner.

BACK AT MY HOUSE, I was finally able to relax a bit. It was different having Melanie there with me, but I was completely at ease with it. After we ate, we sat on the couch. I thoroughly enjoyed having her that close to me.

"So, you really think that coin from your dad is more than some token he came across?" she asked.

"Jeez, yeah, I really do. Thinking back to when he gave it to me, or I guess reliving that moment, I kinda see it differently."

"You know, in all the years I've known you, I don't think I've ever heard you talk about your dad at all."

"Yeah, I mean, I guess that's just how I dealt with it. I wasn't even in high school yet, and I was suddenly an orphan. At the time, I think just ignoring that he ever existed was easier than coping with it all."

She slid even closer to me and gave me a hug.

"And now?" she asked.

"I don't know. When I pulled that coin from the box... that was the first time I'd given him any thought in years. I moved on and never allowed myself to think about him. But there is something there. This coin made me realize I need to learn who he was."

"You scared of that?"

"Not really scared, more not sure what I'll find. "

There was a gentle transition in her eyes. I could tell instantly there was more she wanted to say.

"What? Just say it," I pleaded.

"It's just... listen, don't take offense ... I was wondering, do you think this whole becoming a paranormal researcher was in some way your attempt to connect with him?"

"I doubt it. If it were, I think I would've tried to contact him. It isn't like his ghost was haunting me or anything."

As the evening continued on, that conversation stuck

with me. My dad had truly been erased from my adult life, as if he'd never existed. It was almost as if my entire child-hood had been blocked out. I was fourteen when he died. I was fourteen when I had to move in with my aunt. It was as if that was the moment my life began. I'd completely moved on from the fourteen prior years.

At some point that night, I decided I needed to learn what I could about my dad. For certain, I needed to try and find out everything I could about the coin and why he had it. But, for the first time in my life, I wanted to know him as a person.

The next morning, Melanie drove me out to the office on her way to work since my truck was still there. Any concern she'd had about my well-being was gone. The truth was, I felt good. I felt more at ease than I had in a long time. I also felt driven. I wanted to learn more about my dad and that was my sole mission on that day.

After Melanie left, I put my plan together. I needed to talk to Gordon, my dad's friend and former partner. A quick search on my phone let me know exactly where I could find him. Gordon was a supervisor with the Cherokee National Forest Rangers. He worked out of the office in Unicoi, only a few miles away, the same office where my dad had worked. My dad had worked out of that office but still lived in the Forest Ranger Substation where I grew up. Rangers didn't live in substations after the Headquarters was built, but my dad and I still stayed there until he died.

Gordon had been as close to my father as anyone could be. They'd worked together and were best friends. Gordon was the one who had found my father's body. Gordon was the one who came into the substation to tell me the news. Ultimately, Gordon was the one who'd tried valiantly to be my stand-in father figure, a role I never let him have. When my father died, I tried to separate myself from any memory of him, as much as I could. Gordon, despite having my best interests at heart, was a part of that. I couldn't speak to him without thinking about my dad. As the years went by, we drifted apart. I made it clear that I wanted to forge my own path, and despite wanting to be there for me, he got the message.

As I pulled into the small Unicoi office, there was only one thing on my mind. In my head, I kept replaying the vision I had of my father talking on the phone about shutting down the trail. That specific memory had to be meaningful if I were to believe anything about that ceremony and its intentions. Still, I couldn't understand why. Of all the interactions with my dad, why did that one come to the surface?

I tried to push those questions back a little as I stepped into the office. It was a clean and neat office, and I was greeted by a uniformed woman at the front desk.

"How can I help you?"

"I'd like to speak with Gordon Owens for a moment if he's in."

"Sure, I'll go dig him up. Why don't you follow me. You can have a seat in the conference room."

She led me to a conference room where I took a seat. The room was decorated with maps of the forest as well as photographs. A photo hung proudly on the wall. I had seen it countless times before. It showed my Dad and Gordon posing in front of the National Forest sign at Carvers Gap.

11

"WELL I'LL BE DAMNED! The prodigal son has returned!" Gordon's deep voice bellowed as he entered the conference room.

Gordon was a bear of a man. He stood well over six feet with broad shoulders and a barrel chest. He hurried over to me and extended his hand for a handshake. As I returned the gesture, it felt as if he would crush my hand with his.

"To what do I owe this visit? Once you made it onto TV, I figured I would never see you again, especially not here."

"Well, I wanted to ask you about my dad."

Gordon sat down across the table from me and leaned back in the chair, rubbing his mustache.

"He'd be damn proud of you, David," he finally said. "Damn proud."

"I appreciate that, although I had always assumed his goal for me was to be wearing one of those uniforms."

"Sure, you have a family legacy here. You come from a long line of rangers, but your father wasn't that kind of guy."

"What do you mean by that kind of guy?"

"The father that will only accept the path he chooses for

his son. You know Roger, I mean your dad, he was different. He was cut out for being a ranger for sure, and he loved it. But he knew there was more out there. I remember when you were born. We were sitting on the porch of the old substation smoking cigars. I made a joke about getting you a miniature uniform to start your training. That rubbed him the wrong way. He said that he wanted his children to choose their paths. If you ask me, he was always a little pissed off that he had no choice in a career. So yeah, he'd be damn proud of you!"

I sat in stunned silence.

"But something tells me that wasn't what you came out here for, was it?" he asked.

"Yes and no, I guess. I mean, I just know next to nothing about him. After he died, I kinda shut down. So, I'm just looking to learn more about him."

"Yeah, you were a handful back then. Not that I could blame you. No one should ever have to go through something like that. I always wished I could have done more for you back then, but the truth was, I was dealing with his loss too."

"You know, I don't even remember how he died. I just remember the fact that he did."

"Christ, I will never forget that day. He was up at Roan High Bluff that morning. He always had an interest up there. Anytime he could be in that area of the forest, he was. Anyway, towards the end of the day he hadn't checked in. We tried radioing him but got no response. After trying a few times, I headed out that way. I'd been up there with him a thousand times. So, I figured I could've found him better than anyone. Sure enough, I found him on one of the old trails that branched off. When they did the autopsy, they said something about liver failure. Something he'd probably been living with for a while."

"There are a lot of trails up there. How'd you find him?"

"Yeah, a ton of trails, but I knew Roger. In all the time I'd been up there with him he was always going back to the same few trails when he could. Didn't hurt that it had been a wet week, and I knew his boot tracks better than my own."

"Was it that part of the trail leading to that old shelter?"

"Yeah, you know it?"

"Well yeah, I remember hiking that with him. Actually, that reminds me. That was the part of the trail that got rerouted when I was a kid, right?"

"Yeah, that's it."

"I have this memory of my dad talking on the phone to someone about trying to get it rerouted. I remember him saying something about people getting hurt and going missing in that section of the trail. You know anything about that?"

"Aw hell, that was Rog being Rog. Let me tell ya, when he made a decision, he would do anything to make it happen. He wanted the trail rerouted so he exaggerated some things to make his point."

"Exaggerated? So did it happen or not?"

"Nah, I mean, there was that Barnes kid that went missing back then. But there was nothing to say he was even on that mountain let alone that trail. Roger just used it to make his point. At the end of the day, he was the expert on the trails. So he won."

"But if that was a part of the trail he loved, then why would he reroute the main trail away from it?"

"I never did understand that one much. Like I said, he'd made up his mind on it. Honestly, we were so busy back then with a quarter of the staff we have today, we just kinda had to trust each other on matters like that."

There was something about the way he spoke that made me question what he was saying. There was a slight change in tone when he spoke about the trail reroute, a discomfort. I quickly realized that I wasn't going to get much more from him unless I pushed to the point he shut down. There was only one thing nagging at me that I wanted to ask.

"Listen, thanks for taking the time. It helps to hear some of this stuff, ya know?"

"Don't mention it! You're always welcome here, you know that. And if you ever change your mind, I'm sure I have a uniform and a badge for you so you can follow in your old man's footsteps."

"On that, I was curious what ever happened to my house. I mean the substation."

"Ya know, that place has been locked up since you moved out. There is always talk of making it a gift shop or a museum or something, but there's never a budget to back it up. So, it just sits there."

"You think I'd be able to go there one day? I would like to walk through there again and see what I can remember."

Gordon sat back in the chair silently pondering this.

"Aw hell, you know what. I'll give you the key. Don't mess the place up, and get me the key back. But yeah, if anyone deserves to go through that place it's you. Let me just grab the key from my office... Listen, don't tell nobody 'bout me givin' you the key. I'm sure I'm breaking some sort of rule."

As I HEADED out to the substation I thought back to that missing kid Gordon mentioned. This would have been a perfect time to have the research team from my TV show. I did know someone who might help me uncover something. I picked up my phone and called Jim.

"David, how the hell are you?" Jim said.

"I'm good, just home in between recordings. How is everything up at the Villa with Kat?"

"Everything is great, but we miss you. You gotta come back up here sometime!"

"You're right. I will. But until then, I got a favor to call in."

"Anything."

"Listen, remember you had that buddy, the computer guy that got you a bunch of info on Sam?"

"Aw yeah, Paul."

"You think he'd be able to research something for me?"

"Yeah, what you got?"

"I need to find out anything I can about a kid that went missing in Roan Mountain around 1997. The name was Barnes."

"I'll forward the info. and see what he can dig up."

"Thanks, bro. Listen, I gotta run, but I'll call you back when I got some time later."

Paul was a hacker extraordinaire who'd been able to help Jim find a bunch of interesting and hidden information while I was working on the case involving the demon at his Villa. I didn't know what, if anything, I was looking for from him. But something told me I should try.

I pulled up to the substation, my childhood home. Gordon was right, the place was untouched. I had to park on the side of the road as the driveway was chained off. As I walked up, it looked just as I remembered it aside from the fact that the forest was about to reclaim it. Clearly, no one had walked up there in years. I made my way up the creaky steps of the front porch. I put the key from Gordon into the padlock securing the front door. After jiggling it a bit, the lock loosened up and opened. I opened the door of my home and stepped in.

The inside was exactly as I remembered it. On my left was the small living room with the grandfather clock where my dad would sit reading and smoking his pipe. On the right was the dining room that led into the kitchen. That was the exact table I'd been sitting at in my vision. I eyed the old olive green phone hanging on the wall in the kitchen.

I made my way back to the staircase by the door and headed upstairs to my room. My bed was still there, but the room was stark and empty. I ran my fingers along the wall seeing the pinholes from where my Kurt Cobain poster once hung. I vaguely remembered how all of my possessions just appeared one day at my aunt's house.

I walked over to my dad's office. While my room was completely stripped of everything, his office looked exactly like it had the last time I'd seen it, aside from the missing stack of papers and maps that always cluttered his desktop. I made my way over to the dusty wooden office chair and sat down. I stared at the desk for a few minutes, envisioning talking to a childhood version of myself with me being my dad. I opened up the top drawer. It was a mess of rulers and protractors and such, but then something caught my eye. On the bottom of the drawer there was some writing on the wood. I pulled the drawer out further and started throwing its contents onto the desk. Once empty, I could make out the scribble. "11:27 - 250°" was written there.

Something felt important about it. I took out my phone and took a picture of it before putting everything back in the desk and closing it. I stood up and was about to leave when I remembered Gordon mentioning my dad's journals. I walked over to the closet and opened the door. Inside, my dad's uniforms hung and below them was a file box. I opened the file box to reveal a stack of papers, maps, and notebooks. There had to be twenty old composition books with black and white marbled covers. I couldn't begin to scratch the surface of everything in the box at that moment. I decided to take the box with me. I headed out and loaded the box in my truck before I went back to lock up the house.

On my way back home, I thought about the fact that I had no idea what I was after. Yes, there was my vision, but how much more was there to discover? The one topic I hadn't broached with Gordon was the KGC, but I doubted he would have much to offer and that seemed a bit too sensitive a topic for that conversation. I also doubted that the box of papers and notebooks would yield any clues on that front. Yet, I took them.

I found myself being mad at my dad again. I was mad about the puzzle, the secret of the KGC. I was mad at the sheer fact that he'd died without being able to answer those questions for me. I'd spent a lot of time being angry with him in the past. It was exactly why I'd coped by blocking his very existence from my mind. I didn't like being mad at him, but I was. It wasn't my choice, but it was the situation I was in.

My phone started buzzing, and I looked to see Jim had texted me.

"Paul is over at my place. Call me ASAP!!!"

A FEW MINUTES LATER, I trudged inside my house with the file box and sat down to call Jim.

"Hey David, I got Paul here," Jim said. "You're gonna wanna hear this. Let me put him on speaker."

"Uh David..." a voice said. "This is Paul. Like Jim said, I started looking into that name, Barnes. I don't know what this all adds up to, but there is some seriously covered up shit here. I'm talking like JFK style."

"What the hell are you talking about?" I asked.

"Well okay, you gave me the names Barnes and Roan Mountain, right? So I started looking at that. There are two different stories from the same time period. One, the story that was publicly available and then a completely different story beforehand. Let's start with the more public story. It reads that on May 12th, 1997, a seventeen-year-old Jamie Barnes was reported missing to the Johnson City Police. The story says he had gotten in a fight with his parents the previous Friday and had taken off. When he didn't return by Monday, his parents called the police. Then, on June 21st, a guy taking a hike in the woods comes across his body. The reports all show that he died of exposure. He was found only a couple miles from his house in a place called White Rock. So everything seemed to be simple."

"Seemed to be?"

"Yeah, like I said, that is one story. The other story only really matches up on a couple points. Let me walk you through it. This story starts earlier, on May 9th. So, at 11pm on the 9th, a group of kids approach a forest ranger on Roan Mountain screaming about something in the woods attacking their friend. Apparently they had gone hiking and found some secluded spot to drink or smoke up or whatever. That was when something came out of the woods and attacked their friend ...their friend named Jamie Barnes. There are search reports for the next couple days that led to nothing. Then, a ranger finds Jamie's body on a Roan Mountain trail on May 12th."

"I'm a little confused. How can a body be discovered twice?"

"Hell, you know these government agencies. They will do anything to avoid bad press."

"So what, they just kept his body on ice and changed the story a bit?"

"Well, that is kinda what I was thinking. But then I found the autopsy report. This report again falls into the second hidden storyline here. Anyway, despite the initial reports of him being attacked, there isn't as much as even a scratch on the body. No cuts, nothing. The cause of death is listed as liver failure. But here is where shit gets really messed up. So, in a typical autopsy, all of the organs are taken out, examined, weighed, and all that. On this report, it has all of that information. However, when it gets to the liver, everything is just blank. No information. Like it wasn't removed or examined at all, which is fine except for the fact that it listed liver failure as being the cause of death."

"Wow! That sounds pretty messed up, but what makes you think this is more than simply avoiding bad press? I get it, something is amiss for sure, but not sure I see anything all JFK style in this."

"Well, a lot of that comes with how I found the info. See, there are two completely different reports from completely different agencies. The first story comes from the Johnson City Police, publicly available thanks to the Freedom of Information Act, and of course my mad skills to get it without waiting for a request to go through. But the second, that is more hidden. It is all in documents from the National Forestry Division. I don't know how much you know about that, but let's just say the Forestry Division has often been unwilling to comply with that Freedom of Information Act. These documents came from good old fashioned hacking while any FIA request to the department would only ever turn up the original police reports."

"Still struggling to see the JFK cover up there."

"Okay, let me connect the dots for you. A kid goes camping and something happens. The rangers do their job, end up finding him, but they are not responsible for communication with anyone outside. They forward every-thing to the police and other agencies. I mean, it isn't like the forestry division is going to perform an autopsy. Anyway, by the time the parents call the police, his body has already been found. The police know this but say nothing, not until some other government agency conducts an autopsy. The police are just held back by them. Over a month goes by until the police are given this alternate storyline to go off. I checked the name of the guy who supposedly found the body in the police report, a Leonard Gale. He doesn't exist. As a person, he is a ghost...no records, no birth certificate, no residence. However, his name comes up in police reports all over. It's the government's version of John Doe."

"So you're saying the entire police report is false?"

"Exactly. I would bet there was no hiker who found a body. That report wasn't even written by the police. It was handed to them with the body post-autopsy."

"Alright, I mean I love a good conspiracy and even have my tin-foil hat here, but this is a bit much. What reason would the government have to hide something like this?"

"That's the only question left. I don't know, but there is something there for sure."

"Okay, I gotta think this all through. Can you email me those reports? I'd love to look at them myself."

"Sure thing, I'll send them over now, but be careful with

this stuff. It's all hidden for a reason. Don't go stirring the pot too much and asking too many questions. The higher up the chain things like this go, the quicker they get silenced."

"Now that, I can agree with. Thanks."

By the time I got home, the reports had arrived in my email box. I started looking through them. Obviously my interest was piqued when Paul mentioned that those reports came from my father's office. I knew I had to keep quiet about that for now. The first report I looked at was from the police department. Since the body was found in the National Forest, the ranger was listed at the scene of John Doe's discovery. That ranger was Roger Spur, my father.

I opened the second set of reports, the ones Paul said were 'hidden.' Those reports were from my father's office, but the ranger listed on them was Gordon Owens, the same ranger who told me there was nothing to the story of Barnes and that trail. Even more concerning to me was one name that caught my attention when I read the report. The report listed the friends who approached Gordon. Among those friends listed was Derek Soto. I already knew exactly who Derek was. He was the deceased older brother of Austin, Melanie's ex-husband.

12

A GOVERNMENT COVER-UP was the last thing I'd expected to
find in relation to all this. I knew Gordon was not telling me
the straight story, but did it really go this deep? The more I
thought about it, the more I developed a 'What would Linda
say?' mentality. Linda always looked for a deeper connection
in everything. I knew, with this, I needed to find something
connecting everything beyond the surface. While I was
unable to see all the connections, I decided to look where
this started, with Melanie and her cabin.

I knew there was energy there from Robert Mason. That
had to be my next step. Investigate that to the fullest. I sent
Melanie a text saying that I was heading back to her cabin. I
got in my truck and headed there.

I pulled up to the sleepy cottage and started walking up
to the door. As I approached, I heard a car speeding down
the gravel drive. When I turned to look, a beat-up Toyota
skidded to a stop in front of the cabin. With the car still
running, Zeke stepped out and approached me.

The relaxed man I drank with on the porch only a few

days ago looked completely different. He was out of breath and dripping with sweat.

"David, right?" he yelled as he approached.

"Hey Zeke, good to see you again. What's goin' on?"

"Look, did you see a dog down there when you pulled in?"

"No, sorry."

"Shit man, I gotta go find him."

"Wait, weren't you telling me your dog ran away like months ago?"

"Yeah, but he came back...well kind of."

"Kind of?"

"Man, this morning I heard barking so I came out on the porch, and there he was like fifteen feet from my door. Something's wrong with him, though. It's like it's him, but he just doesn't act the same at all. Anyway, he took off a few minutes ago. I gotta find him. I can't lose him again!"

"Let me help! I know this area pretty good. Certainly, another set of eyes wouldn't hurt."

"I gotta run while I have a fresh trail to follow. But if I lose it, I'll come back for help."

"You sure?"

"Yeah, I just gotta go!"

Within a few seconds, his Toyota was kicking up gravel as he sped down the drive. With Zeke gone, it was time for me to focus on the house. I pulled the key out from under the mat and took a deep breath as I opened the door. The house was still and silent. The cabin creaked with every step. I slowly prodded around the downstairs level before making my way to the loft. Something felt different and empty about the cabin. It was as if the negative energy I'd felt before had vanished. I was hoping that it was simply a side effect of me trying to trap the energy upstairs.

Upon entering the loft, I realized it too was still. The negative energy was simply gone. I slowly made my way to the door in the wall and gently brushed away the line of salt. I opened the door, expecting the rush of cold air I'd felt previously. There was nothing. It was warm and still, exactly what you would expect of a normal attic. I knelt at the door, leaning into the attic. After I'd sat there for several seconds, things started changing. A warm glow of light overhead began to overtake the attic, until the entire space was lit brightly enough for me to see everything. The signature of Robert Mason shone prominently in the light.

I crawled farther into the attic to get a better look. Once I was fully inside, the door slammed shut with a loud bang. Panic rose in my chest. The concern was quickly squelched as I sensed no danger around me. I needed to simply let the energy guide me. At that moment, there was an uncomfortable sensation on my thigh. It felt warm, almost burning. As I tried to push past it and investigate the attic further, the burning sensation escalated. It felt as if there was a hot stone pressing into my leg. As the burning intensified, I started rubbing my thigh, trying to brush away whatever it was.

Through my jeans, I felt the source of this pain. The coin in my pocket was hot. I quickly reached into my pocket to pull it out. As my fingers gripped it, my reflexes took over, and I pulled my hand from my pocket, letting the coin fall onto the floor. Searing pain shot through my hand, as if I'd just touched a hot stove. I clenched my fingers into a fist, wincing as I looked for the coin. It was glowing. A brilliant gold light emanated from it in every direction.

I cautiously reached for it, holding my hand slightly above it to see if it was still hot. In the glow of the coin, I noticed something I hadn't seen before. Under Robert's signature on the beam was a circle. Drawn in the same pencil, this circle appeared to be the exact size of the coin. Confident that the coin was cool enough to touch, I picked it up and brought it towards the circle. As the coin neared the beam, the gold glow started to flicker like a light bulb ready to burn out. Then, when it was directly over the circle, a bright white light emanated from the coin. I pressed the coin against the beam with all my might. The white light became blinding. I closed my eyes. Suddenly my body went limp, and I collapsed onto the floor.

I OPENED my eyes to a completely different scene. I was sitting in a leather chair inside an elegant room decorated with dark woods. A fire roared in the massive marble fireplace. As I tried to take stock of everything I was seeing, I made a stunning realization: it was Cloudland. The gentle ticking of the clock was the only sound aside from the crackle of the fire. I turned my head and saw a figure staring out the window with his back towards me. He was dressed in a suit, and in his hand, he gently swirled a glass of whiskey.

"You have finally arrived." The man spoke in a stern yet quiet voice.

"Uh well, I'm here if that's what you're saying."

"Indeed." The man turned to face me. "I trust you understand your responsibility as a protector. You are the one who holds the coin."

"The coin was my father's. He gave it to me."

"Yes, of course he did. As his father gave it to him along with implicit instructions regarding his role in protecting that sacred spot."

I didn't know how to respond. I had no instructions. Only the coin. But I certainly didn't want to reveal that fact.

"Oh, perhaps you don't know your role?"

I swallowed hard. "I am a Sentinel protecting your cache."

As I spoke those words, his face became stern. It was clear that my response was not what he'd been hoping for. He slowly stepped over to the chair facing mine, unbuttoned his jacket and sat down.

"As I suspected. David, this role of protection is something very different from what the Sentinels were intended to provide. It is a role I created for your great-great- grandfather. A role which had been successfully passed down through your bloodline. It makes no difference now though. Things have changed."

"What do you mean things have changed?"

"The world has changed. The KGC no longer has a place in molding its future. Additionally, the precautions we have taken have left me trapped here. I need you to set things right so that I am able to move on."

"Why me?"

"You carry the coin. It is your birthright, a sacred bond forged years ago, but there is more. You are different, unlike anyone I've seen before."

"Different how?"

"You vanquished Samuel, the most powerful of the Sovereign Lords!"

"And now you expect me to help you so you can rise to power and take Samuel's place?"

Robert stood up and walked across the room. He approached the grandfather clock and leaned against it, staring at me. His eyes were fiery with rage. He took a sip of his whiskey. As the glass left his lips, a smirk appeared on his face. Then he threw his glass across the room to the fireplace. The glass exploded when it collided with the marble hearth.

"I am not Samuel. Samuel may have been my brother in the KGC, but our intentions and motivations were quite different. The problem is, you don't know your role."

His words triggered anger in me. If there was one thing I knew, the Sovereign Lords were anything but good people. He may not have agreed with Samuel, but I had no reason to believe he was any better. "Well then, why don't you enlighten me."

"Oh I would love to. But, much like that coin you carry, your role is passed down. Your father must be the one to help you understand."

"My father is dead!" I stood up and approached him as if I was going to fight him. "You know I vanquished Sam, but you don't know that? You want my help? But I can't help you unless I know what the hell you're talking about."

A softer expression appeared on Robert's face. He stepped closer and put he hands on my shoulders.

"David," he said in a whisper. "I am aware of what happened to your father. He died, much like I did many years earlier. Yet I am speaking with you. Your father may have left the world of the living, but his voice is still here. You must find it."

As he finished speaking, a blinding white light overtook the room. I shielded my eyes with my hand. Just as quickly, the white lights began to dissolve like water going down a drain. In a moment, I was back in Melanie's attic. I shook my head and took a deep breath before crawling out of the attic and into the loft. I shut the door to the attic and knelt, looking around the room.

I'd been frozen like that for a few minutes before I realized the coin was clenched tightly in my fist. I opened my hand and put the coin back in my pocket. I looked at my hand and saw that the pronounced relief of the cross on the coin had left an imprint on my palm. As I rubbed the palm of my hand, it slowly started to dissipate.

I looked at my watch only to realize that somehow I'd been in that attic almost two hours. Not ready to move, I took a moment to gather my thoughts about what I'd experienced. I knew it was Robert, and I knew that I had been transported to his room in the Cloudland. But there was something else I was missing. There was something about the scene that was familiar to me. Yet, I couldn't quite place it. Sitting in that room had a comfortable feeling to it, as if I'd been sitting in my own home. There was definitely something there. Yet, no matter how hard I thought about it, I simply couldn't place it.

Frustrated, I gave up for the time being. It was late, and Melanie would be coming to my house soon. I wanted to be there when she arrived. I hoped seeing her could help me clear my head and look at the situation from a new perspective.

BACK AT MY HOUSE, I tried to let go and enjoy a normal evening. Over dinner, I brushed off talking about the cabin or my dad by trying to steer the conversation toward other topics. For a time it worked. Melanie and I talked about her day and for a brief moment it felt like we were normal people.

After dinner, we moved to the couch and watched some TV. Melanie had been resting her head on my chest when a commercial break came on. She sat up and looked at me. Her eyes showed concern, and she let out a sigh.

"When are you going to talk to me?" she asked, slumping her shoulders.

"What do you mean?"

"Ever since you went off the grid for a couple days, you haven't been yourself. You don't speak at all about anything. Not my house, not what's been going on... it's like you're shutting down on me."

"Melanie, I'm not shutting down," I sat up and ran my fingers through my hair. "I'm just... it's just that I don't understand what's happening."

"Oh c'mon David! I've known you forever and you've always headed straight into the unknown without hesitation. That is part of who you are. You don't know, but you figure it out. You step back and look at it in a way that no one else does and that is what causes it all to make sense."

She was right. I never did walk in with concrete knowledge. I was the one who put the puzzle together without a road map.

"Look, this is just different. I don't know how to explain it."

"Different because you realized your dad was part of the KGC?"

"That's part of it I s'pose."

"Who cares what your dad did? That doesn't change who you are. Why are you letting that get to you?"

"It's not just that. It's everything. It's me."

Her face softened. She was looking at me like I was a lost puppy.

"Look, everything in this whole damn case goes back to me." I stood up and started pacing around the room. "It's your cabin, not mine. You are the one with the Sovereign

Lord in your attic fucking with you, not me. But he isn't looking for you; he's looking for me. Everything in this case leads back to me. I don't know how to do this. I help people. I help people understand what is going on and figure out a way to bring closure to hauntings. But here, I'm not helping someone else understand, all I'm doing is looking at myself."

There was a long moment of silence. She bit her lower lip and tilted her head to the side.

"David, sit down. Just talk to me. What happened there today?"

"What happened? The same thing that has happened every damn time I look at anything. It goes back to me and my dad."

Frustrated, I sat back down and tried to get a hold of myself.

"Okay, so this all goes back to you. I get it. I'm just trying to help, y'know? I care about you, and I'm worried about you."

Another long moment of silence passed. I didn't know what to say. I was mad but didn't even know who I was mad at.

"Look I'm sorry," she said, breaking the silence. "Maybe coming here tonight was a mistake. I should just go back to my cabin." Her words were cold and unemotional.

"Melanie, don't go. I'm sorry, I just don't know what I'm doing."

"So what? That has never stopped you before. Why now?"

"Because it's me! When it's someone else, I can pick everything apart and see what makes it fit together, but I can't do it for myself."

Before I could speak another sentence, she wrapped her

arms around me and kissed me. It was slow and deliberate, leaving my mind clear of anything but her.

"You know," she said softly as she pulled away from me, "it sounds like you're a little scared."

"I'm not scared. It's just different."

"Look, I don't blame you one bit. Look at me and my past with Austin. There is so much shit locked tight in that trunk that I never want to open. I've dealt with it. I've moved on. I don't want to relive any of it. But just because I've dealt with it for now doesn't mean it isn't a part of who I am. A new perspective of that time in my life can always provide a different insight."

That was the Melanie from my past speaking. That was the girl who had always connected with me. She wasn't saying anything profound. But what she said aligned so precisely with what I needed to hear. I realized why I had so deeply missed having her in my life. I knew I had to keep digging into my past. I realized, with Melanie by my side, I didn't have to do it alone.

13

THE NEXT MORNING I sat at my kitchen table, the box of documents I'd grabbed from my dad's office open in front of me. I sat there staring at it. Between sips of coffee I rolled his coin idly across my knuckles. I knew I had to dive in and see what I could find. But Melanie was at work, and the more I stared at the box, the more I realized I wasn't ready to take that leap alone.

I found myself distracted by the coin in my hand. Watching as it rolled across one knuckle and then the next, my mind started to drift. It went back to that day in the woods when my dad gave me the coin. What stuck out in my mind was that everything he'd said about it was related to that one area of the forest.

In a flash, I stuffed the coin in the pocket of my jeans. I stood up, took one last sip of coffee, and got ready to leave. I was heading to the trail. Reading and researching often filled the gaps of information, but my real skill was being able to read the energy I felt in a place. The box of documents could wait. I needed to be on that trail to feel where it directed me.

I drove like a bat out of hell. The wheels of my truck were on the edge of losing traction, slipping as I navigated the tight turns of the mountain road. I flew past the turn-off to Melanie's cabin and headed straight up the mountain. It was still early when I reached the parking area at the Gap. The air was crisp and the mountain was silent, aside from a few people who were unpacking to get an early start on a hike. I parked near the trailhead, the same as everyone else. However, my destination was the old trail on the opposite side of the parking lot. To the average person, it appeared there was no trail there. But, if you knew where to look, a few feet inside the foliage, the trail began.

As I approached the overflow portion of the parking lot, I saw one car parked away from the others, near where the old trail began. A car parked in an Appalachian Trail lot was not an odd sight. Typically it was simply a section hiker who was out for a few days and left their car in the lot. But that wasn't a random hiker's car. It was Melanie's neighbor. Zeke. It was the same car I'd watched speed out of her drive yesterday when he went looking for his dog.

A wave of concern overcame me. Zeke didn't strike me as a hiker at all. Zeke was out looking for his dog yesterday, a journey that should have sent him home by nightfall if he was unsuccessful. My head rattled through the hundreds of purely legitimate and reasonable reasons for his car to be there. While they were all possibilities, something felt wrong. I didn't know Zeke at all. I had no reason to assume anything. Yet, the feeling in my gut told me I needed to be concerned for him.

As I approached the brush hiding the entrance to the trailhead, I noticed some of the saplings were broken. It was a sure sign that someone had walked that way very recently. I became hyper-aware of my surroundings, constantly looking and listening for anything. I made my way to the abandoned trail and entered the dark and cool canopy. The path was overgrown but still defined. The old shelter on the trail was a good mile's hike from there. Every step of the hike I looked for some sign of Zeke.

After about a half hour, I made it to a clearing and the shelter, Spearfinger's Shack as we used to call it. It was a simple structure not unlike most of the shelters on the Appalachian Trail. A raised platform with three walls and a roof, just enough to offer some respite from the elements. It was decrepit, but still standing. I set my backpack down in front of the shack and sat down. I took a deep breath, closed my eyes, and tried to absorb everything.

That area of the forest was particularly quiet. The wind still blew and the trees swayed and creaked, but it was devoid of any animal sounds. As I sat there and thought back, that area had always been that way. Like in my youth, that spot felt completely safe. It felt like a small sanctuary protected from the world.

While I sat there, my head streamed through a slideshow of memories that had taken place in that very spot, from going there with my dad, to being there with Melanie. Every one of the memories was peaceful. It was my retreat from the confusing and sometimes painful world after my dad died. Some kids have a clubhouse in the back-yard. The Shack was my variation of that, the one place I was safe, the one place where I was king.

I came to the Shack intending to find direction and a clue to who I was, who my dad was. However, I felt nothing outside of peace. There was no residual energy for me to tap into.

I STARTED to think back to my time in high school when I would come down there. I was the weird, punk kid with my leather jacket and dirty hair. I made it my mission in life to push everyone away, except for Melanie. I built an emotional wall and put it up between me and the world. I was an angry kid and wanted to do things my way. This shack became my escape from the world. The one place I could be me. The one place I could let my walls down. The one place where, when it came to Melanie, I had confidence and a voice. There, no one could mess with me... until someone did. The last time I had been to the Shack was when Melanie told me she was marrying Austin. That was the moment that destroyed my safe place. At that moment, it was as if someone hit stop on my boom box. My anthem was gone and so was my sanctuary.

I slowly stood up and shook off my trip down memory lane. Aside from realizing how misguided and depressing my youth had been, I'd learned nothing by coming back there. I took a deep breath and caught the smell of smoke. There was a campfire nearby.

The scent was coming from further down the trail. Without thinking, I headed in the direction of the smell. With every step, the scent got stronger. I quickened my pace. I took another deep breath and realized it didn't smell like smoke from clean, dried wood burning. It was heavier, almost acrid. I couldn't place it. A little further down the trail, I reached another clearing and the source of the smell.

There was a large fire pit in the center of the clearing. I realized the acrid smell was not of a live fire but the more overpowering smell of a fire being extinguished. The wood in the pit was only partially burned. I stooped down and put my hand over it. It was still hot. The fire had gone out only minutes prior.

"Hello?" I yelled.

I stood unmoving, trying to hear anything in response, be it words or even the snapping of a twig under someone's foot. There was nothing.

The ground was damp and soft, and as my eyes scanned the area, I realized that my footprints were clear. I could even see the logo imprinted on the ground from the soles of my hiking shoes. Yet, my footprints were the only ones there. There were no tracks of any kind, human or animal, leading in or out of that clearing. Yet, the fire was real, and I could still feel its heat. I took a closer look at the fire pit, and my eyes stopped on a blue piece of fabric. It was on the edge of the pit, lying against one of the rocks.

I picked it up and looked at it. It was only a couple inches square and burned on all the edges. Then, the image of Zeke flashed before my eyes. Zeke telling me about his dog before speeding off. Zeke wearing a blue shirt. I shoved the fabric in my pocket and continued to examine the ground around the fire pit. I tried walking as lightly as possible around the pit. No matter what I did, it was impossible to be near the pit without leaving some print.

Even more frustrating to me was the fact that I could still not feel any negative energy there. There was no emotion to help me paint the picture of what had taken place. It was an anomaly. I felt things everywhere I went, but there, like the Shack, there was a lack of energy. Unsure of what to do next, I cautiously walked back towards the shelter, past it, and toward the parking lot.

For the next fifteen minutes, I walked in silence. I didn't hear or see anything. Then, the forest started to come back to life. Slowly, the sounds of birds chirping and animals running in the distance returned. I stopped to have a drink of water. I set my bag down and got out my water bottle. I looked around again for any sign of someone else on this trail but saw nothing. I was beginning to think that the whole firepit was another vision. I reached into my pocket to retrieve the charred cloth to confirm the reality of what I'd seen. It wasn't there.

I put my water down and frantically went through my pockets. I emptied them all and found nothing but the items I typically carried. The cloth was gone, if it had even existed in the first place. My shoulders slumped as I took a deep breath. Defeated and confused, I put everything back in my pockets and strapped on my backpack once again. I stood there motionless for a moment, debating if I should continue to the parking lot or go back to the phantom fire pit.

If it wasn't real, if it was a vision, what was it trying to show me? I racked my brain trying to answer the question but couldn't. I knew visions always had a purpose. Their message may be hard to decipher, but it was always there. I could only feel that this was trying to tell me something about Zeke, but that almost felt too literal.

I continued thinking about it as I headed back toward the parking lot. After only a few steps, I heard the echo of someone else in the forest. The unmistakable sounds of twigs snapping and bending under each step. Someone was ahead of me on the trail, and they were close.

I froze. I resisted the urge to shout out. If it was Zeke, I wanted him to know I was there, but if it wasn't, I didn't want to draw any negative attention. Despite everything running through my head, I stood completely silent and unmoving. I crouched down to keep myself from being visible. I waited and watched.

The steps were slow and steady as they approached, and they did not waver. The only change was the volume, getting louder with each step as they drew closer. I took a deep breath. I was sure the person was upon me or would be in another couple steps. I squinted through the foliage. The first thing I was able to see was a hiking boot and an olive drab pair of pants.

I recognized it immediately. It was a uniform, a ranger uniform. Not wanting to raise suspicion, I stood up.

"Hey, who's there?" I asked.

"US Forest Service. This trail is off-limits," a gruff voice responded... a gruff voice I knew all too well.

"Gordon?"

"Who's there? Step onto the trail where I can see you!"

I swallowed hard and timidly stepped out into the clearing of the trail. Gordon bore down with a look of contempt until he recognized me. His eyes widened but his frustration was still visible.

"David?" he asked removing his hat and wiping his forehead. "What the hell are you doing out here? You know better than to come down this trail."

"Sorry, I just wanted to...uh...be here where he was and see what I could feel."

"You mean like that ghost stuff you do on TV? Jesus, kid. You can't be going down here. You have any idea how dangerous this trail can be?"

In that instant, I didn't hear the voice of a forest ranger, I heard his feeble attempt at being a stand-in father for me after my dad was gone. "Dammit Gordon, I'm not a fucking kid. I can handle myself. Did you follow me here or something?"

"It's not like that. I know you can handle yourself. It's just this trail... you know... it just isn't safe for anyone."

"So you did follow me here, then!"

"No! I had no clue you were out here!"

I stood silent. The juvenile rage that had overtaken me was starting to fade, and I didn't know what to say.

"Look," Gordon said, "a deputy called in a report of a man going down here. I had to come check it out. I certainly didn't expect you."

"Sorry, I just felt I needed to be here, and I kinda go to another place in my head when I'm trying to feel something. You just caught me off guard."

"I get it, but I gotta get you out of here. C'mon, let's get back to the Gap."

I started to walk with him back down the trail. "Hey, aren't you like the boss of the department? Shouldn't one of the new rangers be checking out random people out here?"

He stopped walking and turned to face me. "This trail is...it's not right. I lost my best friend, your dad on this very trail. I'm not gonna risk losing anyone else. If a ranger needs to go down here, I'm the only one who will do it, on my command."

"I get that. But it's just a trail. You said it yourself the other day. Dad... well his liver failed. That would've happened here, on any other trail, or even at home. It just happened."

He looked down at his feet and his shoulders slumped. "There is more to this trail than that. Your dad wanted it closed off for a reason. I may have not agreed with him or even understood why, but I knew him, and if he felt this trail wasn't safe, I had to believe it. Years later, I came down here myself and stumbled on that old shelter. Apparently, it had become a local hangout for kids. All I could hear in my head was your dad's voice saying it wasn't a safe place. It became a bit of a personal project for me from that point forward."

"Did you have any other issues out here?"

"No, nothing. It was just a thing I felt I had to do. Look,

do me a favor. I know you're just trying to feel all your ghost things back here. I get it. But you gotta leave this trail alone. Nothing has happened out here, but it's closed down and it needs to stay that way. I gave you the key to the substation. I'm trying to help you, but you gotta do this for me. Okay?"

Gordon was lying. I knew, from the reports and his sudden change in demeanor, there was so much more to this story, but it was clear I was going to get nothing else from him. While part of me seethed with anger at his lies, I took a deep breath and just agreed with him. For now, I needed to get out of there and figure out how I could return without him.

We started heading back down the trail. With every step my anger became stronger. Just when I thought I would not be able to bite my tongue any longer, I heard a dog bark. I jumped at the sound and turned toward it. Ten yards behind us, a dirty, mangy dog stepped onto the path. He stood tall and stoic. He bared his teeth as if he was protecting his owner.

"David! What's gotten into you?" Gordon said as he grabbed my shoulder.

I turned to look at him. He was staring down the trail towards the dog. I turned back towards the dog but nothing was there. It was just the overgrown trail. I shook my head and looked again. There was nothing there.

Crossing paths with Gordon on this trail had overwhelmed my thoughts. His evasiveness and my attempt at understanding everything made Zeke completely slip my mind. Seeing that dog on the trail brought Zeke to the forefront. I returned my attention back at Gordon who appeared concerned.

"Jeez, I thought I heard something," I said. "Just got spooked."

"Let's just get you out of here already. I hate this damn trail."

"Wait!" I yelled. "We can't go!"

Gordon rubbed his chin, looking at me with raised eyebrows.

"There is someone out there," I said pointing down the trail. "It's Melanie's neighbor, Zeke. He took off looking for his dog. I saw his car parked at the entrance to this trail. I think he is down there somewhere."

"Are you sure?"

"Yes! I'm sure he went down there somewhere, but I didn't see him. I just felt it."

"Alright, you get the hell out of here. I'll look for him."

"I can help."

"No you can't! You need to get out of here. I'll call in some backup if I need it, but you need to be gone from this trail for good!"

14

I spent that night at home with Melanie. She had quickly moved from being my client to being my confidant and sounding board for this case. The only problem was that she was far more interested in how everything connected to her house than the greater story. Also, I was so enamored with her that it was difficult to focus on anything else.

After she left for work the next morning, I thought everything through. I realized I was headed in many different directions. I wanted to help Melanie, but I found myself focused more on my father. As much as I wanted to avoid consulting Linda again, I realized I needed some help. I drove out to the office and took a deep breath as I walked in.

Linda was meditating in the conference room. Her head jerked to the side to look at me, and a large smile appeared on her face. She was absolutely beaming when she stood up and hugged me. "I thought you would avoid talking to me as long as possible. I'm so glad you changed your mind. Please, come sit with me."

I hesitantly sat down with her in the conference room.

"Go on, tell me what you've seen," she prodded.

"My dad. This is apparently all about him. He had something to do with protecting the forest for the KGC. That's how I'm connected to all this."

She responded only with a nod, showing me she already knew.

"Look, I get it. My dad ties me into everything, but that doesn't help me at all with Melanie and her house. I need to focus on that for now."

"Your dad, Mel's house, the forest... they are all the same thing. These are not separate cases."

"I get it, but now I am down some wormhole trying to learn about my dad and not doing a damn thing for Melanie."

"Be patient. Follow where the case leads you. You know this, David." She paused and looked at me with a disappointed expression as she held out her hand. "Let me see it please."

"See what?"

"I can feel it with you. What have you found? Please, let me see it."

I knew exactly what she was referring to. The coin my father had given me. Linda had this gift to feel objects in the room even if they were out of sight. I'd seen her do it before with Kat. It was unnerving. I obediently reached into my pocket to retrieve the KGC coin and handed it to Linda. She held it tightly in her fist and closed her eyes. After a few seconds she began to nod as if she was listening to someone give her instructions. She opened her eyes and handed me the coin.

"What did you see?" I asked.

"You are lost, David."

"No shit I'm lost. Why else would I be standing here asking for your help?"

"I saw nothing that you don't already know. The trouble is, you know it yet you refuse to look. "

"You have anything to say that might be a little more helpful?"

"Tell me what you did over the last few days."

"What I did? What do you mean?"

"Your days, where you went, what you did. Please. Walk me through it."

"I went to the Ranger station, and then I stopped at my old house and picked up some stuff."

"Your old house? What did you do there?"

"I told you. I just grabbed some of my dad's old stuff and looked around a bit."

"And what did you feel while you were inside?"

That question left me without a response. The truth was, I'd felt nothing, although I didn't want to admit that to Linda. After an uncomfortable silence, she sighed and grabbed my shoulders.

"Listen to me, David. You are a very talented investigator and can uncover tremendous insights using that skill, but you didn't set out to be a private investigator. Your investigative skills only bring true insight when you combine them with the gift you have to feel. Normally, you let your feelings guide your research. Now, you are ignoring your skill, ignoring what you sense. I don't have any help for you beyond what you already know. Right now, you need to look inward and allow yourself to truly absorb everything."

At that moment, I realized precisely what she had been trying to get me to understand this whole time, and I knew exactly what I needed to do next.

"Ahh, so you do understand," she said as if she could actually see the synapses firing in my brain.

"I do. Thank you."

I gave her a hug, then stepped back and looked at her.

"You think he'll talk to me? I mean, I'm not like you."

"He has always been speaking to you. You just never understood where the voice was coming from. It's about time you have the conversation directly."

I said bye to Linda, got in my truck, and drove back to the old sub-station where I'd grown up. I was going to talk to my dad.

I PULLED off the road in front of my old house again. I approached the door, clearing my thoughts. I was there to contact my dad. I was unsure of what would happen. I had always been able to feel a presence or energy. However, communicating with a presence was something I'd rarely done, and when I did, it was reluctantly. This was my father. This was so different than anything else I'd done.

I thought about what I wanted to achieve. There were so many things I would have loved to talk to my dad about, but this was my one chance. I needed his help in understanding the case. As I approached the door, I tried to force all those thoughts out of my head so I could just let happen whatever was going to happen. I took in a deep breath as I unlocked the door and stepped in.

I was greeted by the loud clang of the grandfather clock finishing its hourly chime. I instinctively looked at my watch and realized it was 10:17 am. There would be no reason for the clock to be chiming then. I stepped into the living room and looked at it. It stood in the corner of the room, untouched and unmoving. A thick layer of dust covered its surface, and the pendulum sat still.

"Dad?" I spoke as my eyes darted around the room. "It's me. I'm home now."

I stood silently, waiting for some sort of response. When none came, I took a deep breath, approached the couch and sat down. I let my mind go back to my childhood growing up there. I remembered watching TV on that very couch. I started remembering the hours I'd spent playing The Legend of Zelda with my butt on those cushions. I brought my attention back to the present. Just then, the TV sprang to life showing a familiar episode of Boy Meets World. I stared at it for a moment, wondering what I was seeing. Then my gaze drifted to the clock. I saw him. My dad was standing there, fastidiously cleaning the grandfather clock and winding it. I started to remember that routine of his. Every week he would spend an hour messing with the clock.

"Hey, dad!" I yelled.

He stopped and turned his head to look at me.

"In a minute, David. I need to finish this." He returned his attention to the clock.

His blowing me off like that was an experience I was very familiar with. I wasn't sure if I was experiencing it or just reliving a memory. I continued to watch him. After he finished wiping down the exterior, he set down the rag and opened the front to wind the clock. I realized that, despite seeing that routine every week, I'd never really watched it. As he wound the clock, I noticed the clocks hands. According to the clock, it was precisely 11:27. I'd seen that time before. It was written in his desk. I wondered if this was a true vision or my manifestation from that. Then, I noticed something else. When he finished winding the clock, he closed a small compartment inside it. Then he re-set the clock according to his watch and started the pendulum. Finally, before shutting the glass door, he pulled something out of the inside of the clock and put it in his pocket.

As my mind started to focus on what my dad put in his pocket, the entire scene faded away. My dad was gone. The TV still sat covered in dust. The clock was silent.

"Dad, I'm still here. Talk to me."

I could feel pangs of adolescent rage build up inside of me as it always did with my dad. At that moment, I felt like I had when I'd come home, proud of a grade, only to be ignored by my dad. He was all I had, but he was never really there, especially when it came to anything I cared about.

"You know, this is just like you! The moment something matters to me, and I need you, you aren't there! You left me with nothing. Raised by mom's sister who only made sure I was fed. And then there's Gordon. You know that asshole can't even speak honestly with me about anything? You know what? I'm done with this. I should have never come back here. The only damn thing I've learned is that you, the one person I should've been able to trust, were a part of an organization that did nothing but spread evil across the country."

I stood up and pulled the coin from my pocket.

"The KGC. Do you know how many lives they destroyed to keep their way of life? And now I find out you were one of them!"

Tears streamed down my face. In a matter of moments, I'd unleashed every ounce of pain and frustration I'd bottled up since I was a kid. I pulled back my arm and threw the coin at the clock. The coin hit the glass pane on the door. I expected the glass to shatter, but it didn't. The coin bounced off with a clang. It flipped in the air as it landed on the carpet in front of me. I fell to my knees and pounded my fists on the ground until I just couldn't anymore. I raised my hands to my head and wiped my eyes. I tried to regain control over myself. When I looked up again, I saw Robert Mason.

THE IMAGE ONLY LASTED AN INSTANT. By the time I stopped to rub my eyes and get a better look, it was gone. In that brief moment I understood what I was there to find. It wasn't Robert. It was the clock. The clock that I'd grown up with, that my dad poured so much attention into, wasn't his clock. It was the clock I had seen in Robert's room in Cloudland.

I stood up and made my way over to the clock. It was truly an exquisite piece. The dark hand-carved wood was in pristine condition. I found the brass latch holding the glass door shut and unlocked it. As I opened the cabinet, I thought about the image of my father that I'd just seen. I pulled out a flashlight and began to inspect the inside of the clock. I quickly found the compartment I'd seen my dad closing, but it just looked like part of the cabinet. I couldn't find a latch, a hinge, or anything that would indicate that it was a compartment aside from the small gaps in the wood around what I presumed was its door.

Underneath the compartment I found a circle carved into the wood of the cabinet. I moved the flashlight to examine it. Inside was the embellishment of a cross, a cross that looked identical to the one on my coin. I dropped the flashlight and grabbed the coin from the carpet. I pressed the coin into the circle. It fit perfectly.

Nothing happened.

I let go of the coin, and it simply dropped out, crashing against the weights inside the clock as it fell. I'd expected it to work like Melanie's attic, but there was nothing. I was missing something, but I didn't know what.

I stepped back and looked at the clock. "Of course, the clock needs to be running!" I yelled to the empty room.

I found the key to the clock hanging inside the cabinet and began to wind it. The heavy brass weights slowly lifted from the bottom of the cabinet where they had rested for years. After the clock was completely wound, I put the key back and gently pulled the pendulum to the side. As I released it, the clock came to life. The pendulum swung back and forth and the clock began its familiar low ticking noise.

With the clock running, I retrieved the coin and once again pressed it into the impression in the cabinet. Nothing. Again the coin fell. That time, in its descent, it hit the pendulum causing it to swing off center. I grabbed it and stopped the clock again.

Frustrated, I picked up the coin again and began to roll it on my fingers. Looking at the face of the clock, it hit me. In my vision, the clock was stopped, but the time was set to exactly 11:27. It was set to 8:42 at that moment. I slowly moved the minute hand around stopping at every 15-minute interval to let the clock chime. After finally making it to 11 o'clock, then 11:15, I moved the minute hand to 11:27.

I took a deep breath and fit the coin into the impression. This time, the coin stuck. I heard a soft click. The door of the compartment popped open. I pulled out my flashlight and gently opened the door. Inside was an envelope. I lifted the envelope out and moved over towards the window where I could see it in natural sunlight. It was a US Forest Service envelope, and on the front was written 'David' in blue ink. I sat on the couch and pulled out my knife. I gently cut the sealed envelope open and pulled out the two folded papers inside.

The top one appeared to be far newer than the other. It was a letter from my dad.

David,

I can only assume that by finding this letter, you have learned of our legacy and our role. Much like you, I never chose this task. It was passed down to me from my father. The other papers in this envelope will explain more about the role we have been chosen to fulfill.

That coin you used to retrieve this letter is the key. I gave it to you in the forest because it protects you from the evil that lurks there. The coin is the link between our family legacy and the KGC. We have been sworn to protect people from the area near the abandoned shelter. Many years ago, a terrible evil was conjured on that spot as a guardian. It is very powerful and, unchecked, it would gradually gain power until it could not be contained.

The real role we are sworn to fulfill is to, when the time comes, vanquish that evil. Do not think of this task as a burden, as I have. It is an honor and needs to be taken on for the greater good. As my son, this will fall into your hands. The coin is the only weapon we have to fight this.

Love Always,

Dad

My hands were shaking. I set the letter down and began skimming the other document. It was a bit hard to read, written in a formal script, which had faded considerably. It was signed by Robert Mason.

It outlined an agreement between Robert and Johan Spur, my great-great-grandfather. Robert would employ Johan to watch over that area of the forest. It also mentioned the designation of this part of the National Forest to aid with those efforts. Johan would hold a permanent position within the US Forest Service.

It also detailed a change to their original agreement. Johan's role was no longer focused on protecting the area from people, but on protecting people from the area and the evil that lived there. At the end of the document, it named the evil 'Spearfinger'.

15

BY THE TIME I got home, my head was spinning. I needed to step back before diving into the legend of Spearfinger. Something else was nagging me: Zeke. On my way back home, I drove by Melanie's place. There was no sign of Zeke anywhere. His car was gone and the cabin was locked up tight. I picked up the phone and called Gordon.

"Hey, it's David. I wanted to call you back about yesterday."

"Oh, of course. Look, I didn't mean to freak you out, but as much as I want to give you free reign, I do need to make sure I do my job."

"No, I meant with Zeke. Did you find him out there?"

"Oh...um no. I'm sure it's fine. You said you didn't actually see him on the trail. I'm sure he's just camping out on one of the balds."

"Yeah, of course. Well, let me know if you find anything. Thanks." I hung up the phone.

There was something that unnerved me about Gordon. He was hiding something, I could feel it. I started sifting through the info Paul had sent me about those kids who'd went missing. The one that stood out was Austin's older brother. I was sure I could get some info from Melanie, but I didn't exactly want to jump into any conversation about her ex without knowing what I was getting into.

Following my gut, I decided to research it on my own first. I didn't really know much about Austin's brother, except that he died when I was a kid. With his name appearing in that questionable report, I felt like there could be something there. After a cursory search, I learned that he died only about a month after Barnes did. Unfortunately, with all of that being pre-internet, there wasn't much out there. I started searching for his father, Glen Soto, and a new story started to unfold before me. Glen had a massive footprint on the web, which all centered around one thing: searching for KGC gold.

A founding member of a treasure hunting forum, Glen had assembled an impressive amount of research and information about the lost KGC treasure. From maps to interpretation of symbols found on trees, he had everything. I spent the next couple hours reading everything I could from him on the forum. He stated multiple times how he knew precisely where one of the KGC hoards was hidden in Roan Mountain. I was skeptical. If he'd truly known the location, then he would have dug it up himself. Then I found a post where he replied to other forum members posing that same argument.

"You will only be satisfied with a photo of the loot, which I will never show you. I do know the exact location, but at the moment I have no interest in digging there. For one, it is on protected land and would be highly illegal for me to even remove one small piece from this hoard. So, even if I did dig it up, I would never post about it. Secondly, the area is protected by the KGC. This shit is real, and I lost my son to the search. Until I am able to evade the Sentinels protecting this place, I will leave it be. I will not suffer the same fate as my son."

Whatever the truth really was, he clearly believed that his son died at the hands of the KGC Sentinels. I needed to find more information about what had happened to him. I reached back out to Paul, asking him to research Derek Soto. Knowing information from Paul would take some time, I called Linda to discuss Spearfinger.

"So, how's your dad doing?" Linda said as she answered the phone.

"Eh, same old story I s'pose. He always did make me work for everything."

"And I can only imagine you found something that you need your dearest friend to help you out with."

"You could say that."

"So what is it?"

"Spearfinger."

"Spearfinger again? You do know that you're really expanding here. Spearfinger is not your run of the mill demon or spirit."

"Linda, I know that much. I need to find out what I can about the legend. Especially the part about how the tribe vanquished her."

"You sure? Because if the tribe did such a great job vanquishing her, then I doubt that you would need to learn more about it."

"I know, but... let's just say, I have reason to believe that some powerful association may have conjured her back into existence."

"How sure are you? Rumors of her have been around these hills forever. The information you want will require me to call in some favors."

"Does a signed letter talking about Spearfinger from one of the Sovereign Lords of the KGC help sell you?"

"So it is her then."

"I'm afraid so."

"Let me call some people, but this may be tough. The Cherokee are not exactly eager to discuss things like this with people not connected to the tribe."

"Well, something tells me that if anyone knows someone who can help me out, it would be you."

"I do, David, but it will take some doing. Let me make some calls and see what I can work up for you."

EVEN THE DISTRACTION of seeing Melanie couldn't keep my head from spinning. It seemed Austin's family had been looking for what Robert Mason had hidden. While I had no concrete proof, I was starting to believe that Austin's brother had fallen victim to the evil lurking in the forest.

I had planned on not discussing that with Melanie until I knew more, but she knew something was on my mind. No matter how hard I tried to silence my thoughts and focus on her, she could tell I was distracted, and she began calling me out on it. I started by playing it off. Then I blamed the fact that I'd been digging into my dad.

As we finished eating and began clearing the table, I knew I couldn't hide it any longer.

"Just talk to me," she said grabbing my shoulder. "This is kinda what we do together. We share stuff, you know?"

She was right. I knew that.

"C'mon, sit down."

We walked over to the living room and sat on the couch.

I took a deep breath. "Okay, so you know how I was

looking into my dad and everything that had taken place in that area of the forest? I had a friend pull some police reports for me."

"Right, you mentioned that."

"Yeah, well, what I didn't mention was that these reports focus on people dying inexplicably, specifically in the area of the forest that your ghost is trying to help you find. It seems that spot that you've been looking for is protected by some spirit. There are a few unexplained deaths that seem to be caused by the spirit."

Her demeanor immediately shifted. She quickly pulled up a blanket and wrapped herself in it like a cocoon. Her eyes were darting back and forth.

"Derek," she said in a whisper.

She knew exactly where I was going with this.

"Yeah, he was mentioned in one of the police reports."

"Are you saying that this is all happening in my house because of Austin? Like am I supposed to help him avenge his brother's death or something? These spirits or whatever should know I want absolutely nothing to do with him."

"No, at least I haven't seen anything to suggest that. It's just another weird connection, like the way the haunting in your cabin led me to investigate my own father. Your cabin is active because of the residual energy from Cloudland, and that's connected to the KGC."

"So what do you want to know? she asked. "Since that is where you were going anyway."

"Well, what do you know about Derek?"

"Honestly, I don't know much. He was gone before I ever even met Austin. From what I do know, he was just a kid. A kid not a whole lot different from you."

"Me?"

"Yes, you. David, you are not the same person you were

back then. He was a kid, obsessed with finding the KGC treasure and getting the hell out of here... does that ring a bell at all?" She looked at me and raised her eyebrows. "Anyway, their whole family was after that treasure. Jeez, his dad was obsessed. From what I understand, Derek went out looking for it on his own and got lost or something. They found him a couple days later. Said he died of exposure. But that didn't sit well with his dad. He wouldn't accept for even a second that Derek would have gotten lost in those woods, let alone died of exposure. He had a point. They spent more time on that mountain than they did in their house. They knew how to handle themselves out there."

"Does his dad still obsess over the treasure?"

"Oh yeah! Like I said, that treasure was ingrained in the whole family. But Glen started to get even more obsessed with it in recent years. The search for the treasure started to unite with never believing Derek got lost out there. He started to talk about government conspiracies and how Derek had found the treasure, so the KGC had to deal with him."

"And you think he's nuts?"

"No, not at all. That treasure is still out there. If my cabin taught me anything, it's that. But when it comes to Derek, I don't really know. He was just a kid. Kids do stupid shit. I think he got himself in a bad spot. All I really know is what I got from Glen's ramblings. Austin, he never said a word about Derek. It was one of those topics that you know to stay away from. I still think that is half the reason he... Let's just say he never dealt with it, and he found other ways to deal with his emotions."

She put her hand on my shoulder, finally letting her guard down a bit. Her eyes were wet, and the sight of it alone left me struggling to find a response.

"Wait!" she said lurching forward. "What do you know? What happened out there?"

"Honestly, I don't know a damn thing for sure. I had my friend start searching for the reports on Derek. But even without them, I think there's more to Derek's story." I pulled up the report I had about Jamie Barnes on my phone and handed it to her.

I watched her eyes as she quickly read the report. There was an unbridled intensity in them.

"What the hell? I don't remember ever hearing about this."

"Jamie Barnes, he went missing not much before Derek. Derek was with him. Look there's a whole lot more there, but the one thing I know for sure is that Derek, Jamie, and my father all died in pretty much the same spot. The same spot where Robert is leading you."

———

MELANIE SAT IN STUNNED SILENCE. It was probably only a few minutes, though it felt like an eternity. She read and re-read the report in disbelief.

"You're sure this is all the same location?" she asked, putting the report down.

"As best as I can tell. I mean we don't have precise coordinates or anything, but it all seems to align."

"Wait! You'd mentioned that this spot was the spot you and your family were protecting... that you were protecting it for Robert because it was a cache. That evil or whatever is just another way he protected his cache, right?"

"Yeah, that's about right, except me and my family had been sworn to essentially keep people away from the area, not specifically to safeguard any cache."

"Whatever, listen to me." She stood up and began pacing. "You know damn well what the cache of a KGC Lord is. That is the treasure we have been dreaming of since we were kids!"

"Well, that is the legend, and you're probably right about that."

"Exactly! And if I'm having dreams from Robert leading me to this place, that can only mean he wants me to have that treasure!"

"Hold on a second. We don't know that. Besides, with Spearfinger still out there, anyone seeking that treasure is in danger."

"David, you said it yourself. That coin you carry around protects you from the evil. Stop and think about it. The two of us spent our childhood chasing that treasure. Years later, I buy a haunted house that leads me back to you and continues to lead me to the forest. The forest you just happen to have the only protection from. This is fate! We are back together to claim that treasure for ourselves!"

I realized she had a point. The events that led us both there were uncanny to say the least. That was the moment where it hit me. What everyone had been telling me since I got back into town. I had changed. As much as I wanted to deny that fact, it was staring me in the face. Melanie was right. That treasure was all I had ever dreamed about. Now, there was a chance for all of my childhood dreams to come true.... Getting the treasure and getting Melanie.

The problem was, I'd changed. I still wanted Melanie, but my view of the treasure had changed. It was no longer about chasing riches to leave town. The real treasure for me was doing what was needed to put an end to the evil. Setting the world right once again. Erasing the wrongs of generations who had abused their power of the supernatural.

"Robert expects more from me. For you, yes he may be directing you to that spot, but for me, it is my role to put an end to the evil living there. But maybe the two things are not so different."

"How are they not different?"

"What I'm saying is, why can't I work to take care of Spearfinger? Then once that is complete, we get to discover Robert's cache."

She looked at me for a moment. Her enthusiasm had faded and was replaced with a softness. "Then we won't jump into anything too quickly. We've waited for twenty years for that treasure. We can see this through first."

She kissed me. At that moment I felt closer to her than I ever had. She was my treasure. I couldn't imagine anything making me happier than being with her. Robert's cache was just money, but she was real, and that night I realized she was all I needed.

16

THE NEXT MORNING, I awoke feeling happy and content. The sun was streaming through the window and warmed me in a way that felt different. I felt as though I was in the right place in my life.

Melanie had gone to work already, leaving me feeling less than motivated to get out of bed and face the day, especially feeling as content as I did. I eventually reached for my phone on the nightstand. There was an email from an unknown address.

David, It's Paul.

Okay, so this Derek Soto. Let's just say that everything I dug up before seemed to only scratch the surface. The reports are all similar to the ones about Jamie Barnes, almost identical really. The same people signing the reports, the same story, the same missing time frame. And get this: Derek's autopsy made no mention of his liver, either.

Look, I'm happy to pull some of this stuff for you, but I gotta say you might wanna be careful with it. People don't like someone who is digging up dirt. Just be careful. I pulled some other reports you might find interesting. For now, this is all I got.

If you need me, talk to Jim. He will be able to get in touch with me.

I scanned through the list of attached PDFs until one caught my eye. It was titled "SpurRoger03172002"

I opened it, and saw it was all the reports associated with my dad's death. For the next hour, I read every page of it. The story was drastically different than the one Gordon told me. For one thing, it was not a case of him going silent and Gordon looking for him. According to the report, a witness found him just off the current Appalachian Trail, not the closed trail. Additionally, the witness was Leonard Gale, the same ghost witness who'd appeared in the Barnes' report.

The phone slipped from my shaking hand down onto the bed. I clenched my fist tightly and took a deep breath. I had to stop myself from reaching for the phone. I wanted to call Gordon. I wanted him to answer to me. Paul's words echoed in my head. I knew I couldn't.

I closed my eyes and flashed back to my dad's funeral. The line of rangers carrying the casket from the hearse to the grave site. I remember standing in front of the freshly dug hole, watching them lay my father to rest. Gordon stood behind me, with his hands firm on my shoulders. Most of the timeframe around my dad's death was a blur, but I could see that moment with Gordon behind me with absolute clarity.

I picked up my phone and went through the reports again. I was looking for something. I reviewed the autopsy report. Just like the others, there was no information about his liver. As I stared at the page, Gordon's voice echoed in my head:

"When they did the autopsy, they said something about liver failure. Something he had probably been living with for a while."

The only thing that made my father's autopsy report different from any of the others was that it was signed by the Carter County Medical Examiner, Claire Burton. My dad's autopsy was done locally while everyone else's body was shipped off.

I did a quick Google search for Claire and found that she retired a few years ago and resided in Erwin. Unfortunately, there was no updated information or an address. The name wasn't familiar to me, but I knew someone who would be familiar with it.

———————

"HI SUE ELLEN!" I said as I stepped into the Post Office.

"Well if it isn't Mr. Hollywood," she said, looking up from a stack of papers behind the counter. "Rumor is you ended up getting in touch with Mel."

"I can't hide anything from you."

"From what I hear, you two have really hit it off. You know, that's a smart match. You two should've found each other years ago if you ask me. But something tells me you didn't come here looking for love advice or your mail."

"Guess I can't fool you. I was hoping you could help me out with something."

"You know, you should be coming in here a little more often before you just start asking for things."

"I know. I've just been kinda busy..."

"Kinda busy with Mel," she sarcastically interrupted. "What do you need, Hollywood?"

"I'm trying to find someone, but I can't seem to find her address anywhere. A Claire Burton."

"Williams."

"I'm sorry?"

"Claire Williams. She hasn't gone by Burton since she married John. They live up on Bailey Hollow. Moved up there a few years back."

"Ah, so that's why I couldn't find her. I was using her maiden name."

"What are you looking for? She doesn't seem the type of person that you'd be looking up."

"I found my dad's autopsy report. She signed it. I'm just trying to understand what happened to him."

"Well, you don't have to look too far for her. Her and her friends usually spend all morning hanging out at that coffee shop a few doors down."

"You want me to go in there and just yell for her? I've never even met her. Hell, I don't even have a clue what she looks like."

"Is that shyness I'm hearing from you, Hollywood?" she asked, shaking her head. "Don't worry dear, I will help you out. I was just about to go on break anyway."

SUE ELLEN STEPPED into the coffee shop like a celebrity. There were "Heys" and hugs at every step. Just before reaching the counter, she stopped to get the attention of a woman.

"Claire Williams, what a coincidence. How is everything?"

Claire stood up to give Sue Ellen the obligatory hug. She was older but carried herself with a demeanor of strength. I watched her and Sue Ellen engage in the typical small talk for a moment before Sue Ellen grabbed my shoulder and pulled me next to her.

"Isn't it the damndest thing? David here was just asking

me where he might be able to find someone to help him understand this old medical report he has. You wouldn't mind Claire, would you?"

Claire smiled and gestured towards me.

"Uh yeah," I said, doing my best to sound casual. "I was looking into this autopsy report and not being a doctor, I'm afraid I don't understand everything."

"Autopsy report? From around here?"

"I'm afraid so. My father's. It's quite a few years old. If you don't mind, I can pull up a copy of it on my phone. It'll only take a minute."

"You two get acquainted," Sue Ellen said. "I will grab your coffee, David. Black, right?"

I feverishly flipped through my emails, looking for the autopsy report.

"I'm sorry, have we met?" Claire said. "I seem to recognize you from somewhere but can't place it."

"He grew up here, but lately he spends his time in Hollywood working on his TV show," Sue Ellen yelled from the counter.

"Oh, that's it! Is that really you on that ghost show?"

"It certainly is. Here, this is the report." I handed her the phone.

"Please sit down for a moment while I take a look at this." She gestured to the open seat across from her.

Within moments of looking at the phone, her facial expression changed. Her eyes widened and her lips lost their natural inviting smile.

"David, you realize this is my report, don't you?"

"I'm sorry, what do you mean?"

"My report. I was the medical examiner who performed the autopsy and wrote this report."

"Oh really? I thought the name on the report was Burton." I played dumb.

"My maiden name." She continued to scan the document on the phone. I could see her eyes shift as she read the text until they stopped, frozen for second. She immediately set the phone down and looked over her shoulders.

"Come with me." She grabbed my arm as she stood up. "Ladies, I will be right back."

She handed me my phone and walked out the door of the coffee shop with me trailing behind. Once outside, she again looked around and then turned to me. Her face was stern.

"Where did you get this?"

"I... I was looking into my father's death. It happened when I was young, and I never really knew what happened."

She took a deep breath. Her green eyes were penetrating. "Does anyone know you have this? You realize this document was never supposed to be available."

"No, no one knows I have it."

She stood there briefly staring me down as if she was trying to decide whether to trust me.

"I'll tell you about this report, but not here. Not where people can see us. Listen, my husband is away for a couple days. Let me give you my address and you can meet me there tonight at seven. Don't tell anyone you're going there. If you want to know about this report, that is the only way I will speak to it."

"I'm a little confused here. What's the big deal?"

She raised her hand as if to silence me and again turned her head to see if anyone was watching. "Not here. I understand, you go on your show and have free reign to dig up whatever you need. That isn't how it works here. You don't want to go digging where you don't belong. The fact that you even have that report is enough to scare me. I cannot believe you acquired it without someone knowing. I can't be seen speaking to you about it. Please, I will talk, just do what I ask."

Without another word, she turned and walked back into the coffee shop.

I stood there stunned and confused. Apparently, I should have taken Paul a bit more seriously in regards to his conspiracy stories. It was beginning to be too much. I was a paranormal investigator, not a private eye. Sure, I'd dealt with conspiracies before, especially around the KGC, but those were over a century old. This was way above my pay grade for sure.

Sue Ellen walked out of the shop and handed me a cup of coffee and a napkin with an address written on it.

"I trust you got what you were looking for?"

"Kinda, she is gonna look into it and let me know."

"You know, when she walked in, she didn't strike me as someone who'd be inviting you over. She looked upset. Is there something I need to know about all this?"

"What? No. I don't know... she basically told me she doesn't want to go through this in public and would prefer it if I came to her house where she could speak freely."

"If you say so. But believe me, if I get word that you are spending too much time with her, Mel will be the first to know."

Deciding I needed to hold off on the autopsy report until I spoke to Claire, I started to think about another concern of mine. Zeke.

It had been nearly three days since I'd watched Zeke drive off to look for his dog. He was on that trail. I could feel it. Not the way I felt supernatural occurrences. It was more of a gut feeling. Either way, I was concerned about him. Listening to my thoughts, I began to drive to Zeke's house.

As I passed Melanie's cabin, relief washed over me. Zeke's car was parked right outside his front door. I pulled in and parked. I sat looking out my windshield for a moment. From this perspective something was different. It took me a little bit to realize it, but his car was parked in front of his door, pretty typical for most people. But I had never seen his car there before. Normally he always parked on the far side of the house. That feeling in my gut rose again. Something was wrong, and I knew I needed to find out what.

I walked up to the porch and saw the front door was open, and only the flimsy screen door was closed.

"Zeke? You in there?"

Nothing.

I rapped my knuckles on the edge of the screen door. The wood wobbled in response, and the knock echoed throughout the house. There was no answer.

"Zeke, it's David. Get out here and give me a beer!"

The silence continued. I paced around his porch until I got to his cooler and opened it up to take a look. Zeke had come across as the guy who always had an icy cold beer waiting in his cooler. Yet, when I opened it up, only a few cans of Yuengling sat there floating in warm water. The cooler hadn't been touched since the last time I'd seen Zeke.

Against my better judgement, I found myself opening the screen door and stepping inside. The cabin was an exact copy of Melanie's except his was filled with clutter. I cautiously padded further inside.

"Zeke? It's David. Come on out."

I proceeded to the hallway. The bathroom was a mess and empty. The door to the bedroom in the back of the house appeared closed. I hesitated for a second before approaching it. As I got closer, I realized it was slightly ajar.

"Zeke?" I said as I lightly pushed the door open.

He wasn't there. The bedroom looked like a dirty dorm room, clothes thrown everywhere. Clearly, he wasn't the type to make his bed. The clutter and the mess made it impossible to discern if he had just been there five minutes ago or if he had been gone for days.

I made my way back to the living room. In the corner of the room was a massive desk. On the desk were two of the largest computer screens I'd ever seen. I sat down before them and grabbed the mouse. There was a moment of hesitation, feeling like I was invading his privacy. I quickly realized I had already broken into his house. At that point I was already in too deep to care.

As the mouse moved, the two monitors lit up. There were so many windows that popped up: messenger, email, and multiple browsers. The email window caught my attention. A full screen of bolded unread emails filled the screen. I scrolled down until I got to the messages that had been read. A shiver ran up my spine as I realized that not one email of his had been read since the time I last saw him. His instant messenger showed me the same thing. Wherever he was, he was off the grid and not in contact with anyone.

I started clicking through the various open tabs on his web browsers. The most recent were maps and aerial photos of the area. Then, I found tab after tab open to treasure hunting forums. All of them displayed threads related to the KGC and their missing treasure. I started to look at the room from a different perspective. Books littered the coffee table and desk. All history books. The top one, filled with yellow Post-its marking the pages, was an old book dedicated to the legend of the KGC treasure.

With my curiosity piqued, I started to look through the house even more. I went up to the loft and found two flight cases. Opening them revealed metal detectors. These were not the ones that kids got for Christmas. Zeke's were serious tools. He was most certainly a treasure hunter. There was no doubt in my mind that he'd moved to the area to find treasure. I made my way to the kitchen. The dirty plates in the sink were certainly not fresh. I decided it was time for me to go.

As I stepped out of the kitchen towards the door, something caught my eye. On the counter was a set of keys. They were for his car no doubt but covered in mud as if they had just been pulled out of the ground. Next to them was a business card. I turned the card over to reveal it was a ranger card. Gordon's ranger card.

That unsettled me. Gordon's card lying next to dirty keys. Yet, it was pristine. Even if I'd pulled the dirty keys out of my pocket and dropped them on the counter, my fingers would have enough dirt on them to leave a smudge on the card. Something was off about that. I looked at the sink for any sign that dirt had been washed off someone's hands. When I found none, I returned to the bathroom and did the same thing. While everything was a mess, there was no sign of dirt.

I ran outside to Zeke's car and started inspecting the ground around it. There was only one set of footprints leading to the house from the car. It was a boot, exactly like I had always remembered my dad wearing. Exactly like the boots I'd seen Gordon wear that day on the trail.

17

I RETURNED HOME BARELY able to contain my rage. I was infuriated with Gordon. I still didn't understand how everything fit together or if it even did. It was clear that deaths and disappearances were connected to Gordon, but were they also connected to Spearfinger and Robert Mason? That was the question I could not answer. I decided to spend some time focusing on Spearfinger, or at least her legend.

I pored through countless information sources on the web, but the story they told was all basically the same. I decided I needed to find the source material for all the stories. After some work, I was able to find an old report from the turn of the twentieth century documenting Cherokee legends. It appeared to be the report every other story was drawn from.

Spearfinger, who reportedly haunted an area of the forest, was made of stone with a finger as sharp as a razor. She was drawn to villagers. When the opportunity arose, she would lure her victims close before using her finger to murder them. She was also known as a shapeshifter who would often take the shape of her victims and then be able to lure more victims to her. The villagers who hunted her were always unsuccessful; their arrows would simply bounce off of her stone skin.

As the story goes, the villagers eventually created a plan to defeat her. They dug a large pit and covered it with brush. They lit a fire, hoping the smoke would draw her near. It did, and soon Spearfinger was trapped in the pit they created. However, they were unable to vanquish her. A titmouse had directed a hunter to aim for her heart. That proved unsuccessful, forever giving the titmouse a reputation for being a liar. It wasn't until a chickadee landed on her sharpened finger that the hunters realized her hand was in fact her weak spot. Taking aim, the hunter fired again, and an arrow pierced her hand, which contained her heart. She turned to stone, never to return again.

To me, it all sounded like a fairy tale complete with talking birds. The ghost stories I remembered as a kid made Spearfinger sound more real. There was one detail though, which made the story hit home. She fed only upon the livers of her victims. She would remove the organ with her finger and subsequently dine on it. Her victims often showed no wound from the encounter, but they would die shortly afterwards.

Was my dad really one of her victims? As much as I wanted to deny it, the connection was crystal clear. The only things that didn't fit was her location and the fact that she'd been vanquished, supposedly never to return. There was even mention of where the stone believed to be her remains was located. It was almost 100 miles away from Roan Mountain. I didn't really know how a demon of stone could cross that distance, although I had experienced plenty of unbelievable feats.

I picked up my phone and called Linda.

"Yes David, I know, Spearfinger," she said as she answered the phone.

"Damn, you are good! How did you know?"

"Really? You should know better. I'd promised to help you out with her, and we haven't spoken since."

"So, have you been able to find anything?"

"Not much yet. Like I said, this is a little outside my repertoire. Want me to set you up with an Ayahuasca ceremony, no problem, but hunting down a Cherokee legend is a bit more difficult."

"Ayahuasca? Is that what you had me doing? Jesus, I could've died!"

"Don't be a drama queen. Salestino is a highly regarded practitioner. Anyway, my point is, without being a Cherokee, it is a little hard to get this info, but I have some leads I am following up on for you."

"What kind of leads?"

"Cherokee, my dear. A friend of a friend has been studying Cherokee legends and happens to be one-eighth Cherokee, which is enough to actually talk to the right people on this stuff. He should be calling me back any time. Why the sudden urgency?"

"Well how about the fact that I now believe that my father, among many others, were killed by Spearfinger?"

"Just a feeling, or have you investigated this too?"

"A little of both, I'm still flushing out some details."

"Okay, because everything I know about Spearfinger says she was vanquished. I'd hate for you to be barking up the wrong tree with this."

"Yes, I know she was vanquished, but did you also know that she fed exclusively on people's livers?"

"I did."

"But did you also know that everyone who died in the

woods here, including my father, have no information about their liver listed in their autopsy reports?"

"Ah, so your research does point to her being more than a folk story. I just wanted to double check. You know how at times, when one is emotionally connected... well I didn't want you to be jumping to conclusions."

"It's fine."

"David, I'm worried about you. I know firsthand how hard this can be when it hits so close to home. I just want to make sure your judgement isn't impaired."

"Linda, I'm fine. If you want more proof, I should have it tonight. I'm meeting with the medical examiner who signed my dad's autopsy report."

"Okay, call me afterwards please."

───────

I DROVE up the long drive to Claire's house. It was a beautiful farm house, no doubt a hundred years old. The porch light was on. I parked and walked up the steps to the front porch. As my foot hit the second step, Claire threw open the front door. Her eyes intently stared down the driveway.

"Did anyone follow you here?" she whispered.

"What? No."

"Have you told anyone you would be here?"

"Of course not."

"Okay, come inside and have a seat."

She led me to the dining room where I sat down. She followed with a manila envelope. As she sat down, she pulled some papers out of the envelope.

"Here, this is the report, correct?" She slid the report over to me. "A Mr. Roger Spur?"

"Yes, this is my father's report."

"You know, the only reason I'm doing this is because he was your father. Well, that and I fear you would get into more trouble with me ignoring you. What is it you want to know?"

"I want to know why, ever since he died, I have been told he died of liver failure. Yet, when I found this report, there is no mention of his liver at all."

"Perhaps I should start from the beginning. You see, this wasn't a typical autopsy for me. Usually I would be called in to the county hospital, and I would just come over the next day and go to work. This was different. It was immediate and in a location I'd never been nor ever saw again."

"What do you mean immediate?"

"Just that, it was about seven at night when I got the call. It wasn't a 'come in tomorrow' situation; I had to be there within the hour, no excuses."

"Where was it?"

"Oh, I don't remember the location. It was part of the National Forestry Division. It wasn't a doctor's office or a hospital. It was like a vet's office. I think it is where they rehabbed injured animals from the forest. It was unnerving walking in there through a maze of cages with all these animals getting freaked out."

"So what happened then?"

"I performed the autopsy. This one concerned me. At first glance, there was no clear signs to point to a cause of death. Some scratches and bruises but nothing that would hint at something fatal. Then, as I continued with the autopsy, I realized he had no liver."

She stopped to take a drink of tea.

"I'd never seen anything like it. The liver was removed, surgically. I mentioned it and the officer in charge dismissed it. Said that it had already been removed and sent off to a lab for testing."

"Okay, so there should be a report somewhere about the testing of his liver then, right?"

"I don't think you understand what I am saying. His liver was surgically removed. Yet, when I examined his body, there were no incisions anywhere, not even scars. From that moment forward, I was the only one touching him. I never even left the room. The liver was removed alright, but not by me and not in that office. Whoever removed it seemed to be able to do it without leaving even a hint of an incision. It just isn't possible."

"You mentioned an officer there with you. Do remember who he was? Was he local police?"

"There was an officer present. He oversaw everything. He was also the one who informed me that the liver was being tested. The odd thing was that he was just a forest ranger. He was in charge there, but there was also someone pulling his strings. He was constantly on the phone, both reporting and taking orders. His name was Owens, if I remember correctly."

"Owens? Gordon Owens perhaps?"

"Yes! That's it!"

"Okay, but one thing you haven't told me is why all the secrecy around this?"

"Secrecy is just for self-preservation. Look, this is not how I work. There was nothing about that situation in any way indicative of how I do things. I am extremely transparent about everything I do. With this however, I wasn't given a choice."

"What do you mean?"

"Okay, typically if I work with anyone outside the hospital, it's through the local police. This was being handled by the Department of Forestry. Federal. They run things a bit differently. Due to the sensitive nature of this case and the current investigation, I was informed that the case was confidential, and I was ordered not to speak about it to anyone. That's why I was surprised to see this report on your phone. Every report I have ever written is readily available."

"Except this one."

"Yes! Except this one. This report does not exist. From a documentation level, that evening doesn't even exist. I couldn't log my time, nothing. I was paid in cash that night and told that it was a matter of security due to the nature of the investigation surrounding it. I didn't completely believe them then; I believe them less now. At the same time, I am a doctor, so with HIPAA and all that, confidentiality has always been second nature to me."

We spoke a little longer. Then I thanked her for her time and reassured her that I would never relay any of our conversation to anyone. As Claire showed me to the door, she stopped to offer a parting piece of advice.

"David, I don't know what you're looking for, nor do I know the reality of who is behind all of it. But I have been a medical examiner for many years. Whatever you look to discover in this, it may not be worth your effort. You are not going to bring your father back."

"Thank you. I appreciate that. However, I am not looking to right any wrongs of the past so I can sleep at night. I am trying to ensure that no one else ends up like my father."

I AWOKE the next morning to find a text from Linda telling me to meet her at a certain address at eleven. The address was far, at least a two hour drive. Typical of Linda, she offered no other information aside from the address and the time. In the back of my mind, I couldn't help but think back to the secluded mountain villa where I'd undergone meditation with some medicinal assistance. Despite my apprehension, I couldn't deny that Linda always came through for me.

I navigated the narrow mountain passages into North Carolina and finally arrived at the location, a trailhead for the Whiteside Mountain trail. I pulled up and parked next to Linda's VW. She was standing outside the car speaking with a young man.

"David, this is Adahy!" She gestured to the young man. "I think he will be able to help you understand a bit more about what's going on."

"Please, call me Andy." The young man extended his hand to me.

"Uh, hi Andy, great to meet you," I shook his hand.

"Adahy grew up here and knows quite a bit about the legends of this area," Linda said.

"Linda tells me you are interested in Spearfinger," he said.

"I'm not completely sure, to be honest. Up in Roan Mountain, there has always been talk of Spearfinger haunting the woods. I guess I would like to know more about the legend of Spearfinger, as you know it, before I make any definitive claims."

He looked at me with a perplexed expression, his deep brown eyes wide.

"Are you suggesting that Spearfinger is haunting the woods in Roan?"

"No, I didn't mean that. All I really know is that a lot of people like to apply the Spearfinger story to just about anything that happens in the Appalachian Mountains. I figured, at the very least, I should learn what I could about the legend and then try to figure out what, if anything, is scaring people in the woods up there."

"Well, if people are just getting scared, it isn't Spearfinger. She didn't scare people at all. However, she did feed on people's liver. Unless you have a bunch of people turning up dead without a liver, this is definitely not your haunt."

My heart sank deep into my chest as he spoke.

"Come, walk with me. I will tell you the story," he said.

Linda took that as an opportunity to exit. Andy and I began to walk down the sparse trails. As we walked, he began to tell the story of Spearfinger. Most of what he told me was no different than what I'd already read.

"So given the legend of how Spearfinger was defeated, is it even possible for her to return?" I asked when he had finished.

"In theory, no, not at all. But that is why I wanted to meet you here. There is something I think you need to see."

We walked another quarter mile on the trail until we reached a clearing.

"What I told you is the Spearfinger legend as it was first documented. But the documented story isn't complete. See the documented story always tells of how a rock remains in the place she was vanquished. Not just a rock, but her body, as it retreated back to the form she was created from."

"Yes, I read that too."

"Okay, so let me ask you something. This story has been repeated and rewritten hundreds of times. The story states that the location of her remains is known and still visible today, yet no one states the actual location. Don't you find that a bit odd?"

"I suppose, although I deal with a lot of lore and it is inconsistencies like that which always make these stories get classified as lore and nothing else."

"Well, that was the question that bugged me. I spent a massive amount of time researching and interviewing many of the Cherokee elders in an effort to find an answer."

"And what did you find out?"

"What I found is that this clearing right here," he said pointing to the center of the clearing, "is where she was vanquished. If you look close, there is a rock circle here where the spot was marked."

"I don't understand. I'm not seeing this large rock that is supposed to be her remains."

"Exactly! The elders are insistent that this is the location. All recorded information points to the rock being here up until somewhere around the turn of the century. Then the records describe this as being the known location with no mention of the rock."

"So are you telling me she is gone?"

"I'm not stating anything as a fact. But, I believe she was here and she no longer is. If this ghost in the woods by you started in the early 1900's ...well...I guess this may be a possibility."

I was completely overwhelmed by that possibility. If this was Spearfinger I was dealing with, how would I vanquish her?

By the time I made it back to my car and bid farewell to Andy, I realized I had no cell service in that particular area. After about fifteen minutes of driving, my phone finally found service and started vibrating like crazy with missed calls and messages.

The first message was a playful voicemail from Melanie. "Hey David. Look, it's a gorgeous day out. I'm gonna take the afternoon off work and head out to the Gap. Why don't you join me? We can take a stab at finding that lost gold!"

When I listened to her second message, I realized she was more serious than I'd initially thought.

"Hey, I made it to Spearfinger's shack. Listen, there is something out here. I'm kinda freaked out and holed up in the shack. Please come out here."

The final message had been left only fifteen minutes ago and was nothing but rustling noises followed by Melanie's shrill scream.

PART III

18

APRIL 22, 2001

Roger Spur sat on the edge of the abandoned hiking shelter. It was covered in spray paint and littered with empty beer cans. In stark contrast to the mess of the shelter was Roger. His boots were recently shined, his uniform clean and pressed. The forest was alive with sounds that spring morning. Birds chirped and rodents rustled as Roger listened intently, waiting to hear something different.

Roger jolted as he heard a twig snapping in the distance. He looked in the direction of the sound but was unable to see anything. Soon, more sounds were audible, the unmistakable sounds of a human moving through the forest. As the sounds grew closer, Roger stood up and ran his hands down his uniform.

"Glen?" he yelled. "Is that you?"

The sounds stopped for a brief moment before a voice replied. "'Course it's me. Who else would be stupid enough to come down here?"

Roger relaxed slightly, letting his shoulders drop. Soon, a

large man forced his way through the brush and into the clearing. He was broad and stood well over six feet.

"Why the hell do you insist on meeting me here?" Glen asked. "I told you we could have done this anywhere."

"C'mon Glen. You could use the hike."

"Alright, so if this is gonna happen, I gotta know. What makes you so damn special?"

"What do you mean?"

"You know damn well what I mean. Everyone who has gone anywhere near that cache has turned up dead... 'cept you."

"What do you care? If I don't make it back, your secret dies with me. If I do, you're a very rich man. I've been up and down these hills a million times. I know what I'm doing."

"You sure about that?" Glen asked.

"Of course I'm sure!"

"No, what I'm sayin'...this forest...it isn't like other spots. This forest can read you. Read your intentions. It knows why you are there. You may have been up through these hills a million times but never out seeking the cache."

"Like I said, I'm the one taking the risk," Roger replied as he patted the gold coin in his pocket.

"Alright, well then, I guess this is yours."

Glen pulled a single sheet of paper out of his pocket and handed it to Roger. Roger carefully unfolded it. As he looked at the paper, his eyes narrowed. He looked up at Glen with disdain.

"250°? What the hell am I supposed to do with that?"

"It's your heading. You walk on that bearing true to course from the starting point, and you'll walk right into the damn cache."

"I don't suppose you know the starting point?"

"Of course I do, That's easy. Well, it should be for you anyway. It's the southwest corner of the ol' Cloudland Hotel."

"Jesus, Glen, you know as well as I do, that place was destroyed long before we were born."

"Yeah, yeah, yeah, but the foundation is still there. Find the southwest corner up there, follow your heading precisely from that point, and you'll hit the cache."

"So it's that easy, then?"

"Easy? You're speaking to the man who lost his son in this search. It's anything but easy!"

"Sorry, I didn't mean it like that."

"Yeah, I know..." Glen started to shift uneasily. He pointed off into the distance.

There was a loud thrashing of the trees followed by a stomp so loud the ground seemed to vibrate with it.

"You hear that? Do you fucking hear that?" Glen shouted.

"The hell?"

"It's her. That bitch is coming back for me!" Glen took off in a sprint back the way he'd come. His massive body moved awkwardly, yet with incredible speed, before he disappeared through the brush.

Roger stood frozen in place. His head shifted from watching Glen run, to the opposite direction where the thrashing had come from. The sounds continued and came closer with every second. Roger snatched up his radio off of his duty belt and raised it to his mouth, pressing the button.

"Gordon, you copy? It's Roger."

The thrashing continued to get closer as Roger held the radio to his ear awaiting a response.

"Gordon here, go ahead."

"Glen split. He is on his way up to the trailhead. Make sure he gets out of here okay."

"Did everything go as we intended?"

"Sure did. This should be no trouble at all."

Roger clipped the radio back on his duty belt and focused his attention on the sound in the trees. It was close now. By the way it was moving, it would only be a few seconds before it emerged from the brush.

Roger took a deep breath and stood stoically waiting.

There was one final thud before a hand parted the brush on the edge of the clearing. The hand paused. The only thing visible was a feminine hand. Everything went silent, as if the birds had all retreated in its presence.

"Why do you tease me?" a woman's gravelly voice said. "It's been so long since I've eaten. You know he isn't welcome here. Yet you let him leave before I arrived."

"I told you, I'm not going to provide you with a victim. I'm protecting him."

"Then why was he here?"

"Because, I needed to make sure that he would keep his distance."

"Your games!" the woman hissed. "You better watch yourself. You seek in my realm too, no different than he. There will be a day when you are not protected, and I will be waiting."

"I'm sure you told my father the same thing, and his father before that. Yet, here I am."

"Your father didn't seek. Your father respected his role! You, however, have forgotten your place. Your greed will be your demise!"

19

I CALLED MELANIE, praying she would pick up. She didn't. After five more rings, I left an awkward voicemail pleading with her to call me back. My mind raced. My fingers tightened on the steering wheel as my foot pressed the accelerator. My truck barreled down the two-lane mountain road.

I was doing everything I could to get to Melanie as fast as possible, but I knew it was no use. I was two hours away. If something happened in the forest, there was nothing I could do..

I wracked my brain trying to think of someone, anyone who could help. Linda, even if she was at the office, would never make it down that trail. Zeke had already met his own trouble in the forest, and I didn't even know him well enough to begin with. I realized there was only one person I could call. While he was without a doubt the last person I wanted to call, it was my only available option—Gordon.

After spending only a minute debating it, I picked up the phone and dialed Gordon's number. As it rang, images flashed before my eyes of his business card at Zeke's, of his name on all those reports. I knew he was the enemy, but also my only hope. His phone went to voicemail.

"Gordon, it's David. Listen, I need you. It's Melanie. She went out to the old shack on that trail, and I think something happened to her. I'm a couple hours away. You need to get out there immediately!"

I hung up the phone and froze. I was crippled with fear for Melanie. Sweat started to run down my forehead as my eyes welled up with tears. My trembling hand let go of the phone. I watched it drop in what looked like slow motion, landing on the floor of my truck. My eyes glanced up to see a buck standing in the middle of the road.

I slammed on the brakes and turned the steering wheel away from the deer. The deer's black eyes boring into me was the last thing I saw before everything went black.

WHEN I OPENED MY EYES, there was a searing pain in my head, and a blinding light shone on my face. It took a moment before I could see anything but white. I raised my hand to my forehead and shuddered in pain. The touch left my fingers slick with blood. As my vision began to clear, I saw a blurred shape in front of my car. I thought it was the deer, but as the outline became clearer, I realized it was a human.

"David!" a voice said.

I squeezed my eyes shut and opened them again. The shape became clearer. It was a man in a uniform, wearing a hat. It was my father.

"David, you must wake up now."

"What are you doing here?"

"I'm here to help you, and clearly you need it more than I ever imagined."

"What?"

"Melanie is in danger. You need to help her."

"I know that, Dad! Why the hell do you think I was speeding down this road to begin with?"

"You need to understand what you are getting into before you do more damage."

"Okay, what are you talking about?"

"Spearfinger."

"I know about Spearfinger!"

"No, you don't! You think just because you learned about the original Spearfinger, you have a clue what is actually happening?"

"Seriously, Dad? You didn't belittle me enough in life. You gotta come back to do it more?"

"David, just listen! Spearfinger was raised to protect one thing. By design she was drawn with insatiable hunger for only those who seek the cache she protects. The problem is, when you raise an entity and try to confine it the way Robert did, it doesn't work right. Initially, Spearfinger did exactly what was intended. She would lie dormant until someone came looking for her cache. As time went on though, she evolved. She began to take on more human qualities. She became vengeful. If she was ever denied a victim, not only would she continue to seek out that person but also seek revenge on whoever stopped her."

"That's you, isn't it? That is how you died?"

"David, I spent years trying to protect people from her, but some people wronged her. She started seeking them, moving outside of the confines of her specific location. I intervened to protect them and unknowingly sacrificed myself. She will not stop."

Right there, for the first time, I saw my dad differently. I began to understand why he'd left me. I began to understand that he was looking out for me.

"What does this have to do with Melanie?"

"Melanie is going to stand between Spearfinger and her victim. Melanie doesn't know how to stop Spearfinger. Her actions will end up killing her and the person she is protecting."

I had to go to Melanie, but for a moment, I realized there was something else I needed to say.

"Dad, I'm sorry, I didn't know."

"You shouldn't have known. You don't need to be sorry, but you need to act. Your time is short. Go now to Melanie. I will be there with you."

THERE WAS a flash of brilliant green light. When it dissipated, my father was gone. There was no deer. I touched my throbbing forehead and could feel the blood still there. My truck sat nearly sideways across the road. I began to take a quick inventory of my injuries. I took a look at my head in the visor's mirror. I found some old napkins in my glove box to wipe off the blood. I had a nice gash but nothing that would require stitches. I stepped out of the truck to see if I had hit anything. Everything appeared the same as it always was.

Returning to the cab, I picked up my phone from the floorboard and glance at it to see if there were any new messages. There weren't. There were so many thoughts I wanted to explore and think about, but it wasn't the time. I still had to get to Melanie. I turned my truck on and sped down the road.

As I drove, I began to process everything that happened. I realized that after seeing my dad, I was dealing with multiple versions of the truth: from what Robert's spirit told me, to my father's words to me, to the real world data. There were plenty of consistencies, yet each had a different spin. I realized that Linda was right. I was too close to the case. My emotions were getting in the way of my ability to approach it objectively. The number one rule I had always followed in my investigations was that communications with spirits, much like communications with people, can never be trusted as rock-hard facts. It made sense. In life, people lied and bent the truth to get you to believe their perspective. The first mistake many people make is believing a spirit is more trustworthy than the person was in life. I simply had not paid attention to my rules during this case.

As the miles flew by, my concern for Melanie increased exponentially. The message from my dad was cryptic, and I couldn't make complete sense of it. The only thing I knew for sure was that she was in trouble, and I needed to help her. I pushed my truck to the limits of what was safe to drive. Soon, I was passing Melanie's house on my way to the Gap. I was getting so close that I could barely breathe. My fingers tightened around the steering wheel. I pulled into the Gap and saw her Jeep near the entrance to the old trail. I parked and leapt from the car, sprinting through the brush and down the trail.

The first mile of the trail passed by in no time. Soon, I turned the corner, leading me to Spearfinger's Shack.

"Melanie!" I yelled.

I heard nothing over the sound of my panting breath. I bent over with my hands on my thighs, trying to catch my breath as I yelled her name again. Then I heard it. There was a rustling sound coming from the shack. I approached and immediately saw her inside.

Melanie lay there. She was tied up and gagged. I dove into the shack and tore the cloth gag off her mouth.

"David, you need to leave. He's here waiting for you!"

"What? I'm not going anywhere without you!" I pulled out my knife and began cutting the ropes that bound her ankles together.

"David, please listen! He's coming for you. You need to go now!"

"Who's coming for me?"

There was no response to my question. As I made the final cut in the rope, I looked up at her. Her eyes were wide with fear. She was ever so slightly turning her head back and forth as if to say 'no.' Aside from that slight motion, she remained still. Then I heard the click of a pistol being cocked.

"Well, well, well, David," a whiny male voice said. "You still aren't very bright. In case you didn't figure it out yet, I'm the one who is coming back for you."

I slowly began to turn my head to see my assailant.

"Whoa, there. I wouldn't be moving too much if I were you. After all, you wouldn't want this hollow point to accidentally rip your skull apart, would you?"

I stopped moving. I didn't need to face him. I recognized his voice all too well. It was slightly different with age but still unmistakable. The voice of the one person I truly loathed. Austin, Melanie's ex. I crouched there in the momentary silence, picturing him. His long greasy black hair now thin. His tall, slightly overweight build. The patchwork stubble on his face. The only thing I really couldn't assume without seeing him was whether or not he was wearing his trademark bandana. My fists clenched with rage as I awaited his next command.

"Slowly turn around, but keep your eyes closed. I wanna get a great look at you when you get to see who I am."

"You think I don't know it's you, Austin?" I couldn't contain myself. I slowly turned and kept my eyes shut as instructed.

"Oh, so you really are the smart guy... go ahead, open your eyes and look at me."

I opened my eyes to see the man in front of me. Austin stood there looking even older than I'd expected. There was no bandana, but he still wore the tight black tank top, making him look ridiculous. I half expected to see a pointy guitar under his arm, but there was none. He held the chrome pistol sideways like a gangster on TV. On his wrist, I noticed the same broken clock tattoo Melanie had, a detail I wished I could unsee. I loved Melanie but refused to picture her with him.

He looked like a broken man. The years of trying to sell CDs that no one wanted while trying to find some semblance of income to pay the bills had caught up to him. He was ruined, and as such, unpredictable and dangerous. Despite all this, he was the man who robbed Melanie of so many years. Beaten her and controlled her. I didn't care how broken he was, I could give him no pity.

"WHAT DO YOU WANT, AUSTIN?" I asked.

"You know damn well what I want."

"Actually, I really don't. I mean, it could be Melanie, but seeing as you had your opportunity to take her long before I arrived, I'll scratch that off the list. I don't know. Maybe you just think you'll feel better about your existence by taking me out. Am I at least getting warm?"

"Fuck you!" He hit my cheek with the pistol.

I'd pissed him off. It wasn't on purpose. It was what I always did to him in school. It's probably the reason he'd always hated me. It was definitely the reason Melanie and I couldn't be friends once she was with him.

"What are you possibly gonna accomplish by shooting me? You think you won't get busted for that? What, a good prison sentence is the best future you can come up with?"

"You may die, but if you do, it will be the same way as your worthless father did."

"So wait, if that's the only way I might die out here, that tells me you have zero intention of actually killing me. Why not put the gun down then before something stupid happens?"

"Shut up!" he shouted, waving the gun in my face. "You'll talk when I ask you to."

"As you wish," I said, raising my hands to show my compliance.

"You're going to give me what your father promised my dad. You are going to walk into that forest and get me the treasure, and don't even act like you have no idea what I'm talking about."

"Fine, let's talk about it, but put the damn gun down first."

Austin reluctantly complied and lowered his pistol.

"Okay, now that you've done that, what the hell are you talking about with my dad and your dad, and what makes you think I actually know where the treasure is? I mean, I know it's out there somewhere, but that's it."

"You really don't know anything do you?" he said,

following his words with a bellowing cackle. "You're not finding the damn treasure. You're retrieving it for me."

"You know where it is?"

"I know where it is, my dad knows where it is... hell, even your dad knew where it is."

"Then go get it yourself!"

"If only it were that easy. Last person who tried to get it was my brother, and you know how that worked out for him... Oh wait, someone else tried.... Who was it? Oh yeah, your dad. I'm in no hurry to follow in their footsteps."

"My dad was nothing like your brother. He could care less about the treasure out there!"

He burst into laughter, and his lips curled up on the edges, making him resemble the Joker. I wanted nothing more than to punch him in that moment.

Austin gathered himself before speaking again. "Okay, okay, you're not this stupid. You have to know, right? Think you're gonna catch me on something? Your dad was more obsessed with that treasure than anyone. Problem was... he was too stupid to find it on his own. My dad wouldn't go near this forest after my brother died. So he cut a deal with him. My dad told him where it was. He went to retrieve it."

I slowly lowered my hands a bit. "That's the story you heard, anyway. Let's say it's true. Say my dad did go out there with a heading from your father, and let's assume that's why he died in this forest. What the fuck makes you think I'll be any more successful than he was? Christ, he spent his life out here. I've barely been out here in the last five years."

He paused and looked at me with that dumb stare. It reminded me so much of when I sat by him in classes. It was like he was waiting for his brain to process before he could respond. I hated him so much.

"See, there you go trying to be all tricky. There is a secret to this forest, a way to get by that beast out there. It's a secret I think you know. I'd bet my guitar collection and dirt bikes on it! The best part is, it doesn't matter if you know it or not. I don't care about you. If you end up just like your dad, it doesn't affect me at all. In the off chance you really don't have a clue, oh well!"

At that moment something happened in the forest. Large flocks of birds took flight out of the trees. Austin didn't seem to notice anything until the ground shook. There was a massive thud back about a hundred yards in the distance. It was followed by silence.

Austin's eyes narrowed, and his jaw opened as he looked towards the sound. Then came a thrashing in the brush. Still far away, but it sounded like a large animal ripping through every branch in its way. At the sound of a second thud, Austin holstered his pistol and turned back to me.

"Well, here's your test. I'm getting the fuck out of here. If you and Mel make it out of this, I'll find you."

He took off in a sprint down the trail, leaving Melanie and I to deal with whatever was coming for us.

The thuds seemed to be getting louder and closer together. I found the knife I'd dropped when Austin interrupted me while cutting Melanie's ropes.

"It's Spearfinger, isn't it?" she said in a dazed voice.

"I don't know what the hell it is, but I don't want to stick around to find out!"

I prodded her to move, but she stood paralyzed with fear.

"Melanie, we gotta get out of here!"

I pulled her arm, trying to get her moving down the trail. The thuds were close now. Only a few yards beyond the clearing.

"Melanie, move!"

Just then there was another thud, followed by absolute silence.

Melanie's eyes were wide, like that moment when Austin was standing behind me. I turned to follow her gaze. The brush at the edge of the clearing began to rustle. Then a hand was visible. I took a deep breath and swallowed hard.

A figure made its way slowly through the brush. Then it faced me. It was a face I recognized immediately. It was Zeke.

20

Zeke silently stared at me. He was dirty and looked like he'd been living in the forest since I'd last seen him. His clothes were torn. As he looked at me, his eyes appeared vacant.

"Zeke!" I said, slowly approaching him. "What are you doing out here?"

He gave no response and continued to stare at me. Finally, he raised his right hand as if to say 'stop'.

"This isn't the first time I was denied a meal," he said in a low, guttural tone. "Do you really think this action will serve you better than it did your father?"

"Zeke? What the hell are you talking about?"

"My calling. Those who come seeking do not leave this forest. That is, of course, when humans do not intervene. He will come back, and when he does, you best not protect him. You wouldn't want my blood lust pointed toward you as well."

"Who are you and what happened to Zeke?" I yelled.

"My name is U'tlun'ta. I was brought here to protect. I'm bound to this earth, only able to feed on those who seek.

Zeke, he came seeking. That's how it works, how it has always worked. That man who was here, he seeks too. Yet, you chose to stand between us, denying me what is rightfully mine."

"How did I deny you anything?"

"You came. You stood between us. You are protected. I am not only bound to this forest. I cannot cross he who has the coin."

I reached into my pocket and retrieved the gold coin. It felt warm in my hand.

"You mean this?" I asked holding up the coin.

Zeke recoiled at the mere sight of it. He held up his hand and writhed as if it was causing him extreme pain. "Stop! Put that away!"

I complied and put the coin back in my pocket. Immediately, Zeke stopped moving and stood straight again.

"What did you mean when you mentioned my father?"

"Your father was the last person to use that coin. Your father tried to control me. To deny me."

Zeke stretched out his left hand and waved for me to come closer. I hesitated but stepped towards him. As I moved in closer, I was overwhelmed with his stench. He smelled like a rotting corpse. I could hardly breathe. I wrinkled my nose, trying to avoid inhaling the smell of that thing.

"Come closer. As I said, you are protected. I will not hurt you yet."

I stepped in even closer. Close enough to stare into the hollow dark eyes.

"I warned your father once, much as I have warned you today. He denied me. He tried to control me. To keep me from my calling. He wanted to choose. He wanted to protect. I warned him."

"What was your warning?"

"I told him that I will not be denied. That a time would come when he was without that damned coin, and when he was, I would be waiting. My calling is to guard from anyone who seeks. I can see within people. I can feel their intentions. Your father tried to fool me. No matter what he showed everyone else, deep inside, he was a seeker. In the end, he got the punishment all seekers do."

He paused as if waiting for some knee-jerk reaction from me. I had none.

"I see you are the guardian I have been waiting for," he said as he began to step backward into the brush. "Do not repeat the mistakes of your father."

He was gone. By the time his last word was spoken, it was as if he had been absorbed into the forest. I wanted to chase after him, but I knew it would be of no use. I turned to Melanie who had not moved from her spot, staring wide-eyed at the events that had transpired.

"Are you alright?" I gently rubbed her shoulder.

At first she recoiled from my touch before mentally confirming it really was me.

"What was that, David?"

"I'm pretty sure that was Spearfinger... well, Spearfinger in the form of your neighbor. I think it's safe to assume Zeke was one of her victims."

"So that thing really did kill your dad."

"Yup."

"But that makes no sense. That coin was your dad's. If he had the coin, he would have been untouchable."

"That is assuming he had the coin. My dad gave me that coin almost a year before he died."

I didn't make the connection until I said it out loud. I was the reason my dad had died. He had given me the coin to protect me, but then he had been without the coin and Spearfinger had punished him. It was a lot to take in, and initially I didn't feel guilt. I just felt deep sorrow.

"Forget about Spearfinger for a minute. What were you doing down here with Austin?"

"I called you. I came out hoping you'd meet me. I camped out here at the Shack. I was making a fire, and then he snuck up behind me and grabbed me."

"I will take care of him. If he wants me, fine, but he can leave you out of it!" A rage boiled inside me. I had always hated Austin, but now, after he'd tied Melanie up like an animal, I would not be stopped. "Let's get the hell out of here."

MELANIE REMAINED in a shocked state of silence when we arrived at her cottage. As I pulled in and parked, I couldn't help but stare out at Zeke's house. I had talked to Zeke in the forest, but he wasn't Zeke. He was a creature of the forest. I hadn't really known him before, but it still bothered me. Less than a week ago, he'd shared a beer with me on that porch. Now he was gone. I'd seen him go. I could've stopped him. Of course, at the time I'd had no clue what he was getting himself into. It didn't make it any easier. A part of me felt responsible.

As I stood there staring at his cottage, an image popped into my head. Gordon's business card in Zeke's house. Gordon had been there the day Zeke disappeared. He had been in his house. Gordon knew something. Why was Gordon at the center of everything in this forest? And...

"Why the fuck didn't he show up?" I yelled towards the house. "Why didn't he call?"

Melanie jumped back at my sudden outburst.

"David? Who are you yelling at?"

I clenched my teeth and seethed with rage. "Gordon! He has something to do with all of this. I called him, but he never even showed up."

"You don't need Gordon." she said as she wrapped her arm around me. "If you ask me, you took care of everything by yourself."

For a brief moment I was able to relax. My shoulders drooped, and I unclenched my fists. She was right. I had handled it. Yet, that didn't change the fact that Gordon didn't show. I was mad, but I could deal with him later. Melanie squeezed me in her arms briefly before grabbing my hand and walking me into her cottage.

Once inside, she grabbed a blanket from the pile in the corner and retreated to the couch. She sat up with her back on the arm rest, put her feet up on the cushion and curled into a small ball. She looked helpless there, still in shock, a blank stare in her eyes. I tried to sit as close to her as I could despite her detached demeanor.

I gently rested my hands on her knees. I looked at her with a somewhat defeated smile in the hope that I could see something in her eyes. There was nothing. After several agonizing minutes, she spoke.

"Austin is in danger, isn't he?" Her face still bore the emotionless stare.

"From me or that thing in the forest?" I replied in a feeble attempt to bring in some levity.

She didn't respond, which was enough for me to realize that my humor wasn't welcome yet.

"Yeah, I think he is. If he ever returns to the forest, anyway... but I think we are all in danger to a certain degree.

Hell, your neighbor fell to that thing. It needs to be stopped."

"She cannot be stopped," she replied in a monotone voice.

"She will be stopped. I promise you that." My hands gently rubbed her knees. I didn't have a clue what was going through her head. There were a thousand plausible reasons for her to be in shock at that moment. It nagged at me that I was clueless to which one it was. "Why don't you get some sleep. I'll stay here and try to figure out what to do next."

She nodded in silent agreement. I moved to let her stretch out her legs. Kneeling next to her, I covered her with the blanket and kissed her on the forehead. I stayed kneeling there in my own distant silence. My stare was broken when I saw Melanie's body gently twitch. She was asleep, very soundly asleep.

I stood up and walked over to the adjoining loveseat where I sat down. My head drooped into my hands as I tried to make sense of everything that had happened in the last day. I pulled my phone from my pocket and looked at the screen. I had a text from Gordon.

David, call me when you can. There is something you need to see, alone.

My fingers tightened around the phone. I was enraged but forced myself to take a deep breath. If I was going to call him, I needed to keep my cool. Melanie was still in a deep sleep. I watched as the blanket on top of her rose and fell with each of her breaths. The calming rhythm helped me to regain my composure. After a few minutes, I stood up and walked out to the front porch.

I dialed Gordon's number and took a final deep breath, both dreading the impending conversation but also wanting it over with. It only rang once before I was greeted with his familiar voice.

"David, where are you?" he asked.

"I'm over at Melanie's"

"Are you able to talk privately?"

"Yeah."

"No, without Melanie. I can't have her listening in."

"It's fine. She's asleep."

"Okay, look, about today…"

"What about today? Where the hell were you?" I balled my fingers into fists as my rage began to boil.

"David, there is something you need to understand."

"Well, I'm listening."

"I need to show you. Can you meet me at the substation? I assume you still have the key."

"Just tell me why I should bother meeting you."

There was silence on the phone.

"Look, I was there. That is what I need to show you." he said in a strained voice. "Melanie…. well…she's not what you think. You are in danger, David."

AT the very least Gordon had succeeded in getting my attention. I didn't trust him. However, I acknowledged that he certainly had a lot of knowledge that was important to me. I had to play nice with him, and I hated playing nice. I was always much better off being me, which was why I struggled with my job of a lifetime, the TV gig.

If I was going to play nice with Gordon, I figured I needed a plan of my own. When I was convinced Melanie would not be waking up anytime soon, I wrote her a note saying I'd be back in a few minutes and headed to my truck.

Behind the front seat, I pulled out my leather jacket and put it on. It was warm, but I hoped that the cool breeze would be enough to make wearing the jacket not seem completely out of place. I unpacked one of the voice-recorders that I'd used in Melanie's attic and placed it in my jacket pocket.

As I sat down in my truck and started the engine, I giggled at the absurdity of my master plan. An out-of-season jacket concealing a voice recorder in the hopes that Gordon would say something incriminating. I realized that even if he did, I wouldn't know what to do with the recording. Blackmail was not a part of my repertoire. As insane as the entire plan was, it was the best one I had. Additionally, focusing on my ruse allowed me to not succumb to my rage toward Gordon.

When I reached the substation, Gordon's truck was already there waiting. I switched on my recorder and walked up the steps to the porch, hearing the familiar creak under my feet. I opened the front door and found Gordon sitting on the couch in the living room, his legs crossed.

"Come, have a seat," he said.

"I think I'll stand. You said you have something to show me."

"I see you started up the clock when you came out here." He gestured to the clock across the room.

"Yeah, the house didn't feel right without the constant ticking."

"You know that clock was very special to your dad. Actually, your entire family."

"Yeah, yeah, I know. It was passed down a couple generations. It was the only nice thing that my family had when they first moved into this house. I've heard that story a hundred times."

"I believe that story is completely true, but did you ever

hear the story before that one? The one that explains how a simple man could acquire such a magnificent piece of horology?"

"I haven't heard it, I've seen it! It came from Cloudland… Is this really what you called me for? To talk about the damn clock?"

"Not at all, but I do feel the clock helps build a greater understanding of the situation."

I was frustrated and impatient, yet I let Gordon continue. I could still appreciate the information.

"Enlighten me." I sat down in the chair nearest Gordon.

"This clock was built long before your ancestors took possession of it. It was commissioned and built for Robert Mason."

I perked up at the mention of Mason's name.

"Ah yes, I assumed you'd be familiar with him," he said. "It wasn't for Robert to have in one of his houses. He actually commissioned this clock to adorn the private drawing room at Cloudland where he stayed."

"Like I said, get to the point. I know this already."

"Even more interesting is how your family came to take possession of it. The story, as your father told it, started back with your great-great grandfather, Johan Spur. He was a trusted confidant of Robert's. In fact, Robert had this house built for Johan."

"Wait, I thought Johan was part of the Forestry Division." Now he had my attention.

"He was. That role was created by Robert."

"Okay, so Robert gave him a job."

"Listen, David. Robert didn't give Johan a job. Johan had a job working for Robert. Robert had this National Forest created. This was the first substation here and Johan was the first person to live here. Do you know anything about clocks?"

"This historical trip has been great, really, but enough about the damn clock."

"This clock was not merely commissioned to tell time. It was built to guard secrets and protect them from anyone seeking to find them. Perhaps you are familiar with some of the hidden panels within this clock."

"Yeah, you know, I think I'm one step ahead of you there."

"Okay, then tell me this. What can be so important that not only is it hidden, not only do multiple generations of a family strive to protect it, but an entire National Forest is created to facilitate its protection?"

"C'mon Gordon, we both know damn well what is out there. What I don't know is what you wanted to show me... or better yet, maybe you'd like to answer some questions of mine."

Gordon furrowed his brow and looked at me with extreme seriousness. I wanted to hold back my cards as long as I could, but he was pushing me over the edge.

"Fair enough. What would you like to know?"

"Why don't you tell me what really happened to my dad."

"I'm afraid you know that story already."

"Yeah, no thanks to you! What I don't know is why you covered it up."

"David, what do you think would happen if word got out that some untamable beast was loose in the forest, eating people's livers? The entire department would be shut down. If the department was shut down, there would be no one to follow through with the purpose for which it was originally created." Gordon stood up and began to pace the living room. The floor creaked and groaned in response to every step. "Look, I may not have been part of your family's legacy, but your father was my best friend. When he left, I took on the role of protecting that area of the forest, which is exactly why I called you here today."

He sat down and rubbed his chin. After a moment, he reached over to a laptop lying on the couch and opened it.

"Look, I told you that I have taken special precautions in protecting that area. I've also set cameras up in that area of the forest. I knew someone was there before you even called."

"Then why the fuck didn't you do anything?"

"David, not everything is as it appears. I think you need to watch this. I saw what happened when you went into the forest. I saw what you saw. Austin tied up Melanie. But I also saw this first." He handed me his laptop.

21

THERE WAS one video file on the desktop of Gordon's laptop. He clicked on it, and the video began playing in full screen. The camera angle was of the back corner of the parking lot near the entrance to that trail. The image was black and white, but still remarkably clear. In the bottom corner of the video was a date and time stamp.

"Here, let me fast-forward this a little," he said as he moved the video forward a few minutes.

I saw Melanie's Jeep pull into view. She pulled in and parked right in front of the path. She got out of the car and walked to the back of the Jeep and stayed there. The Jeep blocked her from the view of the camera; however, both sides of her Jeep were clearly visible, so I knew she hadn't left the frame. A few moments passed until another car pulled up, first slowly driving past her, then parking further down in the lot. It was an old Camaro. It had tinted windows, making it impossible to make out who was driving from the view of the camera.

The door opened and Austin stepped out. As he exited the car, there was a huge grin on his face. He turned around to grab a backpack from inside his car and then walked behind Melanie's Jeep. While Melanie was still blocked from the camera's view, I could still clearly see Austin. The two appeared to talk for a few moments before they both walked to the start of the trail together.

I pressed pause on the video player and froze one of the last frames before they stepped out of the camera's view. Melanie was almost looking directly at the camera at that moment. What surprised me in that image was that she appeared calm and content. It was certainly not the face of someone under duress.

I stood staring at that image, chewing the inside of my lip. I'd spent a large part of this day consumed with rage. Anger against Austin and anger against Gordon. At that moment, the rage inside of me dissipated, leaving me feeling betrayed and stupid.

"So much for sneaking up and holding her at gunpoint," I seethed.

"I'm sorry David, but now you will understand why I needed to show this to you."

"That doesn't explain why you didn't go help them. If you knew they were there, why didn't you step in? You know exactly what is down in that woods. You've always fucking known!"

As I spoke, something deep inside me snapped. The twine holding together every ounce of my sanity quickly unraveled.

"You don't understand," he said.

"No, I don't understand! You sit here on your fat ass and watch people on camera walking towards their death and don't do a fucking thing about it. You could've stopped them. You could've stopped Zeke. You could've stopped my dad! You spend more time covering everything up than you do actually trying to prevent any of it from happening. All you do is watch like it's some sick TV show. That's what really happened when my father died, you sick fuck! You watched him go down there and immediately turned your attention to covering it all up!"

Gordon stood up and snapped the laptop shut.

"What happened to your father was an accident," he growled. "It wasn't supposed to happen."

"But it did happen! And what did you do to stop it?"

"If I had known what was going to happen, I would've. Your father had been down there probably a thousand times, just like you, and nothing ever happened. Why would I think for a second that it would have been any different that day?"

Gordon's eyes began to water. He stood there pacing the room. His giant, chubby hands were incessantly fidgeting.

"Look, I can't go down there. I can go to the old shelter but no further. I have only known two people to ever go down there and return. You and your dad. I've been there before with your dad. I've heard him talk to that woman. He was protected by that coin. What I didn't know was that he had given that coin to you. If I knew, I would've never let him go into that woods that day."

I'd made this realization already, but hearing it from Gordon cemented it. He knew. He knew that I was the reason my dad died. I looked at Gordon. He appeared more like a giant teddy bear in that moment than the overgrown troll I usually saw him as. He looked at me with this, 'Yeah, I know and it sucks' stare.

I was completely defeated in that moment. Everything I felt like I knew had been ripped away. Even Melanie was apparently conspiring against me. With a thousand horrible images going through my head, one took root. All of my anger, pain, and frustration blossomed into one single point: the resolve to end Spearfinger. I realized that it wouldn't change things with Melanie, or much at all really, but the chance to avenge the death of my father became my sole goal and focus.

"How do I end her?" I asked Gordon.

"End her?"

"Spearfinger. Her time ends now, with me. How do I end this once and for all?"

GORDON'S EYES grew wide with fear and shock.

"You don't end her. You stay the hell away from her!" he pleaded.

"No! You said it yourself, talking about this fucking clock!" I stood pointing to it. "My father spent his whole damn life catering to Robert Mason's cause. Where did it get him? In a fucking grave like everyone else. I'm done. This ends now! Are you gonna help me or just sit there and be completely useless?"

I glared at Gordon, admonishing him to help. My face was wet with a combination of sweat and tears.

"I swore on your father's grave that I would protect you and keep you safe. If you think I will stand by while you walk into a suicide mission, you're crazy."

"Then it sounds like you are with me."

Gordon looked at me for a moment. His eyes were red. His mustache bristled, and then he gave me a silent nod. "If I can't stop you, I'll help."

We stood there in a silent and uncomfortable agreement.

"What about Melanie?" I said, breaking the silence. "I don't even know what to think about her."

"I don't know either, All I can say is that her little stunt in the forest was certainly not what it seemed. I would suggest that you continue to act as if you didn't see that video. See where her allegiances really are."

"Speaking of allegiances... since you are now helping me, I need to understand something. You speak about my dad as if he was doing everything in his power to protect this cache."

"That's right."

"Is it though?"

Gordon ran this question through his head, biting the inside of his lip, before responding. "Of course it is. You know that."

"I'm not sure I do. One thing I do know is that Spearfinger is only drawn to those who enter the forest seeking the cache. She doesn't strike me as someone who would turn on her protector. So. before we go any further in this whole thing, I need to know why Spearfinger killed my father."

"I... I don't understand."

"Oh bullshit! It's a simple question, and I'm sure you know the answer. Was there a point where my father stopped protecting and opted to simply find the treasure for himself?"

"David, I'm afraid that question isn't as simple as you believe. Yes, he died because he was seeking the treasure. If that's what you want me to say, there you have it. But there is more to the story than that."

"Well if I'm supposed to trust you, now would be a good time to fill me in."

"Things were different then. The path had only recently

been closed off, and people were hanging around there constantly. There was also a string of disappearances. It had gotten to the point where it was simply a danger to everyone. Your dad met with Austin's dad who, as you know, spent his lifetime seeking that treasure. Your dad pleaded with him to stop, but Glen wasn't exactly a trusting fellow. He believed your dad was trying to get the treasure for himself and that it was all a ploy. There's one thing you need to understand about your father. Yes, he was dedicated to the cause of protecting the cache, but something else overshadowed that dedication in him."

"What was that?"

"Protecting people. Every victim of that beast lay heavily upon his shoulders. He felt personally responsible for each of those deaths. It's exactly why he did things like petition to reroute the trail away from there. Glen's insatiable lust for the treasure forced your father's hand. With Glen steadfastly focused on continuing to search, your dad believed the only way to protect people from Spearfinger was to eliminate what Spearfinger protected. In essence, get rid of the treasure, and with nothing to protect, Spearfinger would move on."

"So you're saying the protector became the hunter?"

"It wasn't that black and white, but yeah. He spent years trying to keep Glen at bay, and even struck a bargain with him, a bargain he never intended to keep. He told Glen he was safe from the beast, protected. Glen shared the location of the cache and your father vowed to retrieve it. He never intended to follow through on that vow. He kept pushing Glen off with obstacles he encountered and such. It worked for a while, until Glen did pretty much the same thing Austin did to you. Held him at gunpoint and demanded the treasure."

Gordon paused and sat back down. His eyes were glassed over. I didn't speak and waited for him to continue.

"You know kid, I'll never know what was going through his mind that day. I've spent every day since then wishin' I stepped in. I know he wanted to protect people and end this all... Aw hell, he chose to give his life for Glen's. He had to know he'd be her next victim. I dunno, maybe he thought he could get away with it. All I know is, that's the choice he made."

I was speechless.

"You wanted to know what happened to your dad, and now you do. Damn good man, he was."

"Why didn't you tell me this until now?"

"Like I said when you came to my office that day, if you choose to follow in his footsteps, that is a choice you need to make on your own. I'm not gonna force you into it, even if there is a whole family legacy behind it. I've lost too much to that beast already."

THE GRANDFATHER CLOCK continued to tick in its steady rhythm as Gordon and I sat there, both emotionally exhausted.

"You think it would've worked?" I asked with hesitation. "You know, removing the treasure. That is, had he not given me the coin."

"Aw kid, don't you go blaming yourself for this!"

"That's not what I'm asking. Would it have worked? If Glen or anyone else found that treasure, would she be gone?"

"That's the part that has bugged me about it. I don't really know. It sounded like a good theory back then.

Truth is, we never knew. We always saw Spearfinger as being contained in the forest. What we didn't know is if she was confined to one location... or if it was all based on proximity to the treasure. Say Glen got the treasure. Who's to say she wouldn't have followed him, killed him, and then been loose in town? I've always assumed your dad realized it wouldn't work, and that's why he gave you the coin."

"I'm not following."

"If you had the coin, no one would be protected, no one would be able to get in there. Giving you that coin allowed your dad to keep the treasure safe."

I pinched the bridge of my nose trying to get a grip on all of this.

"You know, I talked to Robert." I said.

"Robert Mason?" He picked up his head giving me all of his attention. "You mean like on the TV show, the whole ghost thing?"

"Yeah, something like that. At Melanie's place. Hell, that's how all this started. Anyway, he told me that my role had changed, and that I needed to put an end to Spearfinger."

"Did he tell you how to do it?"

"I wish. All I know is the legend of how she was vanquished by the Cherokee."

"And I s'pose you think it can be done the same way now?"

"No, I don't. I'm still working on how. Point is, it's time to put an end to this once and for all."

"What do you need from me?"

I thought about that question for a moment. I hadn't even figured out a plan, let alone Gordon's role in it.

"For now, answer my calls, and let me know the second

anyone sets foot on that trail. Right now, I gotta deal with Melanie."

I left the substation and mentally pushed aside as much of that conversation as I could. I needed to deal with Melanie and try to pretend I never saw the video he'd showed me. It sucked. If there is one thing I'd never had, it was a poker face. I knew Gordon was right in being vigilant around her and acting like nothing had changed, but I had my doubts as to whether I could pull it off.

As I was driving off, worrying about how to play this, the full weight of her betrayal hit me, and my heart sank. Before that moment, I don't know that I had even stepped back far enough to realize just how much I cared about her. I pulled over and tried to compose myself. I was not going to make the same mistake my father had. I would not protect Austin.

As I sat there fuming, I started to form a vengeful plan. Yes, I would play dumb to Melanie. I would play dumb so that I could ensure that Austin was on the front line against Spearfinger.

I arrived back at her house just before sunset. As I parked, I couldn't help but to look out at Zeke's place. I thought about him talking to me in the forest. The person I'd spoken with was certainly Spearfinger taking the form of Zeke, but did that mean Zeke was still there, still alive while Spearfinger used his body? I believed the answer was no. I knew in my gut he was dead, but part of me wanted to believe that there was a chance to save him as well.

I quietly walked into the house. Melanie looked as if she hadn't moved. My note was still on the counter. I balled it up and threw it away. I looked over at Melanie sleeping there. She was so peaceful, so beautiful. The woman lying there couldn't have betrayed me. I loved her. Despite the video Gordon had showed me, I felt there was more to the story.

Throughout my life, she'd caused me a lot of heartache. More than everyone else combined, but none of it had been malicious.

With her sleeping soundly, I chose to turn my attention to the other person in that house that I needed to speak with... Robert.

I gingerly walked up to the loft and opened the attic door. I knelt in its opening and peered into the darkness. It was completely still. I turned on my phone's flashlight and examined the timbers to find the spot I'd used my coin the last time. I gently rubbed my fingers across the area and took a deep breath. Robert had always come to me. I had never summoned him directly. I hoped I was not making a mistake.

I pulled out my coin and squeezed it tight in my hand. Swallowing hard, I pressed it into the wood timber. As I did, the lights went out, and I was thrown into complete darkness. The general feeling of space was changed. I couldn't see anything, but I felt like I was falling. The air was sucked from my lungs as I tumbled into emptiness. I squeezed my eyes shut and gritted my teeth, praying for the out of control feeling to stop. Then it did.

It ended suddenly with my body slamming against the earth. After a moment of shock, I realized I wasn't in Melanie's house. I felt grass against my face and arms. I moved to my knees and opened my eyes. I was in a clearing in the forest. The moon shone brightly through a gap in the trees. As I took a deep breath, my lungs filled with the acrid smoke of a fire nearby. I stood and walked towards the smoke. Just beyond the clearing was a holler. I could see the orange glow of a campfire through the trees. Sitting on a log next to the fire was Robert.

22

"I SEE you've returned for my help," Robert said. "It's all right, come closer. Sit with me by the fire."

I cautiously stepped into the holler and approached Robert. Despite the surroundings, he was still dressed formally, wearing the same suit he was the last time I'd seen him. The only thing that had changed was the addition of a fedora on his head.

"I appreciate you calling on me." He stood and extended his hand in greeting. "I admit, after having dealt with my brother Samuel, I expected a certain degree of apprehension and caution from you."

"Samuel wanted to kill me." I reached for his hand and shook it. "You, at least from what I've been exposed to, want the opposite."

"I suppose that's true. While we were united within the KGC, we were indeed very different people. I realize though, you have not called upon me to talk about Samuel. So why have you come?"

"I need to destroy Spearfinger. You are the only one who knows how."

"Yes indeed. I'm sure you are aware that when we brought her out of retirement, we also instilled a few restrictions. Most notably, the protection granted to anyone with that coin. In addition, I made sure that she could also be destroyed should the proper circumstances arise."

"And what are those circumstances?" I asked as I took a seat on a log.

"Spearfinger is an extremely dangerous entity. With that, she has proven to be the perfect form of protection for that cache. What has changed is the purpose of saving that cache.

I have been trapped here for an entire lifetime. Able to observe the changes in the world. The KGC and our work was simply misguided. It was fueled by lust and ego. We created an entire army to preserve and fight for our way of life. My time here has shown me how wrong we truly were. How wrong I was. Putting an end to Spearfinger is my final act of atonement.

The original intent was to preserve that for the time when the KGC could rise again. I fear that will never happen and should never happen. If the cache is not being preserved any longer for the KGC, what purpose is there in keeping it protected? At this point, her very existence poses a huge danger to innocent people. Too many lives have been lost protecting the cache. You are correct. The time has come for it to end."

"So, how does one vanquish her?"

"I'm afraid that is the difficult part. You must understand, when she was conjured, loyalty to the KGC superseded everything to our members. With that in mind, I felt that in order to ensure that she was only vanquished at the correct moment, it can only be done by the most loyal of members."

"So the coin? Because I have the coin, only I can vanquish her?"

"Yes, but there is more. The coin is only part of the equation. In an action of true loyalty, there must be a sacrifice to her. She will often take the form of her victims. This is an in-between time for her. In order to take that form, she also becomes more vulnerable. In fact, when she has taken the human form, she can be killed as easily as a human. So yes, it requires the coin in order to get close enough to her to kill her, but it also requires the sacrifice of a person whose form she can take."

"She is already in human form. I spoke with her today in the form of Melanie's neighbor. No one else will have to die!"

"David, she will only appear in each human form once. In addition to making her vulnerable, it also requires a large amount of her energy. If you spoke to her in human form already, you will never see her in human form again until she has a new victim."

"How is this an act of loyalty? It is right now, just because I have the coin. But had anyone else gotten the coin they could accomplish the same thing without any loyalty."

"You are very correct. There certainly is more to it than what I've stated. She can only be vanquished by the act of sacrifice. However, accessing the cache, well that is another story for another day I'm afraid.

"So that's it. I must make sure she kills someone else to stop her? There are no loopholes to this rule?"

"I'm afraid not. As I said, I needed to ensure the decision to vanquish her was not stepped into lightly. I'm sorry for this, but it is the only way."

"That's really some shit! This is your atonement? I have

to sacrifice someone so you can move on? Can't you sacrifice yourself?"

"I'm afraid it doesn't work that way. It's true, I will be released from this earth. No longer bound to the hotel and this forest. Moving on is not always a good thing. I'm afraid that what awaits me beyond this earth will be anything but pleasant. My fate was set in stone long ago. There is no use avoiding it any longer. However, you are not ending her for my benefit. You are ending her because I cannot, and she needs to be stopped." He stood up and walked up to me. He looked me straight in the eyes and continued to speak. "David, I'm afraid this needs to happen quickly. She is hungry. The longer you wait, the more victims she will have. I trust you to follow through with this."

After he spoke those words, he turned and walked into the forest. As his body passed through the brush and he could no longer be seen, the flames of the small campfire began to grow. The heat on my face was extreme. I stood up and took a step backward. The flames were now at least three feet tall and continued to grow. As the tower of flames grew ever taller, it started to push out wider as well. I continued to step backward until my body was stopped by something. I turned to look, and the holler was enclosed in a rock wall on all sides.

I frantically started to run along the perimeter looking for an escape. There was none. There was no break in the rock wall. I was trapped as the fire continued to spread out towards me. I pushed on the rock wall. It wouldn't move and was hot to the touch. When the flames were only inches away from me, there was a loud crackling sound in the sky. The fire flashed hotter and brighter than anything I'd ever seen. I was blinded by the flash of light. I felt the heat quickly dissipate and fade away.

I opened my eyes and found myself standing in the center of Melanie's loft.

I SPENT a few moments examining my hands and my body for any sign of the inferno I had just witnessed. Realizing I had escaped unscathed, I padded over to the edge of the loft and looked down. Melanie was still sleeping peacefully on the couch. Looking at her, I was conflicted. Part of me wanted to curl up next to her and forget about everything else. The rest of me was a jumble of emotions from heart-break to rage.

I headed down the stairway, exhausted. I opted to sit in the chair across from the sofa. At the very least, I wanted to be near her when she woke. I emptied my pockets on the coffee table and took off my shoes. As I sat there and tried to let go of the day, my head began circling around the conversation with Robert. I had to choose. I had to sacrifice one person to end Spearfinger. The choice was simple: Austin. There was no other option that was nearly as satisfying and would truly bring closure. Austin would die, and because of that, everything would be right again.

With that thought, I slipped into a deep sleep.

When I opened my eyes, the cabin was filled with bright natural light. I groggily looked at my watch and realized it was just after noon. A flash of panic that I was late for something jolted me up. It took a few moments to realize where I was. When I did, all I could see was the crumpled up blanket on the couch where Melanie had been sleeping. She was gone. I scrambled to look through the house. There was no sign of her anywhere. I stepped out onto the porch. My

truck sat exactly where I had parked it the night before, but
Melanie's Jeep was gone.

I stepped back inside to try and figure out a plan, and
then I remembered that Melanie's Jeep had never been
there. We'd left it at the Gap the day before when I'd driven
her home. I patted down my jeans looking for my phone
when I realized I'd left it on the coffee table. I ran over to
the table and picked it up and found the battery had died.
After unsuccessfully searching the house for a charging
cable, I ran out to my truck and plugged my phone in. With
my phone slowly getting enough of a charge to power up, I
tried to imagine where she would have gone. Either she
walked somewhere or Austin picked her up. The only
places within reasonable walking distance were town or
the Gap.

The hair on the back of my neck stood up at the mere
thought of her heading to the Gap again. She might have
woken up and wanted to let me sleep, heading out to the
Gap to retrieve her Jeep. Without knowing how long she'd
been gone, it was impossible to even guess. I was too impatient to wait for my phone to come back to life. I hopped in
my truck and started driving to the Gap. There was only one
road up there. If she'd hiked up there to get her Jeep, I'd
either pass her on her walk up or see her Jeep drive by on
the way down.

I sped up the mountain, taking the hairpin turns and
switchbacks far faster than what was advised. Only a few
minutes later, I reached the top and found her Jeep parked
in the same place it had been yesterday. Overcome with
frustration, I parked next to it. I grabbed my phone and realized that it had finally powered on. I called her phone and
waited for it to connect. It rang once and immediately went
to voicemail. Her phone was turned off. I tried calling three

more times just to be sure, but every time I got the same result.

I laid down on my steering wheel in defeat. I wasn't content believing she headed out to town, but I didn't have any other ideas and waiting around for her was not something I could handle. I sat up and looked out my windshield. In front of my car was the trail that headed down to Spearfinger. As I stared out at the small section of trampled brush hiding the trail, something caught my eye. In a tree, pointing directly at my truck, was a mounted trail camera. Gordon's camera!

I picked up my phone and called Gordon.

"Hey, can you access the camera on the trail?" I asked. "The one you showed me the footage from yesterday?"

"Yeah, hang on. Anything in particular I should be looking for?"

"Melanie! She left while I was asleep, and I need to know if she headed down there."

"Let's see, been a busy morning there... Looks like there was a beautiful 14-point buck over there just after seven this morning... some birds of course... oh here we go."

"What did you find?"

"That's your girl. She went down there at 10:18 this morning. No other captures, well other than you sitting in your truck now. It looks like she's still down there. Want me to check the camera I have set up over by the shack?"

"No. No need, I'm going down there."

"Be careful! Call me if you need me!"

"Wait, Gordon?"

"Yeah."

"Was she alone?"

"Yeah, no sign of Austin this morning. Look, I'll keep an eye on the camera and let you know if I spot him coming."

I LEFT the truck and took off in a sprint down the trail. Fueled by a dangerous combination of fear and rage, I headed to the shack with abandon. The trail was mostly downhill, letting me cover ground quickly. Leaping over the small patches where water crossed the trail while dodging low branches, I made incredible time. I could see the turn in front of the shack was just ahead. I stopped to catch my breath so that I could approach as silently as possible.

The forest was quiet and still. It was also damp. The smell of the wet forest floor was overpowering. My shirt was wet from sweat as I began to creep towards the shack, watching every step to remain as silent as possible. My senses went into a state of hyper-alertness. I was keenly aware of every sound. I expected to hear some sign of Melanie up ahead, but there was nothing.

As I approached the final turn before the shack, I paused. My hand instinctively reached for the knife I carried in my front pocket and rested, ready to wield the blade in an instant. I took a deep breath and stepped into the turn.

The shack appeared to be empty. I looked at the ground and saw a set of footprints leading there. They appeared to be Melanie's. Now less focused on remaining silent, I walked up to the shack. It was empty. There was nothing to suggest that anyone had been there since last night.

I looked back at the footprints. They did lead to the shack. It was clear she spent some time there. The tracks moved every direction in front of the shack as if she had paced back and forth there for a bit. There was one line of tracks that broke out of that pattern and traveled out beyond the clearing and into the brush. Without hesitation I followed them. If Melanie had gone that deep, she was in trouble. Despite what had happened yesterday, I was not willing to let her be my sacrifice.

The brush was thick and wet. It was impossible to follow footsteps so I resorted to looking for any sign that someone had been through there. I was able to spot a few patches where it looked as if the small branches had been trampled. The brush gave way to the canopy. The tall trees blocked out the sunlight. There, with no foliage growing below ten feet on the trees, I was able to clearly see what lay ahead. I looked for any sign of Melanie. Off in the distance, I saw something unnatural. A bright orange backpack leaned against the base of a tree. Melanie's backpack.

I jogged up to the pack, but there was no other sign of her. I looked again through the trees, not knowing which direction to go. I couldn't find any sign of a track. Then I heard something. It was very faint, but it sounded like someone crying.

My head jerked towards the direction of the sound. About ten yards in front of me was a large moss covered boulder. I started walking towards it.

"Melanie!" I yelled.

I heard a loud sniff in reply, and then a disheveled Melanie appeared from behind the boulder. She was shaken, and she wobbled as if her legs were going to give out. Her eyes were bloodshot and her face was wet with tears.

"David, you...you're not supposed to be here."

"Neither are you! C'mon, let's get out of here.

"David, stop!" she screamed. "You cannot be here. You need to leave now!"

"I'm not leaving without you. You know it isn't safe out here. You need to come with me."

"You don't understand. She's coming. She's coming now, for you! You need to run!

As she spoke, the ground shook with a massive thud. It sounded like someone was ripping the massive trees out of the ground and tossing them aside.

When the ground trembled, Melanie lost her footing and collapsed onto her knees. I sprinted up to her and grabbed her arms, trying to pull her to her feet.

"You have to listen to me," she said, sobbing.

I ignored her, scooping her up in my arms. Her fists pounded on me, and she screamed for me to stop. I continued to carry her. There was a constant sound of rustling trees behind us, getting closer at every moment. I made it past where her backpack sat and continued forward, walking as fast as I could. She stopped punching me and laid there limply in my arms. We made it to the brush and back to the clearing by the shack. I laid her body down on the floor of the shack.

"Is this person here under your protection?" a loud witchy voice screeched.

I looked back and saw a figure standing there. A long wrinkled finger extended out from the brush. It was a foot long with a jagged, yellowed fingernail at its tip.

"Yes, she is here under my protection!" I shouted to the figure.

"I'm not speaking to you."

"Yes, he's under my protection," a quiet and broken voice behind me said.

I turned to look and saw Melanie holding out her hand towards the figure.

"I told you to run! Why didn't you listen to me?" she snarled.

I turned back to the figure in the woods, and it was gone.

I looked back at Melanie, still standing there, still sobbing, still holding her fist out. As I looked at her, she slowly turned her hand and opened her fingers. In the palm of her hand was the coin. My coin.

"I'm sorry" she whispered as she collapsed on the ground.

23

"GORDON, send someone down to the shack," I yelled into my phone. "I need to get Melanie to a hospital. She's unconscious, and I won't be able to carry her all the way to the Gap!"

"I'm sending help now," Gordon replied. "But you gotta realize it's gonna be awhile. They can't exactly drive an ambulance down the trail. Not to mention the fact that I have to lead them so we don't have some EMT's tangling with that beast."

"Aw hell, I might as well just carry her. It's a hike, but I'll get her out of here before someone else gets here."

"Just stay with her! Help is on its way. The last thing anyone needs is for you to injure yourself while trying to be the hero. Just rest and wait. As long as she's breathing and her heart rate is solid, you guys will be alright."

"Yeah, got it." I hung up the phone in frustration.

I looked at her lying there. A tear rolled down my cheek. I was confused and mad at her, but I loved her. I feared for her. She had been with Spearfinger, I knew she had the coin, but I couldn't let myself believe she was safe. I wasn't ready to let her slip away like my dad. The coin was still clutched in her right hand. I gently peeled the fingers away until I could grab the coin.

I thought back to the night before when I'd slept in her cabin. She was sound asleep on her couch. I'd pulled my phone, keys, wallet, and coin out of my pockets and put them on the coffee table before I fell asleep. She must have grabbed it there. When I'd woken up to find her gone and my phone dead, I'd never even noticed that the coin was gone.

I took a deep breath and shook my head as I put the coin back in my pocket. I put my fingers on her wrist to check her pulse. It felt normal. I looked at my watch, then down the trail. I balled my fingers into fists and quickly released them.

"Fuck it!" I said to no one in particular.

I took a deep breath and wrapped my arms around Melanie's limp body. I was going to carry her out of there. There was no way I was going to wait for someone to find us down there. I lifted her easily, adrenaline coursing through my veins. I spent a moment repositioning her in my arms, and I quickly started to make my way back up the trail.

The first few hundred feet went smoothly. Then, as my arms and my back started to burn, I looked for a place to lay her down for a moment. I quickly realized that wasn't an option. I knew that it would take far more energy to pick her back up than it did to carry her. If I put her down then, I'd be done. I had to power through.

I took each step slowly to ensure my footing. My gait was short to conserve as much energy as I could. I kept my head up and eyes focused on the trail ahead. I knew the trail like the back of my hand. Yet, I found myself playing mental games.

"That tree, right up there, once you pass that you're almost done," I'd say to myself. I knew the Gap wasn't just past that tree, but I needed to focus on my progress. Two thirds of the way up, I found a large rock. I leaned back on the rock for a few minutes. It was the best I could do to relieve the pain in my lower back for just a moment. My shirt was soaked through with sweat. I continued and fought the pain. Doing anything else would have meant stopping indefinitely. I couldn't reposition her or my arms around her. The slightest shift and I would've lost my grip. I had no choice but to continue.

The sky darkened, and there was a heavy mist in the air. I gritted my teeth to fight off the pain I was feeling and continue forward. The last turn of the trail was in sight. As I trudged forward, my phone started ringing. Unable to answer or even silence the phone, it became another annoyance. I hoped that it was Gordon calling to tell me that help was coming. I made my way past the final turn and faced the last incline of the hike. That gave me a renewed sense of resolve. My tired, heavy feet slowly trudged toward the end of the hike.

Nearing the top, I saw a figure plunge through the brush separating the trail from the parking lot. Blinded by the constant flow of burning sweat in my eyes, I could only make out the silhouette of a man, but I knew it was Gordon.

"Gordon, down here!" I choked out.

The figure quickly descended towards us, navigating the uneven footing with ease.

"Dammit, David!" he yelled as he took Melanie from my arms. "You will never listen to me, will you?"

"No way I was gonna wait for someone to make it down there to help!"

Gordon moved up the trail with ease while carrying Melanie.

"Listen, the EMT's are up there. Do me a favor and shut up about what happened down there. Story is you two were hiking and she passed out. That's all we know."

I followed Gordon through the brush. The flashing red and blue lights of the ambulance were blinding as they reflected off the mist in the air. I made it as far as the hood of my truck before I collapsed. Knowing Melanie was being cared for immediately drained the adrenaline that had kept me going. Every ounce of energy I had was gone. I was exhausted.

LATER THAT EVENING, I sat in the waiting room at the Johnson County Hospital. Gordon bitched me out for letting the coin out of my sight and not listening to him. I waited for the first word on Melanie's condition. I was covered in mud, and I stank yet there was no way I was going to leave until I found out if she was all right.

I was furious with her for so many reasons. I felt completely betrayed; however, the moment she collapsed all of that disappeared and was replaced with concern for her well-being. I wanted to pace, but my legs were so tired that I wasn't sure if I could stand. The silence was killing me though. I forced myself to slowly stand, and on very shaky legs, I walked over to the small gift shop. I grabbed a bottle of Cheerwine and made my way to the cashier.

I patted down my pockets and pulled out a five dollar bill. It was completely wet, soaked with what I could only assume was sweat. I hesitantly handed it over to the young blonde woman.

"Sorry, I... It's been a long day."

"It's fine, I understand completely," she replied cheerfully.

She handed me my change, and I started to walk out.

"Excuse me." she called out.

I turned back to face her.

"Is there a problem?"

"No, it's just... Are you David, from... you know... Paranormal Archaeology?"

"Yeah, that's me," I said, smiling slightly for the first time all day.

"I can't believe it's you. I've seen every one of your shows. I love that stuff!"

"Thank you!"

"You know, you should really get in touch with Renegade Jack! It would be a dream come true to see you two collab on somethin'!"

"Sorry, Renegade who?"

"Seriously? You know Renegade Jack, the Youtuber? You can't tell me you have never seen any of his videos. You guys would be perfect together!"

"I'll be sure to check him out, but right now I gotta get back to..." I gestured to the waiting room, "I guess sitting on my ass."

I paused and saw a display with phone chargers and cables and such. I picked up a set of earbuds and set them on the counter.

"Since I'm waiting here anyway, I might as well check it out now."

The woman beamed with excitement as she rang me up for the earbuds.

I sat back down in the waiting room and pulled out my phone to search for Renegade Jack on YouTube. I landed on a page that had hundreds of videos, all with hundreds of thousands of views. The subject matter of the videos seemed to vary, covering everything from urban exploration to haunted houses. They all featured super spammy-sounding headlines like "Millionaire Gangster's Abandoned Home" or "My Ride with the Infamous Hitchhiking Ghost."

I was about to forgo watching any of these videos, even though I had nothing better to do, then one title caught my eye. "Hidden Confederate Gold on Appalachian Trail." The thumbnail image for the video was a cheesy photo of the Appalachian Mountains with a giant clipart image depicting a pot of gold superimposed on top of it. With great reservation, I started the video.

The video launched with a full panoramic view of the Carver's Gap parking lot. Then Jack entered the scene. He was super excited and could only be described as zany, wearing ostentatious sunglasses and speaking like a teenager hopped up on energy drinks. As I continued watching, what really caught my attention was the fact that he was not just some kid who heard a rumor of the KGC treasure. He spoke with accuracy and authority on the history of the area. He stood at the foundation of the Cloudland Hotel and intricately described the opulence and the layout of the hotel that had once stood there. Whoever he was, he was intelligent and had done his research despite his goofy persona.

As the video played on, Jack described how the hotel, among other things, was the cornerstone for finding the hidden cache.

"The treasure could only be found by standing in the private study of the hotel and following a straight path based upon a specific compass bearing. That bearing has never been disclosed and is believed to be lost to time. However, standing right here, I know it is out there. I can feel it. One direction or another, if you travel a straight line you will walk across the KGC's cache! Smash that like button! Hit subscribe to see where I end up next! This is Renegade Jack." He smiled as the video image faded out.

I pulled the earbuds from my ears and set down my phone. Had this been any other day, I would have certainly reached out to Renegade Jack. However, on that day, my mind was more focused on Melanie. I took a sip of Cheerwine and rubbed my legs, trying to coax some energy back into them. Out of the corner of my eye, I saw an older woman in a white doctor's coat approach the reception desk. I watched intently as she spoke, and the receptionist looked up and pointed my direction. The doctor then approached me.

"David?" she said.

"That's me."

"Hi, I'm Dr. Weaver. I'm the E.R. doctor overseeing Melanie's care."

"Is she okay?"

"Yes, she is going to be fine. It appears she was just extremely dehydrated. I have her on a saline drip. She passed the battery of exams with flying colors, including the liver enzymes. I wanted to ask you about that. When she was admitted, the EMT said the Forest Ranger on site was concerned about possible liver failure. Any idea why that would have been a concern?"

"I don't have a clue," I lied. "All I know is she passed out on the trail, and I thought she was gonna die. I'm no doctor."

"Interesting. Well whatever the reason, her liver is fine. I can take you to her room if you are ready to see her."

THE DOCTOR ESCORTED me to Melanie's room. She instructed me to try to keep her calm. When I stepped into the room, Melanie was sitting up in the adjustable bed and appeared to be awake and alert.

"David! I can't believe you're here!"

Her voice held a hint of nervousness, combined with excitement. Following the immediate surprise of seeing me, her eyes dropped and her expression changed. She looked sullen and sad.

"Look, I don't know what to say. I know you're probably here to yell at me and tell me to stay out of your life... and I deserve that..."

"Actually, I'm here because I was worried about you!"

"I'm sorry! I never intended for you to follow me down there. You were never supposed to be in danger."

I took a deep breath and bit the inside of my lip. I didn't know what to say. I didn't know how I felt. Up until that moment, I was concerned for her safety. But as she brought it up, the pain started to bubble up inside me. I just stared at her.

"Say something! Please David, tell me what you're thinking."

"What I'm thinking?" I said as I began pacing the room. "I want to know the truth!"

"I woke up, and I just saw that coin laying there on the table. You were sound asleep, and I thought I could end this all without you ever knowing. It was a stupid idea."

"End what exactly?"

"The treasure... Austin. You know he won't stop until he has it. I just thought with the coin, I could get it and never have to worry about him threatening you again."

That pushed me over the edge. Whatever restraint I'd had was gone with that statement. In my head I heard

Gordon tell me to not let her know that I'd seen the video. Part of me wanted to listen, but in the end all I could do was give him a mental middle finger as I stepped over the edge.

"Oh for me? That's right, I forgot I'm the one he pistol whipped. And that happened after he snuck up on you and tied you up, right?"

"Yeah, I'm the one that passed out, but I still remember that," she said defensively.

"And here I asked for the truth. So... where were you two planning on flying off to once you got the cache?"

"What are you talking about?"

"Stop with the bullshit! Look, I know the story you told me, but I also know that you two walked down there together. That you planned this ahead of time. So, by the time you stole the coin, let's just say I wasn't exactly surprised. Hurt, angry, ashamed, annoyed. I was a lot of things, but not surprised."

"It's not like that."

"And I should believe you why? Oh, because you have been so fucking honest with me? Jesus Melanie, you sat there while that asshole pointed a gun at my face as part of a plan you had with him, and you want me to believe you?"

"Let me explain. Austin, you don't know what it's like... what he does if I..."

"No, you've explained enough... I just want to know one thing. You owe me that much for hauling your ass out of there today. How long have you been planning this? Were you ever really interested in me or was this all part of a long-term scam?"

I was enraged, and I couldn't contain it anymore. I looked at her with disdain and watched how my last words impacted her. It was like a blade slicing through her heart. She didn't say a word. She didn't have to. Her lip quivered as a stream of tears ran down her cheeks. All she could do was shake her head as if she was saying 'no'. My words had done their damage. In that moment, I realized that whatever reason she'd had for doing this, it was clear she didn't want to hurt me. It was clear that the feelings she had for me were real.

She was hurt. The woman I loved, I had just destroyed. She had lied and betrayed me. I was perfectly within my rights to fight back, but I had gone too far. She was broken. We were broken. Nothing could change that. I stood there staring at her for what felt like an hour. Tears were now running down my cheeks as well. The inside of my lip screamed in pain from my teeth locking onto it. I couldn't do anything but leave. In that moment with her destroyed, I turned away and walked out of the room.

I jogged down the hallway to the exit of the hospital. I couldn't stop. I kept running until I reached my truck in the parking lot. I jumped in and sobbed until I couldn't cry anymore. I was holding the steering wheel with white knuckles, praying that holding onto it would keep me from going off the edge. Then I saw my phone. I took a few deep breaths to regain some composure and called Gordon.

"Gordon, I need a favor, no questions asked."

"What do you need?"

"I need you to meet me. Bring me my father's service revolver you kept after he died. I need it loaded. This is ending tonight!"

24

I ARRIVED at the substation before Gordon and waited in my truck. I wasn't planning on going inside. There wasn't a need to go in there and relive more memories. It was damp and humid outside, and a thick fog covered the ground. I stared out the windshield as the headlights of my truck illuminated the fog around my old home. I turned off my lights. The last thing I needed was to draw any unwanted attention. Emotionally, I was standing on the edge of a razor. At the moment I was fine, but it would take nothing at all to push me over that edge.

I looked at my watch. It was exactly two in the morning, the time I'd told Gordon to meet me. My eyes watched the sweeping second hand of my watch. With every moment that passed, I became more and more anxious. I finally saw approaching headlights in the fog. The ranger truck pulled up and parked in front of me. I stepped out, standing in the light of his truck and waited.

"Dammit kid, you look like shit." Gordon said as he stepped out of his truck. "You sure you need this now?"

"Yeah. Tonight is my only chance."

"Look David, I brought your dad's service piece like you asked, but you gotta understand, right now this is looking like the worst decision I have ever made."

"I said no questions asked."

"I'm not asking a damn thing. I'm talking. You never said nothin' about me not talking. Since you won't let me ask any questions and you need that piece, I s'pose, you have no choice but to listen."

I sighed in frustration and held up my hands.

"Fine, give me your damn speech."

"I don't know what the hell you are going to do out there, but I know one thing that you should understand. Whatever you plan to do out there with your dad's gun...well, I can't help you. I can't protect you."

That little nudge was all that it took for me to stumble emotionally. "First off, I never asked for you to protect me. Secondly, if you could cover up the death of my dad and everyone else for this long, I am pretty fucking sure you can cover up whatever the hell you want."

"How do you think this works? You think I can convince anyone that a man lying in the woods with a massive bullet hole in his skull died of natural causes? Look, all I am saying is, the minute this thing gets fired, you're on your own. "

"Message received," I said flatly.

Gordon looked at me with hardened eyes for a moment. I knew he was concerned. I knew he was disappointed. I didn't care. I also knew that Gordon wouldn't stand in my way. He took a deep breath as his shoulders slumped in defeat. He went to his truck and came back carrying my father's Beretta M9.

"I trust you know how to use this?" he asked.

"Yup."

"All right." He handed the gun to me. "Like you asked

for, it has a full clip, but I ain't giving you a spare clip. Whatever you are planning on doing, you have fifteen shots to do it in and no more. You sure you know what you're getting yourself into?"

"I know how to kill Spearfinger. I am going to end her tonight."

"It's that easy? Just shoot her? Pretty sure that's been tried. You can't tell me that none of her victims ever fired a couple rounds into her before."

I checked the clip in the M9. It was full as promised.

"No, it's not that easy at all, but I know how to kill her, and I will kill her."

"All right, all right. Just know you don't have to do this alone."

"Thanks, but I do need to do this alone," I said as I slid the M9 into my waistband. "Hey Gordon... one other thing. Make sure you shut down those cameras for a while. Pretty sure anything they record will only create unanswerable questions for both of us."

I left Gordon standing there, not really caring what he thought about any of it. I didn't care what repercussions I faced. I was hyper-focused on the task at hand. As my truck entered the deserted streets of Roan, I slowed down to try and compose myself. I knew that once I started it, I couldn't stop until I saw it through. I tried to step back and think logically, but I couldn't. I pulled off the main street in town onto one of the few side roads. I drove as slow as I could to not draw any unwanted attention. When I got within a short distance from my destination, I killed the headlights and continued on at a snail's pace.

Up ahead was the secluded dirt driveway, leading through a junkyard that surrounded an old run down trailer. I parked my truck a few hundred feet away from the trailer and turned off the truck. There were a few lights on in the trailer, but I knew no one was awake. I sat in the truck for a few minutes just watching and listening. Once I was confident that I'd arrived unnoticed, I pulled out the M9, ensured the safety was off and there was a round chambered.

It was time to pay a visit to Austin.

THE MOONLIGHT REFLECTED off the windows of the rusted trailer as I approached. I tightened my sweaty hand around the M9 and gently reached for the handle of the aluminum screen door with my other. I held my breath as I pulled the door open, expecting it to creak loudly. It didn't. I stepped into the dingy living room. I scanned the room, looking for anyone. It was empty. I closed the door silently.

Under the orangish glow of the overhead light, the room was a mess. Empty bottles of Jack Daniels covered a poor excuse for a coffee table. The yellow couch was deeply stained. On it was Austin's prized possession, a black Dean guitar complete with blue lightning bolts. A cord from the guitar traveled to the other side of the room where a giant amplifier stood where most would have a TV. Numerous other guitars hung on that wall, making it look like a junk yard from a 1980's metal video.

I made my way to the door on the other side of the room. Everything beyond that doorway was dark. I gently stepped inside. There was a short hallway that led to the bathroom and the bedroom. Both doors were open. I held my breath as I stepped further into the hallway and then through the doorway to the bedroom.

As my eyes adjusted to the darkness, I could make out

the majority of the cluttered room. Lying in the center of the bed was Austin. I could see his chest rising and falling under his white tank top. I inched closer until I was standing directly over him. I tightened my grip on the M9 and in one fluid motion brought it down on his skull.

"Fuck!" he screamed.

His body shot up. In an exaggerated motion to cover his head with his hands, he toppled off the side of the bed. He thrashed on the ground for a few moments before rising to his knees with his hands on his head.

"I'll fucking kill you, motherfucker!" he yelled.

I stepped back and ran my free hand up the wall until I felt the light switch. I flicked it on and stood there motionless with the gun pointed straight at Austin's head. In the light, I could see the blood covering his hands and dying the top half of his tank top red.

"You will do nothing other than what I tell you to do, understand?" I spat.

"David? You piece of shit! You know you're a dead man, right?"

"Shut up, stay on your knees, keep your hands on your head, and turn around!" I ordered.

He complied. I ordered him to slowly put his hands behind his back. I cautiously approached while putting the gun in my waistband. I began tying paracord around his hands, securing them behind his back. I'd expected him to try to bolt or to turn and face me, but he didn't. Despite what I'd already done, he clearly didn't feel threatened by me.

"Stand up!"

"Alright smart guy," he sneered as he stood. "So tell me, what are you going to do now? I mean, we both know you don't have the balls to kill me, and if you don't, there isn't a damn thing you can do to stop me from coming after you. I feel like a smart guy like you would've thought this out better."

I stared at him. His wicked smile taunted me.

"Oh you didn't think this through... you idiot! You're just pissed off cause that bitch of yours set you up, and this was the best plan you could come up with. Alright, you got me, dick. Whatcha gonna do with me now?"

"Walk outside!"

"Hey, I let you tie me up without even trying to sucker punch you. If I'm goin' outside, you think I can get some shoes?"

Dammit, not only was he cocky but he was also making sense.

"Fine, put on your damn shoes, but I'm not helping you or untying you."

He sauntered across the living room and awkwardly stepped into a pair of old basketball shoes.

He shrugged his shoulders and started walking towards the door. I followed closely behind with the gun trained on him. He got to the front door and kicked it open, nearly knocking it off its hinges.

"Where to now, bossman? Got some secluded trailer out in the forest somewhere you're gonna try to lock me up in?"

"Go to my truck."

"Ah yeah, there you go. Drive me out of there, take me to your makeshift jail cell you think I won't get out of. How long do you really think you can keep this shit going?"

"I'm not locking you up. I'm giving you exactly what you've always wanted."

"Really? You're gonna blow me? Listen, I appreciate it an' all, but you're not really my type."

With every word he spoke, he pushed me further and

further toward the edge. It wasn't possible for me to hate any one person more than I did him.

I forced myself to remain silent. We got to my truck, and I opened the door. I gestured with the M9 for him to get in. For the first time I saw a hint of fear in his eyes. Behind the cockiness, he was truly unsure what I was capable of.

"Really man, where the fuck are you taking me?"

"I told you already. I'm giving you exactly what you always wanted! Tonight you are getting that horde of KGC Gold."

I stepped in the truck, started it, and sped off into the night.

———

I PULLED up to the entrance of the trail and parked. I looked over at Austin. The bleeding had stopped, but his face was covered with orangish dried blood. He didn't look scared or in pain. He looked bored.

"Get out." I ordered.

Austin turned to look at me. He was grinning.

"Look, I gave you too much credit. Now I realize you don't have a clue what you're doin'. First off, how the fuck am I supposed to get out of your truck with my hands tied behind my back? Secondly, you don't have a clue where the gold is!"

I didn't respond. He was right. I was in way over my head. The fact that he was right infuriated me even more.

I leaned over him to open the door of the truck. "Now...get...out!"

He exited the truck. I grabbed a flashlight and walked up behind him.

"Down the path," I said.

He shrugged and started making his way through the brush. "See, unless you've found the gold, and I mean actually touched it with your own hands, this trail is useless. It runs near the gold, that's for damn sure, but you can't find the gold from here."

"Just keep walking."

We silently trudged down the trail. Something about Austin's cockiness concerned me. I didn't know where the gold was, and he knew it. Yet, he willingly followed along. I was missing something. That fact scared me. I was too far gone, though. I had to see my plan through no matter what he was doing.

After an agonizing walk, we made it to the shack. Austin sat down on the front edge of the shack while I took a sip from my water bottle.

"Okay, you got me here," Austin said. "How about I make you a deal?"

"You're the one tied up and you're trying to make a deal with me? Fine, let's hear it."

"You go on and get that gold. You get the gold, bring it to me, and I let you walk out of this forest alive tonight."

"You know I'm the one holding the gun, right?"

"I told you, you ain't got the balls to pull the trigger. We only stopped here 'cause you don't have a damn clue where you're goin'. You're stuck, smart guy. You either have to kill me, or well... yeah you killing me is the only way you even get out of here tonight without taking my deal."

"Don't assume you know everything."

"I know you still believe that your shitty knots will hold me. If I wanted to get out, I'd have been out long ago."

His yellowed teeth shown behind his grin.

"You're full of shit!" I seethed in anger. "Get up! We're getting the gold."

I directed him through the brush following the path I had gone through with Melanie. We made it through the brush and into the canopy. It was darker now, but the surroundings still seemed familiar enough for me to find our way to the rock I'd found Melanie hiding behind.

I swept the forest back and forth with the flashlight beam. I felt like we were heading in the right direction. Everything looked right, but I couldn't find what I was looking for. Melanie's orange backpack should've been midway to the rock. When I'd carried her out of the woods, I'd left it behind. I wasn't seeing it anywhere.

Despite not seeing the backpack, I could feel in my gut we were getting close. I just had to find that rock and wait for Spearfinger to take Austin as her victim. Knowing the entire situation was on the verge of being finished gave me the solace to continue forward.

"You know we're walking in circles, right?" Austin said.

"Just shut up!"

He was getting the best of me. He had successfully gotten me to lose my laser-focused resolve; I started questioning everything I was doing. I kept moving forward, kept looking for the backpack. But he was right. I was certainly walking in circles now. Just as I was about to stop, the beam of my flashlight illuminated the edge of a very large rock. I'd found it. I trudged forward with Austin by my side.

"So now what, smart guy? I'm pretty sure I don't see any gold... and if it's buried, you didn't bring even a shovel. Are you really this stupid?"

"Why don't you tell me why you let me take you here. You seem pretty confident that you can escape and overpower me whenever you want."

He looked at me with a huge grin and let out a laugh. "That's pretty simple. I need you, or at least that coin of yours, to get the gold, but I also really want you dead. This little plan of yours is accomplishing everything I want!"

I stared out at him, unsure of what he meant.

"This trail you took me on, your forest ranger buddy has video cameras all over it. So... now there's video of you taking me down here, tied up at gunpoint. There isn't a fuckin' jury in the world that will convict me for anything when I walk out of here alone."

I stared at him in complete silence. *Why isn't Spearfinger coming?* I thought. The forest was getting brighter. I could tell the sun was starting to rise. I second guessed myself, thinking maybe Spearfinger only appeared at night. I knew this wasn't the case and quickly discarded the thought.

A chill went up my spine as I saw his arms move slightly. He shifted his weight so slowly it was nearly unnoticeable. I tightened my grip on the gun. My palms were sweaty. I couldn't shoot him. I knew that. I was supposed to let Spearfinger have him and then shoot her. I knew he was moments away from attempting to escape, and I didn't know how to stop it without shooting him.

The motion in his arms was less guarded. He knew I wouldn't stop him. I gritted my teeth and took aim. My finger twitched as it hovered above the trigger. I took a deep breath and tried to calm my nerves. As I did, I lightly relaxed my grip on the gun. No matter how much I wanted him gone, I couldn't shoot him. I closed my eyes for a split second and the earth shook violently. In the jolt, my finger pulled the trigger and the gun fired. My shoulders slumped as I saw the empty shell eject from the gun and tumble onto the ground. I closed my eyes, knowing I'd failed.

25

"YOU MISSED! YOU'RE STANDIN' what, three feet away from me, and you fire into the dirt?" Austin screamed laughing.

I opened my eyes to see him standing there. He had escaped from the paracord and raised his hands in the air triumphantly, flashing metal horns like he was on stage, but there was something else. Out of the corner of my eye, I saw something move on his left side. I squeezed my eyes shut quickly and shook my head. When I opened them again, my jaw dropped in shock.

Standing next to him was Melanie. She stood there stoically. Austin, in his celebration, hadn't yet seen her. She didn't move.

"Melanie? Why are you here?"

Austin dropped his hands and tilted his head in reaction to my words. He slowly turned to look around until he saw her next to him. He wrapped his arms around her, pulling her close to him. Her body was rigid and almost unnatural.

"See, I knew you were on my side. Sorry about, you know, having to threaten you and all to pull one over on

David. I shoulda known you'd be on my side. No hard feelings. Just had to cover my bases."

Austin kept looking at her, waiting for a response. None came. She stared out at me in a way I've never seen. Her eyes appeared hollow. There was no emotion at all. The sight made me shiver.

"Are you protecting him?" she finally said in an almost monotone voice.

"Protecting him?" Austin asked. "Baby, you know what's up. We did it!"

It took me a moment to understand exactly what was happening. She wasn't asking Austin. She was asking me. That wasn't Melanie.

My heart went cold. I didn't know how or when, but Spearfinger had taken Melanie. Spearfinger herself was standing before me in human form... In Melanie's form. Melanie had become the sacrifice. I instinctively raised the M9 and looked at Melanie. It wasn't really her, I knew that. But no matter what, it was the woman I loved. I lowered the gun.

I couldn't do it. I'd never be able to do it. I didn't care if Spearfinger ruled the forest forever if it meant I needed to sacrifice her.

"Are you protecting him?" she asked again.

I needed to respond. If I said no, she'd kill him. Another victim, but it wouldn't bring Melanie back. I wracked my brain to come up with some sort of solution. Some way to bring her back. I came up with nothing. My hands began to shake. I fell to my knees. I buried my head in my hands. Anger began to overtake the sadness. I rose back to my feet and pulled the coin from my pocket. I gritted my teeth and squeezed the coin in my palm.

"No, I'm not protecting him. Nobody is protected anymore."

Austin backed away from her. I could tell he was looking for an escape. I put the pistol into my waistband and approached her. Her head slowly raised as I got near. With one swift motion, I grabbed her wrist and yanked it upward.

Her face twisted into a smile. "You have no power over me. Release me now!"

As I held her wrist, I took the coin in my other hand and pressed it into her palm. The moment the coin touched her skin she winced and jerked back. Her head flung backwards, pulling me towards her. I missed her and fell off to the side, tumbling on the ground. The coin flew into the air and landed near my feet. I dove for the coin. Snatching it off the ground, I clutched it in my hand and turned my eyes toward her.

She was now winded, gasping for breath. She'd changed. The hollow eyes were replaced with Melanie's vibrant green ones. Those eyes locked onto me. Tears began to form in them. Melanie was back. She raised the hand I'd put the coin in and inspected her palm. Her fingers began to curl inward as if she was holding an invisible ball. Her hand shook, the muscles in her fingers strained. Her breath became deep and deliberate.

"Melanie, come back!" I yelled. "I know you're in there!"

Her head twisted at my words. She threw her hand down to her side.

"Enough!" she howled.

Her voice wasn't Melanie's. It was piercingly high pitched and raspy. As I looked at her, I saw the green in her eyes dissolve as darkness overtook them. Spearfinger was back.

"I don't protect him," I shouted. "I protect Melanie!"

"Melanie is gone."

Her head jerked to the side as she looked at Austin. He froze in fear. I stepped backwards.

"Come here, Austin. I did rather enjoy your brother's liver. Families should always stick together. Let me help you."

She stepped closer to Austin. He turned to run, and in his haste, careened into the trunk of a tree. He bounced off of the tree and fell backwards. Spearfinger stepped closer, standing directly over him. She raised her hand to the sky and forcefully extended her index finger. She knelt next to him and pinned him down with her other hand. Ready to plunge her fingernail into Austin, she froze. The deafening sound of the gunshot echoed through the forest.

I IMMEDIATELY REACHED for the gun still tucked in my waistband. I looked at Melanie and watched as she slowly collapsed. Her crumpled body lay in a heap next to Austin. Austin pushed her body away from him and quickly got to his feet. He looked at me.

"It ain't worth it. None of this is worth it. Stay the hell away from me!" He turned and sprinted out of the forest.

I dove towards Melanie and rolled her on to her back. Her head hung to the side. My hands brushed her hair out of her face. I closed my eyes as my hands gently stroked her cheeks. I took a deep breath and turned my head toward the direction the shot had come from. My vision was blurred from tears, but I was able to make out an approaching figure in the distance. There was a rifle on his back, its barrel sticking up above his shoulder. It was Gordon.

I stood up and charged at him as fast as I could. As I

neared him, I dropped my shoulder and slammed into him. The force knocked him off his feet and flat on his back. He groaned in pain and struggled to breathe.

"You killed her! You fucking killed her!" I screamed.

"Wake up kid. That wasn't Mel! That was Spearfinger! If that were Mel, she'd be alive. I shot her hand!"

I turned back to Melanie. There was a violent look of resolve on her face. She slowly got to her knees. Her dead eyes never moved from me. She slowly brought her hand up in front of her. She slowly examined her hand.

"Oh shit. According the Cherokee legend, her heart was in her hand! That should've killed her," Gordon said.

"The coin," a voice said.

"What?" I replied.

"I just thought, if you shot her hand... she'd die," Gordon stammered.

"No, about the coin!" I yelled.

"David, use the coin," the voice said.

"I didn't say anything about the coin..." Gordon continued.

I'd stopped listening to him. Another voice was guiding me. It was the familiar voice of my dad. My focus was on the coin. Where the hell was it? I patted down my pockets. It wasn't in my hand anymore. I must've dropped it when I dove for Melanie. I started running back toward her. As I got closer, I spotted something glowing on the ground in front of her. It was the coin. I dove for it and picked it up. I turned to face Melanie. Her eyes bore into me as I moved. I saw her hand. Gordon had shot it, but there was no blood. Just ragged pieces of blackened flesh where the bullet tore through. I grabbed her wrist and slammed the coin down into her palm. I pulled her up. Her face was within an inch of mine.

"Spearfinger, your time here is done. Leave and never return."

I continued to squeeze the coin into her palm with all of my strength. She opened her mouth as if she was going to speak, but nothing came out. Her head began to twitch. Her dead eyes widened, and she turned to look up at the moonlit sky.

In that instant, there was a massive crash and everything turned white. It was as if a bolt of lightning struck me. I was blinded by the flash. The ground shook. There was a sound of rocks tumbling.

My vision started to come back. All I could see was a massive dark shape forming in front of me. As my vision became clearer, I saw a black cloud spewing from Melanie's mouth and forming a large rock in front of me. Suddenly, there was another crash of lightning. I was blinded again, but this time everything was silent. I couldn't see, and I couldn't hear. I could only feel. I immediately became aware of a warm liquid running down my hand.

My vision came back into focus. I could see blood dripping from my hand and trailing down my arm. It was Melanie's blood. I opened my hand to see her delicate hand, now covered in blood, a bullet hole in its center. I stumbled backward. Melanie's limp body fell into my arms. I wrapped my arms around her. Her bloody hand fell limply to her side. I squeezed her body as tightly as I could.

I laid her down in front of me. My hands touched the side of her cheek.

"Don't leave me Melanie," I choked out. "Not now."

I leaned in and kissed her. Her lips were still warm but lifeless.

I held my face next to her and squeezed her body as tightly as I could. My body trembled. I couldn't let go. I felt her body twitch in my arms. Just once. Then again. I could feel her muscles tighten. I felt her chest heave as I heard her take in a giant breath. I gently let go as I pulled back to look at her. Her chest was now alive, rising and falling as she breathed. I cupped her face in my hands and kissed her on her forehead.

"Please, wake up," I whispered.

Her eyelashes began to flicker. Gradually she opened her eyes. Her green, vibrant eyes. Her pupils dilated as she looked at me.

"David?" she asked, confusion in her voice. "What happened? Ow! My hand! What happened to my hand?"

"GORDON, SHE'S ALIVE!" I shouted as I knelt at Melanie's side.

"You're lucky you're still alive after you tackled me like that," he said.

Melanie raised her hand in front of her face, looking at it for the first time. Blood was still running down her arm. "There's a hole in my hand. There is a goddamn hole in my hand!"

Gordon stepped up and gently grabbed her wrist. He wrapped a bandage around it tightly. "Sorry 'bout that. I didn't have much of a choice. Frankly, y'all should be thanking me."

Melanie just stared at him with wide eyes and a confused expression.

"What do you remember?" I asked.

She blinked and shook her head.

"I left the hospital. I wanted to talk to you. I tried calling you a thousand times and you never picked up. I needed to explain what happened. I realized you'd come back here, so I left. I remember a fire. I saw some smoke and could smell a fire burning close by. I assumed it was you. So, I started walking towards the smell. And then... she... that thing! She was standing in front of me. I remember her hand driving into me, and that's it. Until I saw you standing over me. But what happened? My hand! Did you seriously shoot my fuckin' hand?"

"Again, sorry 'bout that." Gordon said as he tightened another bandage around her hand. "Look, I'm all fer catchin' up, but you've lost a lot of blood not to mention the infection you're gonna get if we don't get you to the hospital."

"Wait, is that her?" I asked, pointing just past Melanie.

Behind her was a rock roughly the size of a person. It was clean and jagged on the edges as if it had just been set there.

"Spearfinger?" Melanie asked.

"That's her alright. She looks exactly the same as when I first met her," a voice said.

I looked at Gordon, who was looking at me. My eyes darted over to Melanie's. She was wide-eyed and looking not at me but past me. I turned around. Robert stood there, a smile on his face.

"I knew I invested wisely in your family," he said.

His lips curled as he looked at the ground. He bent down and picked up the coin. He raised it up near his face and rubbed his thumb on the top of it as if he were polishing it. Then he blew on it and flipped it. The coin spun through the air before Robert's hand snatched it. He stepped closer to Melanie.

"Excuse me, if I may, would you mind showing me the wound."

Gordon nodded his head and unwrapped the gauze he'd put on Melanie's hand. Once the gauze was removed, Robert gently lifted her hand.

"Alright, this may hurt for just a second, but trust me, okay?" Not waiting for an answer he gently placed the coin in Melanie's palm and closed her fingers around it. She winced in pain.

"Okay dear, open up your hand."

Melanie opened her hand slowly. As she did, Robert removed the coin. Her hand was perfect. The wound was gone.

"There, see, all better," he said as he flipped the coin again, that time towards me. "You best hang on to that. You'll never know when you'll need it again."

I caught the coin and immediately put it in my pocket. Robert pulled his golden pocket watch from his vest and looked at it shaking his head.

"Time is short. I'd say we have an hour and a half before the sun has completely risen. Follow me."

"Follow you where?" I asked.

"I have something to show you. Consider it my payment for a job well done."

Gordon looked at me and shrugged his shoulders. Robert turned and started walking through the woods. We all stepped in and followed.

"Robert, I thought you said someone needed to die in order to kill her."

"I never said die. I said a sacrifice needed to be made. It looks like you chose to make the biggest sacrifice you could. Truth is, I didn't believe people could come back after she took them over. Lucky for you, it appears they can."

We trudged through the forest up the mountain. Soon, we were high enough that we approached the tree line. As we stepped through the last row of trees, we emerged in a dense fog. Robert continued moving forward. I couldn't see more than ten feet in front of me.

"Guess this is why they named it Cloudland," Robert said as he continued moving forward.

Soon the fog dissipated, and as it did, I realized we were standing in front of a massive building. I recognized it immediately from the photos I'd seen. It was the Cloudland Hotel. It was real and right in front of us. Robert never slowed. He walked up the staircase, onto the porch, and opened the massive door.

We all stepped inside as Robert held the door for us.

"Hurry now. Take the staircase up and then into the double door in the center." he said.

We all walked in the very real building that hadn't existed in almost a hundred years. The dark wooden staircase was covered in a beautiful red carpeting. I walked up the stairs with Melanie and Gordon following. At the top of the stairs stood an ornate dark wooden door. I took a deep breath and turned the handle. I stepped inside to a large study. The clock from my house was against the wall, and my father sat in the center of the room. He looked up as I stepped inside. He smiled and walked up to me.

We stood there in silence for a long moment. After all I'd been through, I had no clue what to say to him.

He stepped closer and wrapped his arms around me. "I'm proud of you son."

There was so much I wanted to say, but in that moment nothing mattered. The years of frustration and sadness disappeared. I felt like things were finally set right. After a moment, he stepped back and looked at me.

"Thanks, Dad," I whispered.

"I suppose I owe this guy some credit too. Who knew you were such a good shot?"

He extended his hand to Gordon, giving him a hearty handshake.

"Thank you for completing my mission," Robert said. "With Spearfinger gone, we can all finally move on."

"But what about the cache?" I asked. "Now it's free for someone like Austin to go dig it up?"

"He'd need the heading first. Roger, what's the bearing?"

"Precisely two hundred and fifty degrees from that window!" my dad replied.

"Wrong!" Robert said.

My dad turned his face to Robert in confusion.

"David, there is nothing buried out there. There is a cache somewhere, but what was hidden here in the forest was just a red herring. My concern was more about the worthiness of the person seeking the cache. Spearfinger could not be defeated except by the right person. The coin was the key to her demise and is now the key to everything else. I have no doubt that a time will come when you will know exactly how to use that coin again! Until then, keep it safe."

Robert shook my hand again and my dad hugged me once more before everything disappeared, and we were left standing on top of the mountain.

EPILOGUE

AFTER THE CLOUDLAND Hotel disappeared before our eyes, the three of us were changed people. The reality was, with Spearfinger gone, a lot had changed. But for us as individuals, everything was different. With Gordon, I'd spent so much of my life never giving him a chance. I'd never appreciated him. At times I'd even hated him. When we were left standing there on the mountain, we just looked at each other for a moment and then shook hands. The handshake led to a hug. That was it physically. But at that moment we both gained a new understanding and respect for one another. It was unspoken, but it didn't need to be said out loud. We just knew.

With Melanie, that was a little more complex. We had work to do. The one thing which was crystal clear however, was how we felt about each other. We drove down the mountain and headed to her cabin. The ride was spent in an awkward silence. Once at the house, we were both exhausted and needed rest, but above that we needed to talk. She explained what happened with Austin. That he had been harassing her and threatening her. She felt as

S. A. JACOBS

though betraying me was the only way out. It might have worked, too.

She had betrayed me and broken my heart. All of that needed time to repair. The one thing I had no doubt about was the fact that it would be repaired. I was hurt but not in doubt. We had been through some things, things which helped us both understand just how important we were to one another.

With Robert having moved out of her cabin, that seemed like the ideal place for us to start our lives over together. In the months that followed that day, I sold my house and moved in. We made a return trip to Spearfinger's Shack. There, we had a small service for Zeke. Just the three of us. Soon, his cabin was cleaned out and put on the market. I made the decision to purchase it, in addition to the other empty cabin next to Melanie's. The two of us renovated them and turned the two adjacent cabins back into rental properties. It all just felt right. The two of us hadn't escaped the small town like we dreamed, but we found each other which was a greater treasure than the cache could have ever held.

THREE MONTHS Later

I had just returned home after spending the last week in Los Angeles with my production company going through the proposed plans for the next season of my show. I had still not signed on for another season. I wanted to make the show into something that I enjoyed, and I could be proud of. The producers looked at the numbers and wanted nothing to change. I even floated the idea of working with Renegade Jack whom I'd contacted and found out we did have a lot in common. The producers saw his YouTube numbers and immediately loved the idea... at least on paper. However, they needed to produce it. His brand of single camera, low production just wouldn't fly with them.

It was a long week of tense conversations. I was anxious to see Melanie again. I missed her. With the business of cabin rentals up and running, she was happier than she'd ever been. She had a purpose, she had a job where she was her own boss, and she was successful.

When I arrived home, I found Melanie waiting for me on the porch. She greeted me with a hug and kiss. In that very moment, my phone rang. I was about to turn it off. I was sure it was my producers coming back with yet another offer. But I looked at the screen of the phone. It wasn't my producers at all, it was Charlene, Renegade Jack's girlfriend and producer. I apologized to Melanie and reluctantly answered the phone.

"David, is that you?"

"Yeah, what's up?

"It's Jack. Something's wrong. Something's very wrong." She was more upset than I'd ever heard her.

"What do you mean?"

"He went off to film another video. Some place in New York. But something went wrong. I don't know what's going on, but I know I need to talk to you."

"What do you mean you need to talk to me?"

"I'm sending you a video. Jack uploaded it this morning, like he normally does when he's on the road. So I can start editing them. This one was uploaded and instead of all the notes he normally provides, there was just a short message. It said 'Send David Now!'"

"Where is he, exactly?"

"Shit I don't know, some abandoned place on the St.

Lawrence River. It used to be owned by John Hubbard. But I can't get a hold of him. My calls don't go through, he doesn't reply to my messages. Something is wrong!"

"You sure about that name?"

"Yes dammit, will you help me?"

"Let me watch the video, and I'll call you right back."

I hung up the phone and looked at Melanie.

"Something tells me you're not going to be home for very long," she said, giving me a hug.

"Jack's in trouble, I guess. Wants me to come out there."

"Okay, doesn't seem like that big of a deal, I suppose."

I didn't respond. I just stood there silent for a moment.

"David, what is it?"

"The last time Charlene heard from him, he was shooting video at a house owned by John Hubbard. John Hubbard was one of the Sovereign Lords."

A NOTE FROM S.A. JACOBS

First and foremost, thank you! It's the support of readers like you that keeps David's story going! It's been an incredible journey with plenty more adventure and haunts to come!

I did want to stop for a minute to give you a little background on this story. A few years ago, I had the experience of a lifetime. Fellow writers, P.T. Hylton and Jonathan Benecke, invited me to spend a week hiking the Appalachian Trail with them. Being able to experience the majesty of the Appalachian Mountains was an adventure I'll never forget. We finished our hike at Carver's Gap and subsequently stopped in Roan Mountain. The community of Roan Mountain is truly a wonderful place, which also happens to have some of the best homemade pizza I've ever eaten. I knew Roan Mountain needed to be the setting for this book. While I tried to capture the sheer beauty of this community in my writing, the story also sheds light on the fictitious dark history of the Cloudland Hotel.

It's important for me to make the distinction between the fantasy of my writing and beauty of the real community present in Roan Mountain. My only hope is that you may be intrigued to learn more about the real Roan Mountain and all its splendor. It truly is an amazing place!

On the same note, I wish to recognize the real men and women who represent the U.S. Forest Service. It's only through their hard work that places like Carver's Gap and the Pisgah-Cherokee National Forest are preserved and available to us. It is truly a blessing that we can experience the untainted landscape of our country in this way.

Long story short, if you have the means, visit the real community of Roan Mountain. Stop by the Roan Mountain State Park Visitors Center and buy a sticker while checking out some of the real history of the Cloudland Hotel. Then head up to Carver's Gap. It's an experience well worth your time!

Finally, please take a moment to check out the writings of P.T. Hylton and Jonathan Benecke. Their books have truly amazed and captivated me.

Thanks for reading!

S.A. Jacobs

Made in the USA
Middletown, DE
15 April 2020